POPS
& THE
nearly
DEAD

POPS
& THE
nearly
DEAD

Edyth Bulbring

First published by Penguin Books (South Africa) (Pty) Ltd 2010

Copyright © Edyth Bulbring 2010

ISBN: 978-1-920495-01-5

ACKNOWLEDGEMENTS

I would like to thank James Woodhouse for being a wise and brilliant editor; Mike, Emily, Sophie and Jack for putting up with me – if not my cooking. And my mother, whose stories about her retirement village in Port Elizabeth, and the memories we share of the wonderful man who lived there all too briefly, gave me *Pops & The Nearly Dead*.

For Mom

Things I Know:

Getting
The Knowledge
is grunt work

1

the KNOWLEDGE

My father says that a chap has to be an expert at something. He says that being a kind of general knowledge all-rounder just means that you land up not knowing very much about anything.

Take my friend Buster, for example. His specialty is James Bond – the movies, not the books. Buster's a bit dense when it comes to the written word, but you can ask him absolutely anything about Bond Movies and he can tell you. And apart from this fantastic knowledge, he also has sound opinions on the topic – opinions that you would feel confident adopting as your own if you were in a conversation with members of the opposite sex and wanted to sound interesting.

Buster knows which of the Bond girls is the hottest. It's Halle Berry, of course – except Buster pronounces it like Hell and not so that it rhymes with Sally. It's the cool way to say it. People who are intimate with Halle say it like this, Buster says. He'll tell you she's the hottest – at least once a week. 'Halle is the hottest,' he'll say – which is quite funny when you first hear him say it, or say it out aloud yourself, but not every week.

And Buster holds the view that the latest Bond guy is the best. I'm of two minds about this. I wasn't crazy about the powder-blue swimming trunks in *Casino Royale*. Not the cut you understand – that was just fine for a guy who packs a healthy lunch box – it was the colour I found a bit dodgy. That's not to say I'm a Roger Moore or Sean Connery fan. They were both a bit crumbly at the edges towards the end, and Roger's gums were in a bad way – a complete age give-away (like in an old dog).

I'm grateful to Buster. Because of him, I can hold my own in any conversation about Bond Movies and sound like I really know what I'm talking about. Chicks go crazy for guys who can converse. Absolutely crazy. I know this from this other guy, Themba. He's the expert on All Matters Of A Sexual Nature. And that includes what turns babes on.

But Themba's not as open as Buster and when he does share something he's not as clear and direct. He likes to speak in double meanings and make mysterious hand signals and mouth movements. Most of the time I never understand what Themba's going on about and I don't like asking – you don't want to look like a complete virgin. But what I do understand makes me feel like throwing up or dying from a heart attack. I'm never sure which is the stronger feeling.

My father's area of expertise, however, is not as useful as Themba's and Buster's. He's an expert on Water. He knows where to find it, how to find it, how to clean it, how to transport it, even how it tastes (it doesn't taste of anything). Which you must admit is pretty dry. For Water.

I suppose there are a couple of people who find my father's knowledge useful though, because he keeps on getting job offers in faraway places with strange names. The latest place is called Bangkok. When I told Themba he fell on the ground laughing. I hadn't given it much thought until then, but I admit it's a pretty rude-sounding name.

Where they got it I just don't know. It's kind of hard to imagine a whole bunch of government people sitting around a table considering what to call the capital of Thailand and coming up with Bangkok as a serious option. Maybe they held some kind of national competition, where people had to enter names, and then they pulled one out of a hat and some joker like Themba entered Bangkok and they were stuck with it. That's probably how it happened.

Unlike my name. I was assigned my name before I was born. If I'd been a girl, I would have been called Hermione. Like one of those big-toothed princesses from some random Northern European country – not the Harry Potter girl (she's hot, as hot as Halle).

Hermione St John Goodenough. Pretty ghastly. But not as bad as the one I got. Randolph St John Goodenough. I mean, shoot me. Put me out of my misery.

There's a whole bunch of us Randolphs. My father, his father and his father all the way back along the family tree. It's a tough name to live with. When I meet people I like to say, 'Call me Red, all my friends do', on account of the fact I have hair that looks like bad sunburn. Red. Now there's a name for a real guy. But people tend to go for the easier options – Carrots, Ginger or, kill me now, Randy.

Randy! I mean, Themba has the stats at his fingertips, and he says that guys think about All Matters Of A Sexual Nature every thirty seconds. Well, it's something like that. And it really doesn't help having a name like Randy. It kind of puts me in the percentile of guys who think about it every fifteen seconds.

To make matters worse, Themba calls me Randy Handy on account of the fact that he says that my only sexual experience has been with my hand. Mrs Hand and her five ugly fingers. Themba says it like he knows it's a fact. He has this real expert air when he speaks of All Matters Of A Sexual Nature.

I used to be a bit envious of people who had The Knowledge. Even of my father and his boring Water, because at least he earns a packet and gets to go to capital cities with sexual names. But I'm not any more. Because I too am now a bone fide Expert.

It's a recent thing. Up until a year ago I was an all-rounder. One of the despised who knew nothing of any real value because it was stuff that anybody could know if they watched enough television or read a couple of encyclopaedias. Then, one day, I woke up and discovered that I was an Expert, part of that group of people who others seek out for specialist advice.

To be honest, I didn't feel completely over the moon about it. Because, hey, my area of expertise is not a big crowd puller. It's hardly going to make me the centre of every conversation with the babes and it's certainly not going to make people all hot and sweaty like they get over the stuff Themba and Buster know. But I didn't feel totally peed off either. Maybe it was because of how it happened. Because, you see, The Knowledge didn't just come to me over night. Nor did it come to me from books and movies, like Themba's and Buster's, or from years of serious study, like my father's. I gained my expertise from real life experience. My knowledge is on the ground stuff – like a trade. And even though it's not something that I decided on and then pursued, I worked for it too. I have scars to show for it all. I earned my stripes.

It all happened because of Bangkok. Last year my father received a job offer from an organisation asking him to go and organise some water for the people of Thailand. Not all of them, just some of the ones who live in Bangkok.

To cut a long story short, my father thought this sounded pretty interesting, so he accepted the job and told me and my mother that we were relocating from Nairobi (where we had lived for the past four years) to that place which I will call the capital of Thailand from now on because calling it by its name makes me think of All Matters Of A Sexual Nature. And I don't want to use up more than my quota. It wouldn't be fair – especially if I stole time off some poor bloke in the lower percentiles who only got to think about getting it every fifty seconds.

I was dead keen when I heard. Everybody, even those with hardly any general knowledge at all, knows that the people from the East can't say their Rs. There, in the capital of Thailand, I would be Landy. Landy Goodenough. Or Led to my new Thai friends, like a wrinkly rock and roll star who's still hot. No more Randy or Randy Handy or Carrots or Ginger or any of the other names that define me as the poster boy for contempt and ridicule.

My father's posting to the capital of Thailand was for five years. There were a couple of things my parents needed to organise before I could join them – a house, a school, a car or two, a washing machine, some staff, et cetera et cetera. They said I needed to be patient. They would send for me when they'd sorted out their lives and got settled. In the meantime, I was being packed off to the Nelson Mandela Gardens Retirement Village to live with Pops.

Pops. It's not his real name but it's the one I've called him since I was a baby. Because he's my grandfather. Well, one of them. The old guy on my mother's side of the family. Not Grandfather Randolph. He's called by his proper name: Grandfather Randolph. Nothing more, nothing less. No Randy Handy for him. Although, let's face it, he's not getting any joy anywhere else, as Themba would say.

Themba said spending three months with Pops and a bunch of nearly dead people sounded like being sentenced to life in a monastery without his collection of naughty mags. Buster said James Bond would never have survived torture like this, not in a million years. But I was totally fine with it.

I loved Pops better than any person in the whole world. He had paid me a three week visit every year since the day I was born. I loved him better than taking long showers – even better than the prospect of travelling ten thousand miles across Africa in an aeroplane without parental guidance to see him.

Pops. He is as his name sounds. Full of noise and surprises. Like a cork coming out of a champagne bottle. All fizzed up and bubbled out and zinging into the air. Pop-pop-pop-pop. Pops!

His name is like the sound in my ears as the plane from Nairobi descended towards Johannesburg. Like the sound in my ears as the plane took off four hours later to a place the residents call 'the friendly city' and people who know better call 'the windy city'.

That's where I was sent so that my mother and father could go to the capital of Thailand for three months and get things shipshape before sending for me. Port Elizabeth, South Africa – the place where my story about gaining The Knowledge begins.

But my expertise did not come from Pops only. It came from a whole bunch of other people of advanced age who spent a lot of time doing things that Pops didn't care a sweaty old jock strap for.

And at the end of my stay at Nelson Mandela Gardens, no one ever called me Randy Handy again, or even Landy Handy. That's because referring to my hands became infra dig, like ice in beer or shit on the cricket pitch or using another chap's toothbrush. Mentioning my hands wasn't something that anyone ever wanted to do again, after those three months I spent in Port Elizabeth with Pops and the Nearly Dead.

Things I Know:

Old People are
stingy with the mayo

2

the BRAAI

My first formal introduction to the good folk of the Nelson Mandela Gardens Retirement Village took place the day I arrived in Port Elizabeth from Nairobi. It happened at the Friday night braai.

These little get-togethers were the brainchild of the Village's Entertainment Committee, of which Pops was a long-serving member. A couple of hours before the braai started, I helped Pops with the wood. This was Pops' job. One of the committee members collected the money for the wood from each resident, another bought the wood, Pops picked it up from the wood buyer's house and lit the fires, and the fourth committee member made sure that the braai grills were cleaned and oiled at the end of the evening.

It was six o'clock sharp when the old people arrived en masse for the braai. There were about fifty of them, which was not a brilliant turnout from an aged population of about one hundred and fifty residents. I supposed the others had something more exciting to do.

I learned something about old people that first night at the Village: old people like to eat supper early; they dread having late nights. It's as though they all believe they need to be fresh and at their best for the challenges of the next day. Like there's something really big happening for which they have to be on top form. But then the day arrives and it's pretty much like the one the day before.

The old people arrived at the braai area outside the Entertainment Hall separately and in couples. Then, slowly but surely, they collected into small groups. I could put labels on them. There was a group I called the Lucky Ones – the ones who still had partners, the ones who were still getting it. I tried not to think about it because the thought of oldies going for it like rabbits was really not something I wanted to be dwelling on.

Then there was another group, consisting entirely of single old ladies. They got the name the Sad Singles. I observed them watching the Lucky Ones. Their eyes followed the way the husbands topped up the wives' wine glasses and how the men laid their pieces of sausage neatly on the braai, stabbing them with a fork and turning them every so often. The Sad Singles' eyes consumed this old ritual with miserable envy and just observing them watching the Lucky Ones gave me a hollow feeling in my tummy.

The Sad Singles had to pour their own drinks and braai their own meat, unless they managed to get one of the members of the third group to do it for them. This was the one Pops belonged to – he was one of the rare single males. I called them the Desirables, because even the most useless of this group was considered by the sad single ladies to be better than no one at all.

Pops was quite the charmer and the Sad Singles adored him. It wasn't difficult to see why. He drew people to him like a swarm of wasps to sticky chicken wings. It's the way he was.

For instance, Pops loved dancing. Not that any person who has chosen Dancing as an area of expert knowledge would have considered Pops a dancer of any note. He sort of danced like one of those sad guys at school who thinks that jogging sideways on the spot is hot. Or cool. Or whatever turns the babes on. Except that everyone knows that jogging sideways on the spot is a big turn-off. Except when Pops did it.

Because when Pops danced it was usually when he was having fun and wasn't thinking about chicks at all. He was just thinking about dancing. So if you put on the radio or shoved a tape into Pops' old music system he would be at it. Whether he was ironing his shirts or frying an egg or cracking open a bottle of beer, when he heard the music he wouldn't be able to stop himself. And even though he looked like such a silly old bugger, you would want to be right there in that space jogging and jiggling and having fun with him.

Everybody did.

Then there was the way that Pops dressed. My housekeepers have always bought all my clothes, and my father's too, so clothes to me had always just been something that were washed and ironed and set out in my drawers and cupboards. Before I went to stay with Pops, I always took the first shirt or pair of trousers and I really didn't notice much what I was wearing. But Pops noticed everything about clothes, especially the colours and the way they felt on his skin. He had this really rabid shirt his old pal bought him in Hawaii. He wore it all the time, even though the fashionistas would probably have told him he looked like a tourist who'd been looking for something to spend the last of his foreign currency on at the airport shop. Pops didn't care. He just loved the colourful flowers. He said he felt like he was wearing a tropical garden.

And on top of the dancing and the clothes, the other thing about Pops that set him apart from Grandfather Randolph – who hasn't danced or worn anything more exciting than a viscose mix since forever – was his taste in food. Pops really did taste food. Not just eat it. He wouldn't eat just anything because he was hungry. And he never did leftovers. 'What for?' he always said. 'Why eat it old and saggy when you can eat it young and fresh?' Though when he told me this he sounded so much like Themba when he talked about girls that it worried me.

And Pops liked to eat food with people he liked. So even if you were to offer Pops one of his favourite foods (like peanut butter, bacon, syrup and banana on white toast), if he had to eat it with someone as boring as Grandfather Randolph, or someone who was an expert on Light Bulbs, he would sooner drink water. Tapped – not sparkling. And I don't want to sound disloyal to my father, but that's all Pops ever wanted to know about Water.

But when Pops ate something he liked, hey, he dribbled and drooled and hummed and swayed and he really dug in there, sucking his fingers and smacking his lips, and if you told him he should lick his plate clean, he'd do it. Okay, that's an exaggeration, but the bottom line was that he was a really serious food lover.

So that's my Grandfather Pops. The favourite of the Sad Singles. There he was at the braai, that Friday night in the first week of October, flicking on a sausage here and there and rolling over a mielie. He didn't mind opening the bottles of wine for the Sad Singles or tasting a bit of potato salad (a bit mean on the mayo, I could see) or three-bean salad (lots of mint, very tasty). That's the kind of guy Pops was. He got into things, getting busy, talking and laughing with people. He was quite the crowd puller, was Pops.

Most of the other Desirables stood as far away from the Sad Singles as possible. I expect they thought that braaing someone else's meat and pouring their drinks all the time was a bit much. And I know how they felt because I got to do it all night.

The Sad Singles jumped on me like a group of starving fleas off a mangy old carpet. It was, 'Be a dear, Randolph, and put my chicken wing on the braai …' and 'Turn my pork ribbetjie, won't you, dear?' and 'Watch that my sausage doesn't burn, please, Randolph?'

I was busy that night, it must be said. Old people can be complete slave drivers. But after a while I kind of got into the swing of things. I'd notice that this one's glass was empty and I'd top her up from her half bottle of dry white ('I always just bring half a bottle, enough for a glass or two, don't want to overdo it, now do I, Randolph'). I'd see that this one was looking for the lid of her Tupperware so that the coleslaw didn't spoil ('I can never finish more than a few spoons, but never mind, it will keep for my lunch tomorrow').

I learned another thing about old people that night too, especially the old ladies: they like to talk. Like I was just mentioning the fact that I thought Halle was as hot as hell and that the new Bond guy was by far the best, being on the whole quite appealing in a metrosexual kind of way, and that was the end of me. I couldn't get a word in edgeways after that. It was Sean this and Britt that and Pussy Galore the other. It was quite clear that Sean was still tops with the old ladies at Nelson Mandela Gardens. And they thought that Honey Ryder aka Ursula Andress's white bikini with that large belt and buckle was just the thing – and the look is coming back, hadn't I noticed? Good fashion always repeats, just like anchovies.

I just stood there, nodding and smiling and every now and then plonking a sausage or chop onto a paper plate. They didn't stop jabbering for a good forty minutes. Quite shaken and stirred by it all, not that anybody was drinking cocktails.

Buster was onto a good thing, it must be said. Even when he's as old as Pops he'll be able to pull the chicks with his expertise on Bond Movies.

Everyone was having a riot of a time, when Pops came over and said it was time to go home. I could hardly hear what he said next what with all the howls of protest from the Sad Singles. Oh, not yet, it's still early, you never leave so early. You haven't even had some dessert. Party pooper. Stuff like that.

I think Pops may have said he had a headache or he was feeling a bit wonky, wiped out, but he could see no one wanted things to end so he just sat down on one of those camping chairs, keeping quiet, while the fun carried on. He was looking like he needed a good eight hours sleep, it must be said.

Then I noticed one of the Sad Singles chatting to one of the males from the group of Lucky Ones. She tilted her polystyrene cup as he poured her some Chenin Blanc and plopped in a cube of ice from his cooler box – taking good care of her. He even turned his head to one side so that his good ear could catch what she was saying.

The moment didn't last. It ended with the appearance of the other half of this happy couple. Except she didn't look so happy. 'Peggy, you have got to, *got to* learn how to braai your own chicken and pour your own wine,' she snapped. 'You have got to, *got to* realise that you're on your own now. You need to become self-sufficient. It's sad. Yes, I know, but that's life. You can't expect other women's husbands to do what yours used to do for you.' And with that she grabbed her partner by the elbow and dragged him off.

It wasn't a big deal, hey? I mean, my mother was always

telling me to make my own cup of tea and Weet-Bix for breakfast. Even chuck the spaghetti ready-mix into a pot. It wasn't a big thing. We all have to do it, hey?

But the poor Sad Single took it hard. She clasped her plate to her chest and sat at the edge of the Lucky Ones, not talking or anything, just toying with her glass as she blinked her eyes rapidly. I watched for a few moments, feeling hollow and useless. Then Pops pulled his camping chair over to where she was sitting. I watched him chatting to her for a bit until I could see that he was almost falling off his chair with weariness and I decided it was time to make tracks to bed.

On our way home I asked Pops what the Sad Single's case was. Her attitude was a bit emo, let's be frank.

Pops told me her name was Mrs Peggy Smythe (rhyming with writhe, not with with) and Mr Smythe (Francis), her husband of thirty-nine years, had kicked the bucket about seven months back. Which, let's face it, is a long time, and Mrs Smythe should have moved on, right?

Wrong, said Pops. Mrs Smythe hadn't been to the Friday night braais since Mr Smythe's departure. That night had been her first time out on the town as a Sad Single and it was only then that she'd realised that she'd never braaied her own meat before, she'd always had Mr Smythe to do it for her. She'd been confronted by the fact that Mr Smythe would never braai for her again. Not on this earth, anyway. He had well and truly left her on her own.

It was a tough lesson for Mrs Smythe to learn. That she was alone and that she had to braai her own meat for the rest of her time. And that she should just bring half a bottle of Chenin Blanc to the braais in future. Enough for just two glasses. Enough for just one person.

Things I Know:

Old People cheat at
Scrabble

3

the SCRABBLE GAME

Pops played Scrabble with the Foxcroft sisters – Felicity and Grace – every Thursday afternoon. He'd been doing this every Thursday for about five years.

That's another thing I learned about old people pretty early on in my stay at the Village: they like to have their routines. And they don't like it when they have to change them.

I was taking a walk around the Village the day after I arrived and I heard this one old guy asking another old guy if he wanted to go to the cinema on Wednesday afternoon. And the old guy said no, Wednesday afternoons were when he watered the garden.

I didn't get it. It wasn't like he couldn't water the garden on Tuesday afternoon instead and then catch the movie on Wednesday. Or maybe even water the garden in the early evening when he got back from the cinema.

But that's the way the old people are. They also don't like sleeping late in the mornings. They like to get going, make an early start, get the show on the road, get organised. They say things like that, but then they get up early and are all dressed and ready for the big day and there's not a lot going on.

That's why they have their routines. It makes them feel busy, like they have things to do which they have to get up for in the morning. Otherwise, they'd probably never get out of their pyjamas, except when they had to buy bread and stuff.

Pops wasn't like that. Okay, he had his little things that he always did, like watching the weather on television at seven-thirty every evening. He and everyone else at Nelson Mandela Gardens – the ones that managed to stay awake that is.

Old people are obsessed with the weather. They always want to know if it's going to rain. Every evening the weatherman would tell us that there was an eighty per cent chance of rain. I'm not exaggerating; he said it practically every night for the three months I watched. And every night the residents at the Village would rub their hands with excitement. Then, the next day, the wind would blow the rain out to sea and everyone would say it would certainly rain tomorrow. And they would sigh as though a special treat had been cancelled.

Apart from watching the weather forecast and drinking a cup of tea before bed, Pops wasn't a big slave to routine. He mostly liked to see what the day had to offer. He liked to be surprised. That's what he said.

Except for Thursdays, which was Pops' Scrabble afternoon. And it was to become my Scrabble afternoon too, because after five years of playing as a threesome, the Foxcroft sisters had agreed to admit me to their game as a fourth. It was a great honour. People had been trying to crash this game for years, Pops said.

So, there we were, Pops and me, taking a walk over to Number 37 – Grace's house. It was a short, pleasant walk. The Village grounds were always kept very neat and clean and all the dog owners abided by the rule that no little surprises should be left on the walkways. They always walked behind their animals with a pooper scooper and a plastic bag.[1]

On this particular Thursday, Pops was carrying a little something for the Foxcrofts in a plastic bag. It was two bottles of Pops' pickled onions. He was crazy for pickles – gherkins, onions, anything that had spent a good couple of months drowning in vinegar. He liked to make them himself. He couldn't stand the rubbish you can buy at the supermarket. That's what he said.

All of a sudden, without warning, Pops made a sound like *woomf* and fell on the path. The bottles made a sound like *smash* and then there was broken glass and vinegar and

---

[1] The management had put signs in big capital letters warning people of this rule every couple of metres along the walkway in case one of the residents had a forgetful moment while taking a stroll.

pickled onions all over the path. Pops was on his knees and his favourite olive-green corduroy Scrabble-playing trousers were torn and there was blood running down his leg.

It gave me quite a turn. I was all over Pops, trying to help him up and jabbering away, asking him over and over again if he was all right. It took a while for Pops to calm me down.

Pops said it had felt like someone had jabbed him in the back of the knee, just like mean kids do to other kids when they're standing behind them in assembly during prayers. Your leg buckles and wobbles and you nearly fall. That's how it felt, Pops said, except he couldn't stop the falling part of it.

We went back to the house and Pops got cleaned up. He said he wasn't going to let a little accident ruin the Scrabble game and we set off again with two more bottles of onions.

Grace and Felicity are three years apart, with Grace being the older sister. They lived a couple of houses away from each other in the Village and took turns at hosting the Thursday Scrabble game.

There were a couple of things Pops felt it worth mentioning about Grace and Felicity. The first was that they were both highly – and I mean highly – competitive. If Felicity served tea and jam scones one Scrabble day, then it would be tea, jam scones and some cheese ones the following Thursday at Grace's house. If Grace did crêpes with cream, it would be crêpes with cream and berries swimming in some boozy liqueur the next Thursday at Felicity's. And these heady levels of competition didn't stop at the catering, they went right through to the actual game.

The other thing about the Foxcroft sisters Pops felt worth mentioning was that Grace had a bit of a memory problem. She couldn't remember what had happened five minutes before, but she could tell you very long stories about what had happened in her childhood. There's a name for this kind of memory problem, but I can't recall it. I think what she had could be contagious.

Their highly developed sense of competition combined with Grace's memory problem made the Scrabble game a war zone. I was aiming to just keep quiet and try not to get killed in the crossfire. Pops' tried and tested strategy meanwhile was to sit opposite the two sisters and make soothing sounds to try and keep the peace. That Thursday however, he was looking a bit pale. I supposed it was the strain of the game that was affecting him.

I'm not really a wordsmith, so I found it hard enough to come up with the words, let alone try to figure out the sneaky spots to put them so that I could get the highest score. I found myself staring at the letters and coming up with words like LOINS and PENIS and SEMEN. Which was pretty embarrassing, so I always had to put down really dumb words like LIONS and PENS and MEN. I wasn't a big scorer.

I was sitting at the table and the word in front of me was VAGINA and there was an s on the board, kindly left by Pops, who was trying to encourage me. I could get a triple letter on the v and a double word score, but there was no way, no way in hell I was putting down VAGINAS in front of Grace and

Felicity. So I went for GAVIN.

Felicity groaned. 'How many times do I have to tell you, Randolph. No proper names.' She couldn't resist looking at my letters. 'You ruddy idiot. What about VAGINAS?' she said, grabbing the other letters and putting the word exactly where it was meant to go. So I had to spend the rest of the afternoon looking at VAGINAS on the board, knowing that Grace and Felicity and Pops were seeing it too. Which was pretty horrible, it must be said. I mean, I didn't even want to think about Grace and Felicity having vaginas. They were spinsters, for heaven's sakes. Actually, I was sure they didn't have them. They couldn't have . . .

Pops said that I'd become quite the expert at Scrabble if I watched Grace and Felicity carefully. All I needed to do, he said, was to challenge my Zone Of Proximal Development, which is the difference between what a person can do without help and what he can do with help.

It was a theory developed by a Belarusian psychologist bloke called Lev Vygotsky a couple of years before I was born. But I doubt Lev ever had to play Scrabble with Grace and Felicity because the things I learned at their Scrabble table that first afternoon did some serious damage to my Zone.

The two sisters spent the afternoon throwing the scoring pad back and forth, accusing each other of cheating. Felicity caught Grace using an I tile as a blank. Grace had turned it over – people don't usually check the other side. But Grace got caught every time (and because she didn't remember she'd been busted she kept on doing it).

The afternoon dragged on and Grace hammered Felicity

for MUSLIM ('It's a capital letter. No capital letters!') and Felicity hammered Grace for WASP ('No acronyms, Grace!'). But Grace insisted WASP was an insect and not an acronym, which Felicity knew, she was just saying it to get back at Grace for MUSLIM. In any case it was a discussion they'd had five minutes before but Felicity was just mentioning it again because it made her think it gave her one over Grace. It was kind of funny, but it got sort of spiteful the fourth time she did it.

Felicity did this kind of mean and crazy stuff to Grace all the time. Like she would break up part of a puzzle that Grace had done the day before and Grace would do the same part again and again without realising it. Or she would remove Grace's bookmark and watch her sister read the same chapter day after day.

But Grace would get her own back some times – on days when she had these convenient forgetful moments designed to drive Felicity psychotic. Like when Felicity asked her to buy blackberry jam and she came back with marmalade ('You can't eat scones with marmalade, can you!'). Or when Felicity invited Grace for supper and she forgot to turn up, or came an hour late so the cheese soufflé collapsed in the middle. Or didn't pay Felicity's telephone account, so that the phone got cut off. It was constant war.

I once asked Pops what it was with the two of them. Why did they live so close to each other and see one another every day if they wanted to kill each other whenever the other's back was turned. And Pops said that perhaps that was what kept them alive.

Things I Know:

I'm crap at
telling jokes

4

MEETING REGINA VERSAGEL

Pops always said that a lot of the time the way things happen was 'just life'. There wasn't a lot you could do about it. For instance, you get up in the morning and you dawdle a bit so that you head into town half an hour later than usual. And so you miss being the number four car in the pile-up on the freeway. That's 'just life', right? Or you are having tea at Grace Foxcroft's place and you're feeling greedy so you take the last rusk and break your tooth on a piece of stone you mistake for a raisin. That's 'just life' – it's the stuff that just sort of happens to you without your having much influence over it.

Buster and Themba always said that apart from being buried alive in a village of fossils, I was damn lucky to have a three month holiday by the seaside. Like all I did was surf all day and drink long colourful drinks decorated with tiny umbrellas and swivel sticks. The truth is, that apart from all the cool stuff – the Scrabble, the braais and the other fun and games – I also had assignments. Two assignments a week that I had to email to my tutor in the capital of Thailand, who was preparing me for the Harrow International School I'd be attending once my parents had settled in and decided I could join them. As Pops said, it was 'just life'!

My assignment for the first week I spent at Nelson Mandela Gardens was an essay on Global Warming. Without wanting to sound completely immodest, I am what you could call quite a fundi on the topic – not an Expert as such, but let's just say that I have some insights. But most of my ideas for my assignment had come from the discussions I'd been having with Pops on the topic. He'd got very excited when I'd told him about it and spat and waved his hands around a lot as he'd talked about the Chinese and the Americans and their ruddy big cars and their blinking washing detergents.

Pops' biggest bugbear was the oysters. There was this spot along the Port Elizabeth coast – I can't say exactly where it is because Pops swore me to secrecy (only he and some other aphrodisiac-seekers know of it) – where the rocks were covered with oysters and at low tide you could go and rip them off and eat them right there, all fresh and swimming in salty sea water.

Pops had this calendar which told him exactly when it was going to be low tide and then he'd head off down to this place with just a knife, not even a lemon or a bottle of Tabasco. Oysters au Naturel, he called it.

For as many years as I'd known Pops he'd been telling me about this spot with the oysters and I had been hoping that he'd take me to his magic place during my visit. But Pops said the oysters were all gone. It wasn't like a whole bunch of greedy gutses had got there ahead of us and finished them off – there were always hundreds of them if you knew where to look – it was just that the tides had changed and now the oysters didn't breed there any more. Pops said that this was not 'just life', it was 'just criminal'.

It's a well-known fact – Themba often tells me – that oysters can really get you all revved up. They, along with ginseng and rhino horn, put lead in a chap's pencil, so to speak. But I didn't think Pops was thinking about his stationery set when he started bitching about the oysters. No. It was probably because oysters are chock-a-block full of vitamin D, which is good for old people's bones. That's probably why Pops was so ticked off by the oyster shortage.

Old people have lots of stuff wrong with them – and not just with their bones. Grace Foxcroft suffers from what is known among laymen like me as 'The Disease of Kings' – gout. Her legs and feet swell something rotten when she eats certain foods. Her calves sort of disappear into her feet and she gets something that Felicity calls 'cankles'.

It happens when the uric acid rises in the bloodstream and poor Grace has to put her feet up and lay off scoffing anchovies and beer and shellfish – which is not a bad idea because the last thing Grace needs is ink in her pen, so to speak.

Pops on the other hand is a pretty healthy guy. He says everything in moderation but life. The key to a healthy body is a bit of exercise, a balanced diet and a couple of beers when the sun starts going down.

He also says the way to keep your mind sharp is to do what you love and to love what you do. It's not a Pops original. It comes from a bloke called Wayne Dyer, an American wacko who must have loved doing what he loved a lot because he's been married three times and has eight children.

So Pops tries not to do anything he doesn't love, but when he does have to, like cleaning the bath or eating Brussel sprouts, he does it with a lot of vim and vigour. There's no point doing anything, even the crappy things in life, unless you do them properly, Pops would say.

So, anyway, I had this whole essay on how tidal patterns had been influenced by global warming and how the ruddy big American cars and the blinking Chinese washing detergents were to blame for the drought in oysters along the Port Elizabeth coastline, imperilling the bone density of a whole village of geriatrics (and saving Grace from an attack of gout). I had to email it to my tutor from the Internet cafe next to the fish and chip shop on the sea front. It was the closest one to the Village and an easy walk.

I also used the Internet cafe to email my mother, just to keep her in the loop as to all the goings-on at the Village – I'd sent her some photos of the braai evening (me and

Pops playing at sword fighting with our braai tongs – a gas of a picture). I hadn't heard back from her, but I supposed she was still trying to unpack boxes and get the phone lines connected and all that moving-in rubbish.

My father's a busy kind of guy – what with all those people in the capital of Thailand wanting to bath and water their gardens and stuff like that. But my mother also keeps herself busy. She's known in the industry, as they say, as an 'executive business coach'. It's kind of like she talks to these business executives who get paid a stack of cash but don't know how to do their jobs – and she tells them what to do. Sometimes, when they feel sad or lonely, they email her or call her and she listens and then she tells them that they're worthwhile and not just dumb losers who should resign and let some other guy who knows what he's doing take over the business. She has about thirty clients, so my mother says it's almost like she runs thirty companies around the world from her office at home.

When people ask my mother what she does at home all day, she tells them she is a 'domestic executive', which is the term some women use when they are actually just housewives and don't do anything. But when my mother says it, she says it like it's a joke, which it is (if you consider that she stays at home to work while her clients go to work and do sweet Fanny Adams).

I shouted to Pops that I was heading off for the Internet cafe and he grunted back at me from the sleeper couch on the stoep where he'd been lying for most of the morning – like he had for the past two mornings (since the fall with the bottles of pickled onions on our Scrabble day). He'd probably decided to take it a bit easy, I decided. At his age a fall like that can really take it out of you.

I got a real kick out of the walk down to the beach front. It took about twenty minutes, and as I wandered down the hill I had this awesome view of the harbour. It's one of those harbours that's still working and not just a place where tourists can go and stay at five star hotels and shop for souvenirs and eat in restaurants. It smells of fish and engine oil, and if you go down there early in the morning you can buy fish and squid off the boats.

Pops knew this guy who had a boat and sometimes he gave Pops a stash of black mussels he got off the rocks (from his own secret place) and Pops would cook them in beer. But on some days Pops would just buy fish and chips from the place next to the Internet cafe because he said that the way they did it in batter with all the salt and vinegar was just something he couldn't ever do better at home.

I'd forgotten to put sunscreen on the tips of my ears and on my nose before I left the Village and got pretty much deep fried myself on my walk. This is the thing with Port Elizabeth weather. Most days in October it blows like a Rhino with a head cold, but on this particular Sunday morning the wind had blown itself out overnight and the sun was as hot as Halle.

The Internet cafe was always crowded with people on the weekends – downloading music and porn and sending spam from bogus email addresses (the usual kind of stuff you find going on in Internet cafes). There was a big notice on the wall which said: *Do not use our computers to conduct illegal business!!!* And someone had done a bit of creative work on the word 'illegal' to make it say 'legal'. What a joker!

So I was emailing my tutor the assignment when I felt someone standing behind me. I hate that – creeps who try to read your mail in Internet cafes. So I turned around with a look on my face which would have frozen the nuts off a penguin in the Antarctic. But it wasn't a penguin, it was a girl.

I think you know when it happens. It felt like someone had tied a thick piece of rope around my heart and was trying to pull it out of my chest. That's how it felt when I looked up from the computer screen at this girl.

She said: 'Sorry, I'm not really looking.'

I just stared at her and I couldn't stop. She was the loveliest thing I had ever seen in my life. Her name was Regina. Regina Versagel. But I must call her Reg. All her friends did. That's what she said.

Regina Versagel. Versagel Regina. Regina Versagel. If you say it fast over and over like Red Leather, Yellow Leather, you will get a sense of what could go wrong with the name. You've got to hand it to some parents.[2]

So I said: 'Hello Reg.' And I bet I was the only damn person in the whole world who had ever called her Reg because she gave me such a wide happy smile it was like she'd just been given a thousand bucks free airtime.

I told her my name was Randolph but she could call

---

[2] If Themba had been there he'd have been sharing one of his favourite limericks about the girl called Regina with the designer whatyoumacallit.

me Red. She said: 'Awesome.' Then she said: 'Red'. And I stopped breathing.

I quickly checked my Inbox. My father had sent me a story about how the Americans were going to bomb the moon next year to see if they could find water. *How crazy is this?* was his comment. I sent him a spreadsheet of the week's rainfall in Port Elizabeth since my arrival (zilch) and told him I was only having one minute showers (white lie) to cheer him up.

There was some stuff on penis extensions from Themba and a paparazzi shot of the Bond guy with some new babe from Buster, but nothing from my mother. She was probably still waiting for everything to be set up so that she could get online – her clients would be going crazy from not hearing from her.

I sent my mother an email telling her about my essay on global warming and then attached the full document as well – she would probably want to read about the disappearing oysters and the low tides and Pops' creaking bones. Then I finished up emailing my essay to my tutor and downloaded the next assignment topic onto my memory stick while Regina sat in the chair next to me, looking at me with her bright-green swimming-pool eyes that were twice the size of normal on account of the thick glasses she was wearing. She smelt like cinnamon and baked bread and she played with her hair while she waited, twirling a strand of hair the colour of strawberry jam around and around her finger.

When I was done, Regina asked if I'd like to go to the beach. She wanted to surf and show me some moves on her board.

I froze. My board shorts were still drip-drying in the shower – I had gone for a swim with Grace Foxcroft the day before – and I was wearing my spare: the black, red, green and white striped Speedo.[3] It was two sizes too small – Themba had given it to me as a going-away present when I'd left Nairobi (he'd said that it would pack my crown jewels tighter than a flock of nuns flying economy class to Ireland) – and I would rather have eaten a crate full of worms than swum in it in front of this girl.

I told Regina I'd like a swim very much but regrettably I didn't have my swimming trunks with me. She laughed and said in that case I would have to swim kaalgat – a local word I didn't understand, but from the glint in her eye it sounded even scarier than showing off my Speedo.

I gave the least nervous shrug I could manage, and tried to sidetrack her by asking her if she wanted to hear a joke. It was Buster's favourite James Bond joke and it never fails to bring the house down. Regina said tell it, so I did.

'James Bond walks into a bar and tells a blonde he meets there that he's wearing a state of the art watch that Q has asked him to test,' I said. 'It communicates with him telepathically using alpha waves.'

I was telling Regina the joke and there was a smile playing at the edges of her lips, but when I got to the bit where James tells the blonde that the watch is telling him she isn't wearing any knickers, I felt a hot flush hit the back of my neck. I couldn't say the knicker word to Regina. I just couldn't.

[3] The colours of the Kenyan flag.

I fumbled around for an escape hatch and told her that James is joined by an Irishman, an Englishman and Van der Merwe.

'What about the telepathic watch?' Regina asked.

When Themba tells it the blonde says that the watch is wrong, she certainly is wearing underwear and James says, tapping his watch, 'It's an hour fast.' And then everyone gets it and cracks up. But I didn't tell Regina this. Instead I swung into a diversion about how James gets joined by a racehorse who orders a sandwich at the bar and they watch a chicken crossing the road. To get to the other side.

My face was a cooked tomato. I felt the sweat pouring from my armpits and down my back, pooling in the crack above my Speedo. Then Regina burst out laughing. The laugh came out of her like a hoarse bellow and she got the hiccups. 'You are some crazy guy,' she said.

The way she said it filled me with wonder. I was some crazy guy. Not a loser who couldn't tell a joke without stuffing it up. Some crazy guy.

I looked at her as she burped and hiccupped and wiped the moisture from the corners of her eyes and my heart stopped. I was crazy about her. Totally crazy.

If someone were to ask me now, how it came to be that I got these strange feelings about a red-haired girl called Regina Versagel, I would tell them that it wasn't something that I could have prevented. It just happened. It was 'just life'.

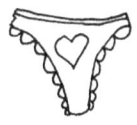

Things I Know:

There's never a
telephone booth
around when you
need one

5

SECRET COMFORTS

I spent the next day haunting the vicinity of the Internet cafe, hoping to bump into Regina Versagel. Pops said I was taking my assignments far too seriously and that too much work made Jack a dull lad.

I didn't have the heart to tell Pops that my name was Randolph, not Jack – his brain was obviously disintegrating from the lack of Vitamin D. Instead, I told him that I was off down the hill to secure him a stash of supplements to make up for the oyster drought. Pops' eyes lit up. 'Fish and chips is a grand idea, Randolph, my boy,' he said. 'Make sure they put the salt on before they add the vinegar.'

I hotfooted it down the hill to the fish and chip shop

which happened, fortuitously, to be next to the Internet cafe. But still no Regina.

Me and Pops ate fish and chips for breakfast, lunch and supper until Pops said if he ate another slap chip his arteries would seize up.

Meanwhile, it felt like my heart was seizing up at Regina's no-show. Everywhere I looked I saw her. Her face was in my bowl of Weet-Bix and milk at breakfast time. Her smile was in the pattern of cracks on the ceiling of my bedroom – which I spent a whole morning gazing at until Pops told me to get off my bed and do something useful. Like, for instance, help Grace Foxcroft find her keys, which she'd put down somewhere but just couldn't for the life of her remember where.

I found Grace's keys in the bathroom cabinet next to her memory pills (where Felicity had probably hidden them) and told her what she needed was a transfusion of omega-3. It would give her brains to rival Einstein.

During the next two days I stuffed Grace with fish and chips (and omega-3, which lives in fish). Grace Foxcroft – you just had to love the old bat. Every time I arrived at the house and suggested another plate of fish and chips she'd say, 'How kind of you to offer, Randolph, I haven't had a nice piece of fish in goodness knows how long.'

So I was coming out of the fish and chip shop with Grace's seventh piece of fish when I saw her. Not Grace, Regina.

'Oh, Red!' Regina said. Then she leaned forward and sniffed me.

I knew the sweat of my labours had stained the underarms of my shirt tea-bag yellow and I wished, oh how I wished that there was a nearby telephone booth where I could do a Clark Kent change-over and emerge with Super Armpits. But if there is one hard lesson I have learned in life it's that there's never a telephone booth around when you need one.

Regina sniffed again. 'Oh, divine,' she said. 'I just love the smell of salt and vinegar.'

So me and Regina sat down on the pavement and ate Grace's fish and chips. Regina ate most of it – that girl had an appetite on her – and while I watched her eat, I told her that I had lived in the United Arab Emirates and Malaysia and Lesotho and Kenya. Then I told her that my next stop was the capital of Thailand, after my parents had settled in.

'But what *are* you?' she asked.

'I was born in Hong Kong,' I told her and added, after a well-placed pause, that Made in Hong Kong was stamped on my ... I faltered. I could not use the arse word with Regina. 'Arm,' I finally said. 'It's on my arm.'

She laughed and pushed me. 'Your arse, silly. It's stamped on your arse,' she said and laughed that hoarse, wide-mouthed laugh of hers. Her mouth was full of half-chewed fish and chips. It was one of the most beautiful sights I had ever seen.

I told Regina my parents were really, really busy and that I had spent most of my time at home with my housekeepers or at school while my mother babysat useless executives and my father did clever things with Water.

I showed her a couple of photos of my housekeepers – Mrs Kibaki from Kenya and Mrs Ntlakana from Lesotho (my favourites) – which I always carried around in my wallet and she said, 'So your parents aren't around much to bug you. Cool.' And I said, 'Yeah, cool.' Even though I thought having parents around to bug a person once in a while might be quite cool as well.

I was just about to tell Regina about my friends Themba and Buster when my cellphone rang. It was Pops. 'Where the blazes are you?' he asked. 'You're supposed to be helping with the Summer Ball decorations.'

I told Regina that I had to go but that I spent most mornings and afternoons, most days, in fact, all the time, hanging out at the Internet cafe.

Regina said cool, she was going surfing but she'd check me around. And then she gave me another push with her greasy hands and set my heart beating like a faulty metronome.

The Entertainment Committee threw one bash a quarter and the last one for the year was coming up: the Nelson Mandela Gardens Summer Ball.

This was another thing I learned about old people. They like to do things way in advance. They never leave things to the last minute. It's as though they suspect that if they don't get things done they might not be around to do them.

Pops was in charge of decorating the Entertainment Hall and he took this job really seriously. As soon as I got back from talking to Regina he had me out on the stoep cutting out stars and circles and all sorts of fancy shapes in coloured paper, which he was planning to string around the Hall.

Pops was good at this sort of thing. He was the guy you wanted on your team if you needed someone who knew how to make things work. Your car breaks down – call Pops. Your washing machine packs up – hey, get Pops. Your light switch is faulty – Pops is your man. In the two weeks that I'd been living with him at the Village there had been a steady dribble of Sad Singles, looking for help with this or that. And when they called, Pops always went around to see if he could help. Sometimes he came back within like ten minutes and said that the thing that was broken couldn't be fixed. And I'd say, 'Oh, she needs to get an expert or something?' And Pops would say, 'No, what's broken can't be fixed.' And he'd say it with a sigh.

Pops had roped in Mrs Smythe to help with the decorations. She was the one who'd lost her husband (Francis) seven months earlier and was finding it hard to get up in the morning. Sometimes I'd see her putting birdseed around the birdbath at two o'clock in the afternoon and she'd still be in her slippers and gown.

At any rate, Mrs Smythe was doing some rather fancy cutting out – a string of paper people holding hands – when Mr Gerald Thorne from Number 18 walked past in the direction of some of the Sad Single houses (you could tell them by their size – they were smaller than the ones for married couples). He did it every day at exactly the same time. I'm not kidding, you could set your watch by Mr Thorne's afternoon walk. And he came back past our house exactly three hours later. Then you knew Pops would be heading for the fridge to crack open a cold beer. It was that time of the day.[4]

When Mr Thorne went by that Thursday afternoon I was thinking about Regina so I didn't really notice him, but Mrs Smythe let out a huge sigh. 'Disgusting,' she said and shook her head. Then she stopped what she was doing and narrowed her eyes in disapproval.

'What's disgusting?' I said, trying to keep the conversation going because it was actually only the second thing Mrs Smythe had said all afternoon. The first was 'Please pass the scissors.' I was trying to get her to come out of her shell a little.

'Gerald Thorne,' she said. 'Every afternoon with that woman. Flaunting it in front of us every day. It's been going on for years. It's sickening.'

I suddenly thought that it was a good thing that Mrs Smythe had been so quiet because she was obviously one of the meanest kind of gossips. And I was particularly glad I hadn't told her about Regina as she would probably have spread my secret around the Village like a disease.

I got the idea of what was going on with Mr Thorne pretty quickly from Mrs Smythe, who once she started on a topic could go on for hours (it turned out). Mr Thorne, the horny devil,[5] visited a certain lady (or not such a lady, depending on your perspective) every day for a bit of old youknowwhat.

---

[4] Pops brewed his own beer secretly twice a year and kept it hidden away in the garage, but everyone always knew what he was up to because he hung the hops out to dry on the lemon tree in one of Grace's stockings.

[5] Note I never used the word 'randy'.

Mrs Bella Dodge was her name and she had been a widow for fifteen years. I agreed with Mrs Smythe – it *was* sickening – as I shoved the vomitous images of Mr Thorne getting carpet burns at Number 27 out of my mind.

Pops stopped sprinkling glitter on the decorations and said one word: 'Bullshit'. Except he said, 'Bull Ess Aitch One Tee,' because Pops always said that swearing in front of women was just plain stupid. But I could see that he was a bit cross. He glared at Mrs Smythe and said something snappish along the lines of, 'That's enough, Peggy. That's enough for the day.' And then he sort of packed her off home, even though there was still tons of stuff that needed to be done.

After supper, Pops called me into the garden. He was looking up at the sky ('It's certainly going to rain …') and preparing to take a leak. So I joined him.

Things happen pretty fast for young guys – a steady *whoosh*, a hearty shake and maybe a confident release of some gas with as much noise as possible. Well, that's what Themba does, the loud fart thing, when he takes his python for a siphon (as he calls it). It's kind of like an exclamation mark, an expression of satisfaction for a job well done.

I stood there and I was just about to shake when I noticed that Pops hadn't even started. I sneaked a glance at him and he had this patient, determined look on his face. He was concentrating like the blazes. So I shuffled my feet to disguise my silence and carried on holding it – it's kind of bad manners to finish first.

We stood there looking at the stars – well, I was looking upwards, I think Pops was giving himself small encouraging nods. Ten minutes later – I'm not kidding – I heard this faint dribble. Then silence. Then another faint dribble. And then lots of mini-whoopee cushion noises; not the triumphant ones that Themba gives, but the ones that say you couldn't help it.

I stared at the heavens and counted the stars – there were about as many as there were freckles on Regina's face. Finally, I heard Pops give his a shake and I followed suit and split a sympathy fart and then we were all home, safe and sound and zipped up.

Before I escaped back inside, Pops said he had a piece of advice for me. 'It's the only advice on life I've got for you, Randolph, my boy,' he said. 'So you can either take heed or chuck it out with the trash.' Then Pops said, with a look full of meaning: 'Beware of women with red hair who wear black underwear.'

I wasn't really sure why Pops had it in for redheads who wore black underwear. My grandmother – his wife of thirty years – had been a redhead, and I was sure that she must have sometimes worn the occasional pair of black knickers. Not that she purposefully rushed out to buy them. She wouldn't have done that to Pops. No. Just maybe a friend or relative might have given them to her for her birthday or something like that.

'Why?' I asked him. 'What's wrong with women with red hair who wear black underwear?'

But Pops just smiled and winked. 'You'll understand when the time comes. I'm just giving you fair warning ... And another thing,' Pops said, as we made our way indoors, 'Randolph, my boy, don't listen to people like Mrs Smythe. They make things ugly. I don't want your ears to be filled with ugliness like that.'

I told Pops okay, but I must admit I was a little obsessed with the idea of Mr Thorne and Mrs Dodge. I mean, if they weren't doing the dirty then what were they in fact doing for three hours every day? Torturing kittens? Swopping stamps? Cleaning the silver? My mind boggled.

I wasn't the only person who was obsessed with the goings on between Mrs Dodge and Mr Thorne. Dozens of eyes followed him on his way to her house every day, but I decided that I would make it my duty to find out what they were doing. Then I could really put Mrs Smythe in her place when she opened her mouth to talk ugly about Mrs Dodge and Mr Thorne. I already knew the widow Dodge by sight. She was one of those ladies whose shape veered very much to curves rather than angles. Quite red-faced and dumpy, but she had a nice smile.

That night I dreamed I was tracking Mr Thorne through a maze. Then I had him cornered. No, it wasn't Mr Thorne. It was Regina Versagel. And she had me cornered. In the jaws of a giant oyster shell. 'This will get you all revved up,' she whispered, offering me a spoon of gooey stuff that looked like old people brain or the stuff that comes out of your nose when you get really bad flu.

I leaned towards Regina; my mouth wide open, my whole

body trembling. Then Regina withdrew her hand and tapped her watch. 'It says you're not wearing any panties,' she said. And I awoke to find myself strangled in my pyjama trousers.

The next afternoon I followed Mr Thorne to Mrs Dodge's house. It was a bit pointless because the curtains were drawn. There wasn't even a crack. But once I start on something, there's almost nothing that can deter me. So, the following day, just a few minutes before Mr Thorne arrived for his daily whatever it was with Mrs Dodge, I knocked on her door and asked her if she had a piece of loo paper for me, my nose was bleeding – I'd had to pick and pick it until I could get a convincing bloody flow.

She said, 'Oh dear! Oh dear!' and rushed for the bathroom.

While she was busy I slipped into her bedroom and opened the curtain just a tiny bit, not that anyone would really see, but it was going to be good enough.

After she'd fussed with loo paper, shoved cold keys down my spine and then finally suggested I pinch the bridge of my nose, I managed to escape Mrs Dodge and positioned myself by her Shasta daisy bush. I didn't know what to expect, but this is what I saw: Mr Thorne walked into Mrs Dodge's bedroom and sat on the bed. It was a single bed. Mrs Dodge walked in and knelt at his feet. My pulse quickened. Oh, Bella, you naughty little pudding! The back of my neck got all sweaty.

Then, as I watched, she took off his shoes and then his socks and started rubbing his feet. Around and around with her thumbs. It was not an appetising sight, it must be said. I've never really understood the stuff about foot fetishes (and even Themba says it's an acquired taste).

They were talking all the time this was going on, but I couldn't hear what they were saying. It didn't look like the kind of raunchy talk Themba says that babes really like. It looked like a conversation about normal stuff, like aching feet and library books.

Then, after about ten minutes, Mr Thorne lay down on his side and faced the wall. Mrs Dodge took off her shoes, lay down next to him and put her arm around his middle. And that was that. I watched for a while, but it was about exciting as watching old people sleeping, so I went and watered Pops' lemon tree and thought about Regina. I counted the lemons on the tree and I decided that if there were more than thirty lemons, then I would see Regina again soon.[6]

Twenty minutes before five o'clock I hit the crack in the curtain again. They were still sleeping and Mrs Dodge was still holding Mr Thorne around the middle. At this point Themba would have been demanding his money back, but it occurred to me that perhaps old people did things that young people thought were strange when really it was what they did as old people. Because the stuff that Mrs Dodge and Mr Thorne were up to was just one of the strangest things I had ever seen.

---

[6] There were thirty-six lemons if I counted the ones lying on the ground.

Guys like Themba spend more than sixty per cent of their waking days and a good part of their soggy dreams thinking of what they would do if they were ever lucky enough to get a girl into a bedroom, let alone onto a single bed. And to be honest some of those thoughts had crossed my mind on occasion too. But here were two consenting adults in a bedroom rubbing feet and sleeping forGodsakes! What a waste.

That night, while me and Pops were watching the fashion channel (Pops just died laughing at the clothes), I told Pops what I'd seen. I made out I was just passing and thought I'd heard a scream. A bit far-fetched, but Pops pretended to believe me. 'It was weird,' I said. 'They're weird. I mean, the foot rub and then the three hour snooze. I don't get it.'

So Pops told me about this experiment where Chinese chimpanzees – they were probably African, but they were living in China – were separated at birth from their parents and were never allowed physical contact with other chimps. The scientists found the chimps didn't grow much and they got sick a lot. One even died from no apparent cause. 'Can you imagine never being hugged or held in your life?' Pops asked. 'Or maybe worse, having known it and then not being able to have it because you're old and all alone?'

I told him I couldn't imagine it (even though my parents prefer not to hug unless it's a special occasion – like the dams are full or one of my mother's clients meets budget). Then I thought of the way Regina had pushed me with those greasy hands of hers. I thought of never being able to see her again, of never having her touch me again with those hands that smelled of chips and salt and vinegar.

Pops put his arm around me and gave me a big squeeze. His hand on my shoulder was a bit trembly. And I sort of got it.

Things I Know:

Old People prefer
Bingo nights to church

6

the BAPTISM

I got to know Brutus rather well during my stay at Nelson Mandela Gardens. Brutus Collins, the nicest old Staffie you could ever hope to meet.

Brutus had a coat as smooth and glossy as black oil and the brownest, friendliest eyes that always seemed to be winking at you. And unlike other dogs, that had collars, Brutus wore brightly coloured hankies around his neck – a fresh one every week.

Mr and Mrs Collins lived in Number 87 and were the oldest couple in the Village. Bruce Collins was ninety-three years old and Sylvia Collins was ninety-one. During the first week of my stay at Nelson Mandela Gardens they had their seventieth wedding anniversary and sent every house in the Village a card with a picture of themselves and Brutus under which the words *Totally Devoted* had been printed.

The card invited everyone to join them in drinking a glass of champagne – well, not the real thing, just the cheaper sparkling stuff – and everyone who was physically able pitched up at their house and toasted Bruce and Sylvia on their lawn. Brutus was there too, wearing his best hanky, and everyone toasted him as well and said what a fine dog he was.

A few days after this happy event, Mr Collins had a stroke and was confined to his bed – it was only a matter of time, Mrs Smythe told me. And not long after that I got this call from Mrs Collins, asking me if I wouldn't mind walking Brutus once a day. She would compensate me for my trouble, of course, but she just couldn't leave her husband's side to take Brutus out to do his business in case he danced his last dance without her.

This was another thing I learned about old people. They don't use words like dead and dying and deceased. Instead, they use the hundreds of happy euphemisms for checking out and cashing in and popping off. It's as though they think that if they say the D words, it will bring bad luck. Tempting fate, as it were.

I considered Mrs Collins' request and agreed. Between Pops and my assignments and hanging around the Internet cafe hoping to spot Regina Versagel I was sure I could fit Brutus in. It was just one walk a day.

So I was around at Number 87 on Sunday afternoon to

pick up Brutus and Mr Collins was up for a change, sitting on the couch in the lounge. He was eating a soft-boiled egg with bread cut into soldiers and I tried not to look too hard at him eating because I don't know what it is about old people and egg, but it's just not something you want to be looking at too often.

Brutus was lying at his feet in the hope of catching an eggy crust but when I came into the room he bounded up to me and started sniffing and licking away at my groin, which was what he did to me every time he greeted me. I was sort of used to it by then and had stopped thinking embarrassed thoughts about what everyone else was thinking – like I didn't wear clean underwear or whatever.

I was standing there, getting my personal work-over from Brutus, when Mrs Collins walked in. She stopped and wrinkled her nose. Then she stared at Mr Collins, who was looking at her warmly between eggy bites, and then at Brutus, whose furry face was hidden between my thighs. 'Oh no, Bru,' she finally said. 'Get out! Get out of here, you smelly old thing!'

Then Mrs Collins started fanning the air and I got a whiff of the worst kind of fart bomb ever made, but I wasn't sure if Mrs Collins was scolding Brutus or her husband, Bruce. It was sort of awkward, so I started to pretend not to notice the whole situation, but then I saw a look pass between Mr Collins and Mrs Collins and I caught on that this was an old joke they had going and I felt kind of bucked that they'd let me in on it. And then Brutus let up on my groin and also gave me his crinkly eyed wink, so I knew that he was in on it too.

Before I headed off for the walk, Mrs Collins took me aside and said that she had something important to tell me. The important thing was that Brutus was going to be baptised – or christened, as she called it – and she was wondering whether I would do Brutus and the Collins family the honour of being one of his godfathers.

I thought Mrs Collins was making another one of her Collins in-house jokes, because anyone with even a tiny bit of religious education knows that animals don't have souls – except of course in the Buddhist religion where everything has a soul. I knew this because earlier that day I'd been doing a bit of research on religions down at the Internet cafe for an assignment on Religious Tolerance (while hoping like crazy to bump into Regina) and I had discovered that Buddhists believe that they start off quite low down the food chain. Only if they behave themselves do they get to be reincarnated as a higher species – if you are a dutiful dung beetle in one life you might come back as the Queen of England in the next.

It seemed my mother had also started taking a keen interest in the religion because the two emails from her that were waiting in my Inbox were full of how aligning the four noble truths with best business practice could help me create good karma and a reincarnated bottom line.

While I was meditating over her wisdom I suddenly felt a breeze on the back of my neck. And then there was this annoying blowing sound in my ear. I looked up from my keyboard and turned around. It was Regina. She pursed her lips and blew at me again, full in the face. Her breath smelled like peanuts. 'You were looking so hot, really hot, Red. So, I thought you needed to be cooled down,' she said.

I touched my face and under my hand it grew hotter as the flush zoomed up my neck. Embarrassed, I jumped up from my seat, knocking my can of Coke onto the keyboard.

The rest of the Internet cafe looked up from their screens and said things like 'shush' and 'forGodsakes', while me and Regina tried to stifle our snorts of laughter as we mopped up the mess. By then the Internet cafe manager was making moves in our direction, so I threw my stuff in my backpack and shut down my mail. 'Come, let's get out of here,' Regina said.

I paused for just one moment as I thought of the advice Pops had given me a few nights before about redheads and black knickers. Just for one moment. Then I decided bugger it and allowed Regina to drag me by the hand out of the cafe, past the growling manager (who'd always said we were not to be 'doing beverages' at our terminals).

Then we were on the street. My hand was hot in Regina's and I found myself panting in short breaths as we ran along the pavement. My heart felt like it was going to burst out of my mouth as we ran.

We crossed the road to the beach and I stripped off down to my swimming shorts, which I had started wearing craftily under my jeans for just in case.

Regina excused herself and went to use the changing room. When she came out she looked like someone who was undergoing an initiation rite or going to war. She had covered herself in sunscreen so thick it was like paint, but the thing that really smashed my heart into the tiniest of pieces that nobody, not even an antique vase restorer or an Olympic puzzle champion, would ever have been able to reassemble was her swimming costume. She was wearing the same swimming costume as Grace Foxcroft. Well, not exactly the same one of course – Regina didn't know Grace then (and even if she had, Grace was three times Regina's size) – but something very similar. It was one of those that had a skirt attached – like something a ballerina would wear – and Regina's collarbones stuck out so that the costume kind of sagged on her chest. When I looked at Regina in this saggy costume I could hardly breathe.

We lay on the sand for a while, so that we could get warmed up by the sun before taking on the Indian Ocean, and Regina did this thing where she burrowed under the sand with her foot until her toes caught mine. At first I squealed like a girl's bikini when I thought it was a sand snake but I soon got the hang of it.

We swam for a bit and then Regina showed me how to body surf. 'Take the wave as it curls. Ride it, Red!' was what she yelled at me each time I got dumped on the beach with a mouthful of sand.

When we came out the water Regina flopped down on some lady's towel by mistake and I had to drag her off to our spot a bit further down the beach. Regina said she was hopeless without her glasses, as blind as a bat. When she said this her eyes flickered sightlessly at me and she gave this funny half shrug like she didn't care, but I could see that she did. At that very moment I wanted to fight and kill anyone who had ever brought on that look; anyone who had ever caused Regina pain. I wanted to put my towel around her and protect her forever.

It was later on that day – as Mrs Collins was making her wacky request for me to do them the honour of becoming Brutus' godfather – that I recalled the way Regina and I had frolicked in the waves that morning. I wondered if Regina had been baptised or whether her soul like Brutus's was in danger of returning as a Buddhist grasshopper. It was no joking matter and I took Mrs Collins' request to see her beloved Brutus baptised to heart and agreed.

Mrs Collins said that Father Christopher had agreed to do the christening at the Collins' residence the very next day. They'd wanted to invite everyone from the Village to attend straight after the Sunday service, as was the tradition in the Church of England, but Father Christopher had cautioned against the full monty. 'He told us that a lot of people wouldn't understand our convictions that animals also have souls and go to heaven, just like you and me, Randolph,' Mrs Collins said. 'Many people are still too stuck in the old ways.'

In any case, Mr Collins was very poorly, so a quiet christening during the week it was going to be. I was to be one of the godfathers while Mr and Mrs Collins were the other two godparents. I'd been chosen because of my special relationship with Brutus and also because I'd been christened in the Church of England – meaning that the promises I would make on behalf of Brutus (that he would live a good and Christian life) would be viewed as a serious commitment from a member of the Anglican community.

The next day I waited outside the Entertainment Hall where Father Christopher usually held the multi-denominational service for people of the Christian faith. It happened once a month on the Sunday after the monthly Bingo evening. Pops always said that there were a lot more people at the Bingo evening than at the church service, but I suppose that is just the way people are – always taking their chances.

Father Christopher walked with me to Number 87 and on the way he told me that what he was doing was really against his better judgement. If the Pope or the Archbishop or even Mr Etienne Groenewald, the Village manager, were to find out that he was christening dogs on the premises it would be tickets for him. But he also told me that he felt as though he had no choice. There he had been, a week earlier, having a confab with Mr and Mrs Collins about funeral arrangements (on account of Mr Collins being so poorly and it being only a matter of time before he shuffled off) when Mr Collins had said that after D-Day he would wait upstairs for Mrs Collins and Brutus – so that they could negotiate their way past the pearly gates together as a family.

Father Christopher had foolishly mentioned that he doubted Brutus would be joining them because of the fact that animals didn't have souls. And that was it. Mr and Mrs Collins had threatened to leave the church and find a more accommodating religion unless Brutus was christened – the more accommodating religion in question being the one where this Pentecostal minister chap had baptised his racehorse.[7]

'So it was a toss up between losing two beautiful souls or making a small compromise,' Father Christopher said. 'I know I can rely on your discretion, Randolph. We will keep it between the four of us – oh, and Brutus as well. He's not going to give the game away. I just don't want to be wasting my time christening all the blasted animals in this place.'

I looked at Father Christopher and I didn't like what I saw. He had a dimple right in the middle of his chin which made it look like a bum.[8] It was pretty disgusting. So was he. He was the kind of bloke other chaps hesitate about sharing a bottle of Coke with, because you know he's going to backwash something horrible into it. Just plain dodgy.

I knew, because Mrs Smythe had told me the night before (when Pops had sent me over to her place to change the light bulb in her bathroom), that Father Christopher lived a very good life courtesy of the bequests he received from the residents – people he sucked up to in the last couple of weeks before they kicked the bucket. It was also well known, Mrs Smythe had informed me, that Mr Collins had a very generous disposition. So I was fully up to date on Father Christopher and how he relied on the generosity of people like Mr Collins, and I knew that he was less concerned with saving souls and more interested in keeping his cash flow healthy.

_____

[7] It had made front page news in *The Herald*, Port Elizabeth's morning newspaper.

[8] The piece of anatomy, not the bum who drinks and sleeps on the pavement.

At any rate, me and Father Christopher reached the house and the christening went off smoothly. Mr and Mrs Collins weren't taking any chances. There was no gentle sprinkling of the water, oh dear, no. They went for total immersion, just to be on the safe side. They put Brutus in one of the metal tubs they had used to keep the booze cold for their wedding anniversary and they filled it with water and dog shampoo – Brutus was due his monthly bath, after all.

Father Christopher said the appropriate things through clenched teeth and I patted Brutus hard on the head to try and keep him from jumping out of the tub because he hated having his bath. I managed to restrain him until the deed was done and then I let him have his way with Father Christopher. There is nothing worse that the smell of wet dog, it must be said.

But when I left Number 87 with a Tupperware of christening cake under my arm, I bumped into a posse of residents making a beeline for the Collins' home. They were carrying cats and budgies in cages (the budgies in the cages, not the cats) and pulling their dogs on leads. One even had a pair of goldfish in a bowl. And they had the radiant look of the newly converted on their faces.

Looking at them I knew that the Collins' metal tub and Father Christopher were going to be kept very busy for the next few months. I also knew I could always rely on Mrs Smythe to spread a secret.

Things I Know:

Popping your zits
before a big date is a
serious no-no

7

the SPOON INCIDENT

Regina Versagel, or Reg to all her friends, was coming to lunch. I had finessed this when I was down at the Internet cafe, sending off my second assignment essay for the week. The topic was Cloning: Is it a good or a bad thing?

Me and Pops thought it was a very, very good thing indeed. Imagine being able to clone Halle Berry. One for me, one for Themba and one for Buster. Oh, and one for James Bond, of course. That would be a Halle of a thing, it must be said.

Pops said he would have settled for a new liver for my grandmother, cloned from the softest, tiniest piece of skin from her inner thigh. Then she wouldn't have slipped off gently into that good night and could have gone boogying with him at the Village's Summer Ball.

On my way out of the Internet cafe, I bumped into Regina – to be honest, I had hung around for about six hours and then pretended I didn't see her when she walked through the door. Regina was sweating like a horse and her hair was all pulled back into an elastic. She told me she'd been at her kick-boxing class, which was why she was so hot and sweaty. I couldn't look at her when she said 'so hot and sweaty'. It made me feel a bit nervous.

After sharing my views with her regarding the cloning of Sean Connery – like when Sean got a bit long in the tooth, they wouldn't have had to keep chopping and changing the Bond actors, they could have just made a younger version (it would have been a blast) – I told Regina how Pops was really a Jamie Oliver clone because he cooked like the TV foodie. One thing led to another and then, suddenly, she was coming to Saturday lunch. You can understand why I appreciated Buster and his expertise on Bond Movies so much. It really made things happen.

As soon as I told Pops what I had done, he decided that he was going to throw what he called a lunch party. A lunch party (as opposed to just lunch) was a function where you invited people who stayed on and on and ended up eating the lunch leftovers for supper. One thing led to another and within a few hours it seemed like everybody else was coming to Saturday lunch too – the whole Village wanted to meet 'Randolph's little friend'.

Pops never did things by half measures. He was an all or nothing kind of guy. So for the next couple of days he chained himself to the kitchen stove and played his entire Madonna collection. Every now and then he'd put his head around the door and shout things like 'a litre of cream' or 'fresh basil' or 'anchovies – the good ones not the ones in tins' and I'd tootle off down the road to the supermarket and get him whatever ingredient he wanted.

I was glad Pops was all excited about things. The previous week, when we had been working on the cloning essay, he'd seemed to get a bit low and had spent a few afternoons lying on his sleeper couch on the stoep snoozing and lolling about.

The deal was that Pops would do the food if I would handle the decor and the ambience, so I spent several hours rearranging things to ensure that the right energy would circulate over lunch.

According to the feng shui principles, one should never have a chime with four dangly bits – the Chinese character for four is very similar to the Chinese character for death. So while Pops didn't have a chime, or a death wish, I added a fifth dangly bit to his mobile of old driftwood that was positioned above the dining room table.

Having made sure that the chi could flow freely, I thought it wouldn't hurt to try and tip the odds in my favour, as it were. A few days earlier, when I had been browsing in a shop close to the Internet cafe (which I had been chucked out of under suspicion of being a potential hacker, given the amount of time I spent there), I had bought a little statue which people in Thailand called Pu-Tai – or the Laughing Buddha. This small chap, who has the tummy of a pregnant elephant, is supposed to bring happiness, good luck and plenitude. I put him on the side table with Pops' pot plant and a bowl of water to attract luck and positive energy.

Apart from this, I had my hands full with trying to decide what to wear. It's a funny thing really, most mornings I got up and chucked on the cleanest, least-creased thing I could find, but what I was going to wear to the lunch party had become a bit of an issue and it was taking up quite a lot of my time. I finally decided on black denims and a white T-shirt. Or maybe the blue denims and the white T-shirt ...

At any rate, the big day arrived and I got my dog-walking chores over fast. Brutus made a magnificent dump on the pathway, which I skilfully managed to shovel under Mrs Dodge's Shasta daisy bush (bugger the scooper: no time, no time). And then I made sure Mrs Vera Jacobson's bottled-up Jack Russel (JR) did his business in double quick time by feeding him a packet of Vienna sausages. I had things to do. I couldn't dilly-dally with the hounds all day.

I had taken JR on as a client after bumping into Mrs Jacobson while walking Brutus one morning. Mrs Jacobson said all JR's brothers and sisters had been squashed and eaten at birth and JR was sadly lacking a young role model (aka me). She would compensate me for my time, of course. With JR and Brutus it was just two walks a day. Not a train smash.

After each walk I would chat to Mrs Jacobson about JR's progress over a few cups of tea and some biscuits. And sometimes she would show me her photograph albums. But that day I told her some other time. I had to run.

I showered twice and tried to resist popping the juicy

chorb on my chin. That's the thing with zits; you think if you squeeze them they will disappear but they just get bigger and uglier and juicier. And even though you know it, you still squeeze them. So eventually I gave in and squeezed the thing. Then I showered again, hoping to calm it down.

After I was done in the shower I slipped into a pair of khaki trousers and a powder-blue T-shirt. I was trying for the metrosexual look, but it wasn't working, so I changed powder-blue for plain white. A bit safer.

Everyone arrived early. 'Where is she? Where is she?' Grace Foxcroft whispered until I told her it was only half past eleven and Regina was expected at one o'clock.

Meanwhile Felicity Foxcroft took one look at my face and dragged me off to the bedroom. She whipped out a bottle of stuff from her make-up bag and started dabbing it on my face. She spent a lot of time on the chin area.

Ten minutes later Mrs Smythe arrived. She sniffed when she saw Grace because she thought Pops liked Grace better and she wanted to be Pops' special friend. I had figured this all out on my own without the benefit of women's intuition because Mrs Smythe always said mean things about Grace.

Mrs Smythe went through to the kitchen to see if she could lend Pops a hand. She told Pops that she was relieved he hadn't cooked anything too spicy, like curry. She didn't like curry or anyone who ate curry for a living.

This was another thing I had learned about Mrs Smythe. She didn't like most people – people who had darker skin than her and who didn't speak English as a first language. I could never quite get a handle on Mrs Smythe's contradictory views. She simply adored her maid (darker than her – but one of the family) and was crazy about the Chinese lady at the takeaway (didn't do much English but made divine noodles). When I had asked Pops about it he'd said that Mrs Smythe suffered from something called Cognitive Dissonance, which was an uncomfortable feeling caused by holding two contradictory ideas simultaneously. He'd added that it wasn't catching if you kept your mind open and got out more.

While I was folding the serviettes (cloth not paper) into swan shapes, Mrs Collins telephoned. She said she and Mr Collins were sad they couldn't be with me on this special day, but Mr Collins was feeling especially poorly. But best of luck anyway with the lunch, dear. They had sent a flower arrangement for the table and a box of After Eight chocolates for coffee after dessert. They were like that, the Collinses, always thinking of others. There were a couple of dozen more phone calls after that from people wishing me well. Everyone was holding thumbs for me.

Grace asked me, 'Where is she? Where is she?' three more times. And then, finally, she arrived.

Everyone stood around Regina and me and stared until I realised that I had to say something, so I opened my mouth and said, 'May I introduce ...' And then for some reason I got so nervous I couldn't say it.

'Yes, Randolph dear?' Grace said encouragingly.

And I said: 'May I introduce ... Vegina Rersagel.'

There was a horrible silence and I felt, as Buster would say, my heart had fallen all the way through my nought. I looked at Regina and she was shaking. She could hardly talk she was laughing so much. 'You are so dead, Gandolph Roodenough,' she said.

Then we were all laughing a bit hysterically and I could see that everything was going to be okay.

The lunch passed in a blur. Everyone stared at me and Regina, like we were something they hadn't seen before or maybe something they remembered from a time long, long ago when their breath didn't smell like old takkies and Lucky Packet sweets.

When they weren't staring, Mrs Smythe laughed too loudly at practically everything Regina said. Grace told Regina thirteen times that she had lovely hair and Felicity asked her about ninety questions. She was like one of those machines you use to shoot balls over the net when you practice your tennis. Questions like: 'Do you have any other friends who are boys? Why? Do you also have lunch with other boys who are friends? Alone?' Things like that.

I was about to intervene when Felicity asked Regina for her telephone number. She did it just like that, so sweet and casual, and not like she'd been spending the duration of the lunch trying to pluck up the courage. She didn't need to say something like, 'I seem to have lost my phone number. May I borrow yours?' (a line that Themba swears by). Felicity just said, 'What's your telephone number, Regina?' As cool as a killer.

Regina recited those magic numbers and I spent the next five minutes trying to finger-paint them with tomato sauce onto a serviette under the table while Felicity carried on with her ninety questions and Pops gazed at her – not at Felicity, at Regina. He only had eyes for my girl. Every now and then, when he caught her eye, he winked at her the way Pops winked, with both eyes closed and his face all scrunched up.

My girl handled them all beautifully. She discussed the number of raisins you needed to put into a bobotie with Pops (a whole packet) and the best kind of fish to braai (yellowtail – never hake). She helped Felicity wash the dishes and didn't mind telling Grace the same thing three times over. She was a big hit with everybody, it must be said.

But the thing I noticed most about our conversations was that I didn't talk about the Bond Movies once. Regina and I found lots of other stuff to talk about. Interesting stuff – like the best way to take the hurt out of blue bottle stings and how to tell if a melon is really tasty before you cut it. And quite a lot of it I'd learned from Pops and the others at the Village. Not expert stuff, you understand, but Regina seemed quite turned on by it all.

No one wanted to go home so Felicity suggested playing a game. There were too many for Scrabble and Regina suggested Spoons. It's a silly card game where you have to collect four of the same kind of card and you have one spoon short of the number of players at the table. When you have four of the same card you take a spoon off the table, but you carry on playing until people notice a spoon is missing. Then they take a spoon until there are two people left without a spoon and when they notice they fight over the last spoon. It's a gas of a game it must be said and everybody laughs and falls all over the place.

I was sitting next to Regina and I watched her closely. When I saw her slyly reaching out for a spoon I reached for the same one. We had to be very quiet as we tried to get the spoon away from each other so no one noticed. Me and Regina did a lot of soft hand fumbling. And as we did this my chest closed up until it felt like I was having an asthma attack.

Later, in round five, Regina had four of a kind again, so she took a spoon. I noticed immediately and I took a spoon too and so did Mrs Smythe and Felicity. We played on merrily, winking at each other and waiting for Grace and Pops to realise what was happening. Finally Grace looked up and caught Regina's wink. Howling at Pops she took the last spoon. She was really laughing hard, because Pops was hopeless and this was the fifth time she'd caught him out.

Pops looked at Grace and the weirdest expression came over his face. It was twisted into a scared, angry snarl. 'Why are you laughing at me?' he said, grabbing the spoon out of Grace's hand. 'You're laughing. Do you think I'm a fool?'

So, of course, Grace laughed harder and everyone laughed with her because we all thought Pops was pulling our legs. But then Pops got up and stormed into my/his bedroom and he didn't come out again.

It wasn't a big train smash because Grace forgot about it after three minutes and Mrs Smythe thought that this sort of meanness was perfectly normal behaviour – her being such a toxic sort of a person – and Felicity had been experimenting with cocktails made from Red Bull and Pops' home brew so she was way past noticing anything anyway.

We carried on playing until everyone left. Then Regina whispered to me, 'Hey, Red ...' I loved the way she called me Red! 'Is your Pops okay? He looked really upset.'

I said, 'Sure, Reg, he's just a big kidder.'

But Pops didn't come out of the bedroom and I had to sleep on the stoep, where I did a lot of thinking about Pops because it was really hard to get some sleep on that lousy sleeper couch.

One of the things I thought about was that the Pops I knew was a really good sport. He laughed harder at himself than anyone else. So who was the spoilsport playing Spoons with me and Regina?

Things I Know:

Old People have
enormous nostrils

8

STOLEN APPLES

The rules governing pets and relatives were very strict at Nelson Mandela Gardens. Residents were entitled to keep cats – spayed and neutered – and dogs – ditto. They just had to make sure that they kept their dogs on a lead when they walked them and that they cleared up after them (the dogs) with a pooper scooper and a plastic bag.

When I lived in Malaysia, I was crazy for a pet. My mother said pets were smelly and too much trouble, but I was determined to have one that I could love and cuddle up to at night.

One morning, when I was at the market with my housekeeper (Mrs Pillai), buying some sugar, I found

Donald. He wasn't a cat or anything lame like that. He was a cockroach, and when I found him stuffing his face at the bottom of a bag of sugar I knew he should be mine.

The thing about cockroaches is that they are quite remarkable in their little ways. Cockroaches fart every fifteen minutes, making them, possibly, one of the biggest contributors to global warming (along with cows). They also have teeth in their stomachs and even if you chop off their heads they can survive for nine days before starving to death.

I kept Donald in a shoebox by my bed and some nights he would escape and I would awake to find him with his head resting on my cheek, nibbling away at my eyelashes. He was affectionate in that way.

In the end Donald escaped one time too many and met his end on the back of my mother's shoe. I didn't even get a chance to say goodbye.

The management at Nelson Mandela Gardens wouldn't have tolerated an exotic pet like Donald – dogs and cats and birds and fish were as far as they were prepared to go. And when it came to keeping relatives the rules were just as strict (minus the pooper scooper and leash) – a week at the most, but no long-term stays.

It made sense. The reason Nelson Mandela Gardens was a retirement village and not a cluster housing complex was because people of around-about the same age wanted to live together. Like-minded people with the same interests and needs. If they wanted to live with a bunch of middle-aged people or with teenagers or toddlers they would be hanging out with their families – not living in a retirement village. It was a lifestyle choice thing, right?

The Nelson Mandela Gardens Retirement Village provided houses for married couples and singles. If you were the former you got a house with two bedrooms and if you were part of the latter you got a house with a single bedroom. Even when your status changed, like when a better half checked out and went onto other things, as it were, the management couldn't take away your house with the two bedrooms. So some of the Sad Singles, who had moved in with partners and lost them along the way, lived in splendour with their second bedrooms. Like Mrs Smythe. Poor compensation, but still, it was better than nothing, hey?

The most envied state was to retain your partner and have the two bedrooms, but second best was to be a Sad Single with a second bedroom. That way you could spend the year telling everyone that a son or daughter was coming to stay for Christmas 'in the spare room'. And when they didn't pitch, you could start telling the same story all over again the following year.

Pops told me there had been this case a few years earlier of a couple who had applied for a house at the Village but although the lady had moved in no one had ever seen her husband. It had caused quite a stir and sparked all sorts of conspiracy theories about his reclusive behaviour – he was mad, he was being kept prisoner, he was ill, he was badly disfigured, he was just shy, he was ugly and shy, he was an alien, he was a mafia don, he was an escaped prisoner, he was a Nigerian drug dealer.

The various options kept everyone at the Village in happy

debate for many months until it was discovered (by the Rules Committee, not the Entertainment Committee) that the lady's husband had passed on three years earlier. Everyone was so mad (probably because they had nothing to talk about any more) that they booted her out of the Village.

I think the reason they made an exception and allowed me to spend three months with Pops was that Pops had one of the houses with only one bedroom, so it wasn't like we were going to be all that comfortable. Another reason was perhaps because Pops helped the Sad Singles all the time – with their leaky plumbing and light bulbs (as well as braaiing their drumsticks). He was also just one of those people that other people didn't want to hate too much, even if they did have a lot of time on their hands.

Pops gave me his bedroom because in any case he liked to sleep on the stoep all year around – spring through winter. It was an enclosed stoep, but during summer, when it wasn't too windy, Pops opened the sliding windows. It was like he was sleeping outside, he said. Well, almost as good as. He got woken up by the birds that came to eat the apples he hung for them under the pepper tree over the bird bath. This was the best way to be woken up. No alarm, or anything like that, just the birds. You couldn't ask for anything more.

Old people are very light sleepers. That's something else I learned while I was staying with Pops. Anything can wake them. Not like young people. For example, I used to be able to sleep through two alarm clocks and my housekeeper yelling in my ear. But after being at the Village for three weeks I think I started to pick up Pops' sleeping habits because the slightest sound woke me. And sleeping on the stoep while Pops did a sulk in my bed didn't help matters.

I got woken up the morning after Regina came for lunch by the birds in the bird bath. They were going mad. Screaming mad. Pops must have heard them too because he came rushing out in his boxer shorts (silky with red-and-purple hearts) with his bum practically hanging out. He had been unusually anxious about the birds for the past few days because there was this nest that had gone up and Pops had been trying to keep Max (the mean cat from Number 52) from eating the chicks.

But it wasn't too serious – or at least that's what we thought at first – it was just that something had come along and eaten all the apples.

Pops said he suspected it was Ozzie Gibson from Number 76. He was in his late eighties and had gone a bit soft in the head – his brain was a bit like a finger biscuit that had been soaked in milk. He'd always had a thing for apples, Pops told me, so maybe he just couldn't resist the fresh, crunchy ones that he had hung out for the birds. Pops said all of this in a matter-of-fact way but I could see that he was a bit worried.

I got me up some courage and telephoned my Regina – I had decided that I would only call her when I had something of significance to tell her. I told her about the little mystery of the apples and we discussed it at great length. I always felt I had to have a talking point, as it were, to keep her interested.

Talking points are quite a thing with old people. They leaped on them like rugby players in a scrum when they found one. Oh, they'd say, their eyes matching the shape

of their mouths, now *that's* a good taking point. And then
it would do the rounds until it got completely worn out and
they would have to find another point worth talking about.

I promised Regina I'd call her as soon as something new
developed and perhaps she could pull in and we could have
a face-to-face discussion and do some brainstorming. And
then play Snap. My voice splintered as I suggested it. Snap.

Regina said absolutely. She'd ask her mother.

I walked around the Village until I found myself outside
the Entertainment Hall. I decided to do some pull-ups on
the old plane tree. If I could just do thirty, Regina's mother
would be say yes and she would be able to come over and I'd
have the guts to ask her to the Summer Ball on Saturday.

If something was going to happen between Regina and
me, it was going to be at the Summer Ball. You know, when
lights are low, bodies are moving slowly to the music and the
ambience is perfect. I would have run a marathon on my
knees if it would have helped my chances.

Sixteen, Seventeen, Eighteen ... And then I was flat on
my back because some old spoiler called Felicity Foxcroft
had pulled me down off the branch, saying that if I carried
on that way I'd get a hernia.

The next morning I heard Pops yelling for me. I was having
the most amazing dream about how the beach sand had
stuck to the suntan lotion on Regina's knees and by the
time I made it to the stoep, a hairy brown arse was already

disappearing into the hydrangea bush. Pops assured me that it was not old Ozzie. Not that I knew why Pops was so certain, but I decided I was going to take his word for it. Sometimes a person can hear too much detail.

Pops grabbed his walking stick and we charged for that hydrangea bush. Pops was yelling, 'Wah! Wah! Wah!' like a war cry and swinging the stick. I was a few steps behind him, trying not to notice the bulging blue veins on the backs of his legs, sticking out from those silky heart-covered boxers. There was something about those veins that made my tummy feel weird.

Pops was about to lay into that hydrangea bush when I saw a small hairy hand sticking out the one side and a long hairy tail flicking around on the other. I was just about to shout, 'Whoa-whoa, Pops!', when Mrs Glenda Klingman from Number 32 beat me to it and shrieked so hard that Pops dropped his stick.

Me and Pops watched as she dived into that hydrangea bush and came out with a monkey. She covered its face with kisses, asking it if it was okay, behaving like it was a small child, not just a hairy monkey.

Pops invited Mrs Klingman and her monkey to come inside and she told us the whole story. Gregory (the monkey) had belonged to her son Miles, who'd been killed in a car accident two weeks earlier. Following the tragedy, she'd taken custody of Gregory.

Pops explained to her gently that she was breaking the Village Rules by keeping a monkey. And she, more than most, should know this because she was on the Rules Committee.

Mrs Klingman looked at Pops like he was a complete weirdo. 'Yes, of course, but I'm the only family he's got,' she said. 'He's my grandchild.'

It was a funny thing actually because Mrs Klingman and Gregory did in fact look like they were related – she had this really hairy face, small brown stones for eyes and her teeth were kind of ground down to little mielie stumps. She also had these very large nostrils. Though, to be honest, I'd noticed during my stay at the Village that large nostrils were an old person thing. I suppose it's owing to all those years of digging and picking that people do in the course of their lives. Since observing this alarming effect I'd been trying to limit myself to a good pick every couple of days.

At any rate, Pops told Mrs Klingman that of course he understood. Then he tried a different approach: 'Glenda,' Pops said to Mrs Klingman, 'Glenda, my dear, you know the rules about long stays. Family members can stay for only a week, no longer.'

Mrs Klingman narrowed her pebbly eyes at Pops. Then she narrowed them at me. 'Randolph's with you for three months,' she said. 'If the Rules Committee can make an exception for Randolph, they can make an exception for another young boy.'

I was just about to point out the obvious to Mrs Klingman – Gregory was a hairy monkey, not a little boy (anyone who hadn't completely lost their marbles could see this) – when Pops gave me a nod that I knew meant shut up.

A little later on in the day Pops explained things a bit to me. It wasn't that Mrs Klingman was stupid, or even nuts, she was just dealing with grief. It was one thing losing a spouse, it was quite another when you lost a child, he said.

Most people sort of accept that you can't live forever. You're going to get old and sick and then one day you're going to cross the river and take a dirt nap. That's the normal way to go if you're lucky. But sometimes things happen that shouldn't. Like you're murdered by a lunatic, or your parachute doesn't open, or you get smacked on the head by a coconut, or you're a guy called Miles who gets hit coming out of your driveway by a drunk driver on your way to buy some milk and bread, leaving behind a pet monkey called Gregory.

People deal with grief in different ways. Buster told me that he'd read that in the new James Bond movie James can't sleep. He's lost weight, drinks a fierce amount of alcohol without getting drunk and is bent on revenge. That's how he deals with losing his true love Vesper Lynd.

Pops said Mrs Klingman wasn't hitting the bottle or bent on revenge, she was just taking a journey through the five stages of grief from denial to acceptance.

I thought of the time me and Regina lay on the beach and the way her toes had wriggled under the ball of my foot like a vicious snake. I recalled the way I'd made her burp when my toes had found the ticklish spot behind her knee. Then I pictured a time when I would never be able to play snake with Regina again. I imagined her telling me she was washing her hair and couldn't come to the Summer Ball with me on Saturday. I felt pretty rotten as I thought these things. I couldn't imagine how Mrs Klingman must have been feeling; probably a trillion times worse.

Pops had advised Mrs Klingman that she should perhaps keep Gregory's existence under wraps a little. But she couldn't, of course, and when Gregory was discovered being over affectionate to Mr Blackie Swartz's mean cat Max (bite marks on the scrotum), the Rules Committee held an emergency meeting and ruled that Gregory had to go (the one dissenting view from the committee coming from Mrs Klingman). Either that or Mrs Klingman had to go and she must take her hairy monkey with her.

Things went to stalemate. Mrs Klingman put her cupboards against the doors in her house and refused to come out. She was prepared for a lengthy siege, having stockpiled hundreds of tins of canned food in her garage in case South Africa went like Rhodesia. That's what Mrs Smythe said. Except I knew Mrs Klingman crept out with Gregory very early in the morning, even before the birds and Pops were up, because the apples were always chomped down to the string.

And in the evening Pops strung up some more – Golden Delicious, fresh and crunchy. He hung carrots and other fruits and vegetables up too. A growing boy needed a balanced diet, Pops said. But he didn't say it in a jokey voice or anything. He said it with a sigh.

Things I Know:

French food sucks,
big time

9

the ALARM

My friend Themba says that there are a million different ways a bloke can tell a chick that he digs her. Some guys do it with flowers – red roses for love, yellow for passion. Other guys do it with poetry and music.

The method of communicating your passion obviously differs according to where you live. It's a cultural thing. In Italy, for example, guys will chew lots of garlic and play the monkey organ outside of your window when you're trying to sleep. It's seen as a big turn-on. In Spain, blokes fight and kill bulls. And in parts of Africa, men give the father of the girl in question a herd of cows to signal their interest.

The animal kingdom also has courtship rules. Take

baboons for example. If a girl baboon likes a boy baboon she will wave her blue arse in his face. Cats and dogs signal their interest by peeing everywhere.

I wasn't crazy about killing bulls or waving my arse in Regina's face, so I asked Themba about something a little more romantic. He suggested I go French. If I considered France's contribution to romance – the French letter, the French kiss, the douche – it was surely obvious that there is no other country more romantic. Or so he said.

Later that afternoon I managed to find a French/English dictionary on one of the shelves in the lounge and it wasn't long before I was putting together phrases that captured the deep feelings I had for my girl. There was: I love you. You are beautiful. You smell like cinnamon. Will you be my girlfriend?

Getting the pronunciation right was causing me a few sweaty moments though. I wanted it to be perfect. It would be the first time – apart from with Halle Berry and Eva Green (aka Vesper Lynd) – that I would tell a girl that I loved her.

The next day I was over at the Collins' – collecting Brutus for his walk – when I happened to mention to Mrs Collins that I was trying to learn the language of love. It turned out that she had been to a finishing school in France when she was a young woman (where, incidentally, she had met Mr Collins) and said she remembered all the important bits of the language. She allowed me to spend the afternoon with her and Mr Collins, and while she fed me French delicacies – escargots (big lumps of rubbery garlic) and truffles (bits of black mould) – I told her over and over again that she was beautiful and smelled like cinnamon. Then we progressed to 'Your moustache tickles' and 'If you don't stop I'll scream and call the manager'.

Mr Collins lay dozing on the chaise lounge wrapped in a blanket, but when I got to the part about screaming and calling the manager his eyes fluttered at Mrs Collins and she winked at him. Then she let Brutus lick her buttery fingers and told him that he was a good dog, in French, and Brutus winked at her too.

Mrs Collins said that I was evidently naturally gifted at languages and perhaps we could progress to some complicated sentence structures. I tried, 'Will you be my date at the Summer Ball?', which was the thing that I most wanted to say to Regina.[9]

Mrs Collins said it was very charming of me to ask her, but she would be staying home with Mr Collins. But perhaps I could ask Regina?

I had, of course, been waiting for the perfect opportunity to ask her. She had been coming over to the Village the past couple of days after school and had taken a keen interest in some of my dog-walking clients, but whenever I had thought about asking her to the Ball my tummy cramped up and my voice shut down.

Regina had adopted a couple of the Sad Singles. She always made a point of playing cards with Felicity Foxcroft, who had included her in her intimate circle of friends (read three). I never figured out what bound these two together

---

[9] As I still hadn't managed to say this simple sentence to her in English, I was hoping to find some courage in the language of the guillotine.

as tight as Mrs Smythe's smile. Perhaps it was because both Regina's grandmothers had gone into the fertiliser business – and Felicity needed someone like Regina who wouldn't play her mean games and could smooth her jagged edges.

While I was perfecting the language of love on Mrs Collins, Mr Groenewald, the Village manager, came around to fix the Collins' buzzer. It had been faulty for a while and Mr Groenewald said he'd rather they were safe than sorry.

The Collins' buzzer was part of a Village-wide safety system that was used by all the residents. Every day between five and eight o'clock in the morning, Nelson Mandela Gardens had a security check-in routine. All the residents from the ninety houses had to press the buzzer on an intercom that connected their houses with Mr Groenewald's office to let him know that everything was fine and well.

But of course, if it was a married couple, then only one of them did it. Or they took it in turns to do it. Or they fought about who would do it. Because, let's face it, for many of them it was one of the big highlights of the day.

Most of the time it was a simple case of 'Good morning, Mr Groenewald, it's Mrs Rosemary Dearden here from Number 29. Everything is fine and well here. Have a nice day.' Though even this was a bit chatty because Mr Groenewald had a board in his office which lit up so he could see exactly who it was who was calling in. You didn't even have to say anything or tell him which house you were belling him from.

But some of the residents liked to talk a bit, so Mr Groenewald got to hear about how Mr Bradley Stutford had slept and how Mrs Clara Single and her poodle Princess planned to spend their day.

I could have told Mr Groenewald that part of their day would be spent with me. Mrs Single had offered me three times the going rate to drop JR and take on Princess as a client when I had initially declined her patronage due to fears of an over-hectic dog-walking schedule.

But I had managed to rejuggle some of my activities to accommodate her (same rate as the others) and after dropping off Brutus, I would walk Princess. Mrs Single said Princess had bad knees, so after five minutes of low intensity exercise I would spend the rest of our time-slot reading the newspaper to Mrs Single and discussing any talking points that might arise. My dog-walking duties were beginning to cut a swathe through my daily plans.

At any rate, Mr Groenewald was a nice guy, so he didn't mind nattering to all the residents for three hours every morning. The residents all liked him a lot and Mr Groenewald never went short of home-made rusks and owned more knitted bedspreads than an orphanage.

He was also a really friendly kind of guy, so if you were going shopping, or taking a walk, or going to the cinema – or whatever outing you were going on that involved leaving the Village – you could check in with Mr Groenewald to let him know you were going out. Just in case you forgot to come back or got lost, which happened to some of the residents – like Grace Foxcroft.

A lot of the ladies would buzz him and tell him that they were going to the hairdresser and then when they got back they might even swing past the office to let him know that they were home safe and sound. And Mr Groenewald always remembered to compliment them on their hair.

But when Mr Groenewald went on holiday the residents had to deal with his deputy, Mr Frik Bernardie. He was a miserable son of a gun, as Pops would say. He cut you off before you could even finish saying 'All is fine and ...' and he never ever chatted. Never. So everyone was always very pleased when Mr Groenewald came back from his holiday.

Mr Groenewald was also very discreet. He had to be in his line of work. I think he probably knew more about each of the residents than any other person in the Village (barring Mrs Smythe, who made it her business to know everything about everyone else's business). Mr Groenewald knew who hit the sherry bottle too hard and who had a gambling habit. He had become, to many of the residents, a kind of priest. He was someone who they could tell stuff to between five and eight o'clock in the morning and everyone felt that their secrets were safe with him.

When Mr Groenewald said, 'Not to worry, Mr Howard[10], next time you go to the shops I'll come with you and we can tell the manager that you took that box of Smarties by mistake,' Mr Howard didn't have to worry that his kleptomania would become hot news at the Village.

Mr Groenewald took his job very seriously and if one of the residents hadn't checked in by eight o'clock he was around at their house quicker than you could say 'heart attack in her bed' or 'fell getting out of the bath'.

If you had a real crisis, you could press the panic button

---

[10] Not his real name to protect his identity.

and it made the most horrible sound, like a car alarm, and then everyone in the Village knew that Number 14 (for instance) had a real crisis.

And even if Mr Groenewald was away from his office, like sleeping or overseeing the garden service or some maintenance work, he would hear the emergency siren and get over to the house in question right away (along with everyone else – who would have rushed over to see what was going on). It didn't happen very often, so when it did, it was something to get excited about, like when it rained.

I never got to make the check-in call. Pops always did it. It was easy as pie for him because the buzzer was right there on the stoep, and in any case Pops was always up by five o'clock and I never made it out of bed before nine. Unless there was a real crisis.

So there I was on Wednesday morning, dreaming about the colour of Regina's underwear (and not only were they black, but they had the hottest pink lace trim), when the emergency alarm went off. For a minute I thought I was back in Nairobi, where car alarms are as common a sound as birds, but then I realised that it was a real crisis and I was out of my bed and running for the front door.

I made it outside and saw that the sound was coming from Mrs Marjorie Denton's place (Number 46), which was two down from us at Number 42. It was easy to see this because there was a swarm of people outside her house and Mr Groenewald was pushing past them to her front door. He didn't look like his normal nice self though – he had this frown that had pulled his two enormous eyebrows down low over the bridge of his nose. To be honest, he looked a bit uptight.

Mr Groenewald used his skeleton key to enter Number 46 and then closed the door behind him. We all waited silently outside. Then, ten minutes later, Mr Groenewald opened the front door and left. Everybody was asking him if Mrs Denton was all right but he just nodded and grunted, so no one was any the wiser as to what had happened. Except I was acting as a guinea pig for Mrs Smythe later that morning – she was trying out a couple of chocolate cake recipes and wanted to know if the dark chocolate was as good as the nutty chocolate – and while I was at it, Mrs Smythe said, I might as well have some tea and a chat. So, because the topic was current, she told me about Mrs Denton.

Mrs Denton was a connoisseur of retirement villages. She had been in five of them over the past seven years (one in every major city in the country). Nelson Mandela Gardens was her fifth since Bloemfontein and after this her next stop would have to be East London. And after East London it would be Durban and then she would probably have to emigrate or die.

Mrs Smythe knew all of this from Miss Meisie Truter, who was a domestic worker who did for Mr Bernardie on Wednesdays (and Mrs Smythe on Thursdays) and who had overheard Mr Bernardie and Mr Groenewald discussing the Mrs Denton issue a couple of weeks back.

Mrs Denton was what retirement villages called a 'problem'. She had been a resident at the Village for three months and she was driving Mr Groenewald mad. At least four mornings a week she'd forget to check in and so he'd have to go around and make sure that everything was fine and well. Except when he got to her place she would have laid a table for breakfast and would be cooking him an egg, or percolating him a nice cup of coffee, and she would say to him, 'Oh, Mr Groenewald, how nice of you to pop in for breakfast!', or something like that – Meisie Truter didn't know the exact words.

'Pathetic, isn't it, the lengths these lonely widows will go to get some male company? Another slice of chocolate cake, Randolph dear?' Mrs Smythe said and I nodded, although I'd already had four slices.

Mrs Smythe poured me another cup of tea and carried on telling me about the Mrs Denton problem. These breakfasts four times a week were becoming a bit much for Mr Groenewald, so he'd been sending Mr Bernardie around to check on Mrs Denton, which had been driving Mrs Denton mad (because Mr Bernardie never sat down and always went away as soon as he saw that she was fine and well). 'Hence the panic button stunt this morning,' Mrs Smythe told me. 'She's determined to get poor Mr Groenewald's attention.'

I thought it was a jolly good thing Mrs Denton wasn't the president of the United States with access to that little red box – those itchy fingers couldn't be trusted with the future of the free world.

I left Mrs Smythe and headed off home. On the way I passed Mrs Denton's house and she was watering her roses. She called out to me that she needed a young pair of taste buds, so I went inside with her and tried her quiche.

While I was eating we talked about the Bond Movies and she showed herself to be quite well informed because she knew that Sean Connery had played Bond in six movies and Roger Moore in seven. It was the kind of knowledge that would have impressed Buster and I could see that Mrs Denton (call me Marjorie) was an intelligent and cultured woman.

Then Marjorie pointed out the photographs on top of her television set and told me about her two daughters and son (in Australia, Canada and Costa Rica), her two brothers (deceased) her five grandchildren (split between Australia, Canada and Costa Rica) and her husband Eric (deceased these past seven years). 'Then there's me. Just me,' she said, and her eyes locked onto mine and they weren't the eyes of some attention-seeking maneater. No. They were the eyes of the loneliest woman in the world (not that I knew all the lonely women in the world, but her eyes were the loneliest ones I'd ever seen).

So I ate some more quiche and then stayed to lunch and ate a fish pie and practised my French – telling Marjorie that she was beautiful and smelled like cinnamon (though I didn't ask her to be my date at the Summer Ball, because she might have said yes and then I'd have been stuffed).

By the time I made it home I was badly in need of a lie down – what with all the chocolate cake and quiche and fish pie. I felt bad as Pops always made a real effort at meal times, but there was no ways I was going to be able to eat another thing for at least ten years.

I didn't want to hurt Pops' feelings about eating other

people's food over his, so I told him I wasn't feeling so hungry on account of the fact I'd just been thrashing Felicity Foxcroft at Old Maid and I never felt hungry after exercise (white lie).

Pops looked at me all worried and said it wasn't a good sign. Young boys should always be hungry – especially after exercise – he said. But he wasn't feeling at all peckish so he wouldn't bother with lunch either and would wait for supper.

I told Pops, 'Okay, fine,' (in French), 'Goodbye' (in French) and went off to the bathroom to practice the language of love in front of the mirror. I asked the chap in the mirror if he would be my date at the Summer Ball and he said yes, he would love to, more than anything in the whole world.

I felt hot with courage. I would call Regina immediately. In ten minutes. Perhaps I'd ask her when I saw her tomorrow. If I managed to juggle five apples for ninety seconds without dropping one.

Later, when I came to think about it, I realised that this was the third lunch Pops had missed in the past week. He hadn't been getting up for breakfast either, not for the past two days. I wondered if he was feeling ill. Surely he would tell me in plain English if there was a problem. He would tell me, right?

And I wondered if Pops was checking in every morning with Mr Groenewald to tell him that all at Number 42 was fine and well. Just that he had lost his appetite. But there was no crisis. No real crisis at all.

Things I Know:

Grace Foxcroft
looks different with
eyebrows

10

the BEAUTY PARLOUR

The next morning me and Pops were off to the Beauty Parlour. Well, okay, it wasn't a real Beauty Parlour, just a bunch of students from the Angela Storm Beauty Academy in town who came to the Village on Thursdays to practise what they were learning. They set up in the Entertainment Hall and charged half price, or sometimes if one of the students was doing it for the first time, as it were, they didn't charge at all.

Practising on old people was sort of risk free, I suppose. It wasn't like if they over-did the eyebrow plucking it was going to make a helluva difference to how the oldies looked, right?

Young people, according to a classification determined by

Buster, are any persons the same age or younger than Halle Berry – who's a real cougar for over forty. The rest are all old. And all old people look pretty much the same to young people. They are wrinkled and speckled, and the females tend to have too much hair in the wrong places (upper lips, legs and underarms) while the males tend to have no hair (on their heads). That's what Buster says.

Themba says there's a damn good reason why old people are ugly. It's so they won't do it any more. Because if they did it as often as young people, they'd probably have heart attacks or do terrible damage to their joints or something. So it really is for their own good that they look the way they do.

I used to think that old people had it easy in the mornings. Like it must take about five seconds to get dressed and ready for the day. Because no one is going to be checking them out anyway, so it doesn't matter what they wear. Right?

Wrong. Something else I learned while staying at the Nelson Mandela Gardens Retirement Village is that old people are really, really vain. Way vainer than young people.

For example, one day Mrs Ida Garton (from Number 54) lost one of her front teeth, and because it was the weekend she couldn't get an appointment with a dentist, so she had to walk around for two days with a gap in the front of her mouth. Whenever she spoke to anyone she covered her mouth, like she had bad breath or something (which she did anyway, but she wasn't covering her mouth to be considerate).

I didn't get it because even when she forgot her gap, and gave her wide-mouthed smile, you could see that having a tooth wouldn't have made her a beauty queen for heaven's sakes. She was just the same either way.

Old people also spend a lot of time changing their clothes. Like two or three times a day – putting on something nice for the walk around the Village before lunch, then dressing down for Scrabble in the afternoon before dressing up again for a braai in the evening. They really do think that other people notice what they're wearing, when most people (young people like Themba and Buster) are of the view that old people could walk around naked for all they cared. Well, on second thoughts, maybe not. They should keep their clothes on. It would be pretty upsetting to see a bunch of old naked people flopping around the place, letting it all hang out.

But because old people like to look nice, the weekly Beauty Parlour visits were really popular with the residents. On a scale of one to ten, I would say that they ranked a big ten. Much more popular than the Friday visits from the Grade 6 kids from the school down the hill, who came and did their Life Orientation projects or Community Service or whatever it was they had to do to earn points for being caring and sensitive to the elderly. Those visits got an eight, I would say.

In fact, the Beauty Parlour was so popular that Pops and me had to book a couple of weeks in advance to make sure that we could get our treatments. And we booked for Grace and Felicity Foxcroft and Mrs Smythe as well. The usual gang.

Pops was having a pedicure and I had booked for a facial, even though I knew that if Themba or Buster ever heard about it I would have to emigrate to the moon – the capital of Thailand wouldn't be far enough away. But sometimes there are things that a guy has to do, and getting a facial was one of those things. Grace said it was a must-do for me so that I could be especially handsome for the Nelson Mandela Gardens Summer Ball. It was on Saturday. In two days' time. And if I could stop dashing to the toilet to throw up, I was going to call Regina Versagel to ask her to be my date.

We arrived at the Hall for our appointments like half an hour early. What is it with old people that they can never be late or on time? Don't they have something better to do?

The students from the Angela Storm Beauty Academy were still setting up but they looked very professional in their white lab coats. The only problem with the mobile Beauty Parlour was that it didn't score high on privacy. It wasn't like there were cubicles where you could have your treatments away from the enquiring eyes of other people (people like Grace and Felicity who were showing a really unhealthy interest in the state of my skin). I also got to know stuff about other people's treatments that, at the end of the day, I really would have preferred not knowing. For a start, I had to watch Pops get a pedicure.

If I had to list all the things that were wrong with Pops' feet, it would be as long as the list of names that Themba keeps of all the girls who've said 'No' to him in the last two years. Here are a few of Pops' foot ailments: athlete's foot, bunions, cracked heels, foot odour, fungus and ingrown nails. His feet were truly disgusting. And I am not exaggerating. I found myself feeling really bad for the young student who got Pops to practise on (Madelaine). I think she was fast realising that Beauty School wasn't as glam as her career guidance counsellor had promised.

It was like a major operation. Madelaine washed and dried Pops' feet and then used a razor blade to cut away all the cracked, horny bits of skin on his heels. Then she clipped his toe nails, trimmed his cuticles and pushed them back. She filed his nails and buffed, polished and painted them with clear varnish. She also plucked out the hair from the tops of his toes. And, finally, she spent a good ten minutes massaging his feet with oil that smelled like girls' deodorant.

At the end of it all Pops was delighted with his new feet, although if the truth be told I thought they looked pretty much the same as they had at the beginning – old and veined and bony.

It was my turn next and as Madelaine made ready to move on from Pops' feet to my face I started to feel even worse for her, because my list of facial problems was as long as Mrs Smythe's list of reasons for why Pops should like her better than Grace.

I'd done a fair amount of research down at the Internet cafe about the various treatments that could make a difference to a chap's skin and mentioned a couple in particular to Madelaine. One of them involved leeches. First you shave your skin and soak it in turpentine. Then, when the pain goes away, you cover your face in leeches and allow them to suck away at your zits – the ultimate acne treatment.

Madelaine said that the training at the Angela Storm Beauty Academy was pretty standard and that if I didn't mind she was going to stick with a normal facial. To be honest, I was relieved – it sounded less vomit-making than smearing my face with dried nightingale droppings (popular with Japanese geishas) or drinking my own urine (popular with Indian holy men).

I lay down on the stretcher bed (on loan from the mobile clinic which came on Wednesdays) and Madelaine put a towel around my hair. She then explained that there were three steps to a facial: massage, steaming and applying a mask. She was adding a fourth element which she called 'extraction'. It came after the steaming and just before the mask. 'It's when she deals with his spots,' Grace (who had suddenly appeared) told Pops.

Madelaine started by massaging this gel into my face. It felt sort of nice until I remembered that she had been handling Pops' feet a few minutes earlier.

When she was finished Madelaine said I must relax for twenty minutes under this machine like a hairdryer on a tripod which hissed hot steam onto my face.

While I took it easy, silently practising saying 'Will you be my date at the Summer Ball?' a couple of million times, Madelaine began on Grace's nails. Poor Grace, she'd been biting them since she was two years old, so there wasn't a lot to work with. They were paper-thin stubs and Madelaine said nail extensions were out of the question. They would fall off in minutes.

Grace got a bit tearful but it wasn't long before she cheered up again and settled for an eyelash tint. She asked for an eyebrow tattoo as well – her eyebrows had been plucked to extinction in the early Sixties and she needed some permanent ones tattooed onto the skin. After all, her eyebrows were the frames to the windows of her soul. That's what Grace said.

Madelaine couldn't deal with all of this and said she was just a first year – eyebrow tattoos were only on the curriculum in the third year – but she'd draw them in with an eyebrow pencil.

After doing what she could for Grace, Madelaine refocused on my face and performed the 'extraction'. I wasn't really sure about this part. I mean, there was something a bit weird about some perfect stranger popping your zits with a couple of cotton buds. Well, not a couple of cotton buds. Madelaine finished half a packet on me.

When Madelaine was finally finished I relaxed some more under a mask of soothing cream, repeating the Summer Ball mantra – this time in French – while Mrs Smythe had her nails done. She got the acrylic nail extensions in Purple Passion (just because Grace couldn't have them). Heaven knows how she thought she was going to wash the dishes or pick her nose.

After the whole thing was over, I looked in the mirror and saw a very red pizza staring back at me. It was my face. Madelaine assured me that everything would 'calm down' after a couple of days and I really hoped she was right and it wasn't more than a couple of days because the dance was happening in a couple of days. Two.

While the others finished their treatments I called Regina and plunged into that battered and bruised French phrase. 'Will you be my date at the Summer Ball?'

Regina put the phone down on me.

I walked ten metres on my hands along the path outside the Hall without falling over and called her back.

She said she was awfully glad to hear from me. Some drunk Frenchman had been trying to sell her a summer package holiday over the phone. I said (very fast) that I was wondering whether she could help me hang the Summer Ball for the decorations. Then I asked a bit more slowly if she would have a moment to offer her expertise in balling me while hanging out this summer.

I was on the point of hanging myself when Regina said she would love to go as my date to the Summer Ball. My tummy felt like I had swallowed a toilet full of leech juice and nightingale poop, but somehow I managed to croak 'cool' before I cut the call and joined everyone else where they were waiting for me at the front of the Hall.

There was certainly something to be said for a bit of pampering. On our walk home I looked at the ladies, and while they really didn't look a lot different, I could see they were on top of the world. They felt beautiful.

Pops, however, wasn't feeling beautiful at all. He had this terrible expression on his face and he was holding his head. He said he had the mother of all headaches and must lie down. It was like, he said, he'd drunk a bottle of mampoer – and then some. His brain felt like it was exploding.

I didn't answer Pops at first. I was thinking about important things. I was thinking about my face. I was thinking about me and Regina's first proper date at the Summer Ball in two days time. I was thinking about whether I could convince the Entertainment Committee to make it a masked ball if my face didn't calm down.

I didn't want to think about Pops at all. Not about his feet. Or his lack of appetite and strange behaviour. Or his headache. I told him Madelaine hadn't started her reflexology module yet so she may have pushed too hard on a pressure point without knowing. Feet can be very sensitive if handled wrongly.

As I said this I caught the expression on Grace's face. She raised her scary Joan Crawford pencil eyebrows at me and gave me a look from underneath her blacker than black eyelashes that said she knew – as I knew – that I was talking codswallop.

Things I Know:

New shoes give
you blisters

11

the SUMMER BALL

Pops said there was no way in heck that I was taking a girl to the dance dressed like *that*. *That* was a pair of black jeans and a black T-shirt Themba had given me for my birthday. It said *Spank me. I've been a bad girl.*

Pops looked at me and shook his head. 'Who *is* this Themba?' he asked.

I started to tell Pops but he said he didn't really want to know *who* Themba was. He just couldn't believe that a thinking person would give such a thing to a friend and that his grandson would ever dream of wearing it.

Pops isn't big on slogan T-shirts. I haven't actually met an old person who is. Themba says it's because most of them can't see very well so they find them intimidating. I didn't think Pops was intimidated by anything, and he wasn't the prudish sort either. In fact, Pops had a tattoo of a butterfly on his left buttock (which he got in his glory days before he met my grandmother). No, slogan T-shirts were a taste thing with Pops.

So that morning me and Pops were off on what he called a shopping expedition, to buy me something classy to wear to the Nelson Mandela Gardens Summer Ball. However, to be honest, I wasn't sure if there was much point as half my face was flaking off and the other half had spawned a crop of genetically modified zits that looked like boils.

We took like an hour to get to the shops ten blocks away. I'm not exaggerating; Pops was driving in slow motion. He stopped at every robot for five minutes and only got going again if someone hooted behind him. And when we eventually got to the mall, Pops said he wasn't in the mood to parallel park, so he took an easy parking spot a ten minute hike from the entrance.

Pops had been doing a lot of things slow that morning. Maybe it was an old people thing. I'd often heard the residents at the Village saying things like, 'I'm not going to rush into it ...' or 'I'm going to take things slowly ...' Perhaps Pops was taking things slow that day.

Inside the mall we made a beeline for a gentleman's clothing establishment called Markham. Pops told me that it had been called Markhams when he was a man about town but had since lost the 's' in a rebranding exercise. But despite losing a letter in its name, he assured me that it was still synonymous with the best in men's fashion. I hoped Regina would be impressed.

We walked out with a linen suit for me. In charcoal. Pops said light suits, unless you were cruising the West Indian islands, made men look like gangsters or estate agents. Which was fine if you were a gangster selling hot goods or an estate agent selling hot houses but if you were a girl looking for a hot prospect, then you couldn't beat a guy in a dark linen suit.

I told Pops Themba's T-shirt would look great with the suit. So Pops bought me a white cotton shirt with a thin grey and blue thread running through the weave. Pops said it was hot but subtle.

The next thing were the shoes. Pops said that shoes were the most important part of any outfit. A person could tell a million things about another person from the shoes he wore. That's what Pops said.

We got a pair of black shoes (Bryant Oxford from Florsheim) with a breathable lining and a leather upper shaped in a sleek profile for a sharp level of distinction (according to the sales guy). The shoes told me that I was shiny and bloody uncomfortable.

Shopping was a tiring sport. I knew I was a bit buggered and Pops looked like he could do with a snooze, so I suggested that we hit the tea shop. Pops shuffled down the passage – his feet must have been playing up – and I shuffled along with him to keep him company. Between me, with my leprous face, and Pops, with his headaches and walking problems, our Madelaine was a real credit to the Angela Storm Beauty

Academy.

In the tea shop Pops couldn't make up his mind what to order. He said he couldn't read the blinking menu. He took off his specs a couple of times and gave them a brisk old wipe on the tablecloth, but it was no good. 'It's all down hill once you reach sixty-five,' he said.

Eventually I ordered Pops a slice of death by chocolate and a double espresso. While we waited for the waitress to bring our food and drinks Pops told me that he had something on his mind. He had been making noises like he wanted to have a real D&M (deep and meaningful) when we had been shopping. It was Regina Versagel and me, and the kinds of things that could happen between the two of us in a dance environment (that's between me and Regina not between me and Pops) that he wanted to talk about.

I told Pops I had heard it all from Themba, and as he (Themba not Pops) was the expert on All Matters Of A Sexual Nature, I thought I was sorted. Pops said he didn't want to talk to me about the stuff that Themba knew. He wanted to talk to me about the stuff Themba wouldn't know anything about. Now this interested me. To have an edge on an expert like Themba ... I told Pops to continue.

So Pops talked. He talked about the first time he met his wife, my grandmother, and what he thought and what he felt and how it all happened between them. It was a long story and Pops told it ... slowly.

Unfortunately, I couldn't see Themba paying me good money as a professional consultant for this kind of Intel. In fact, Themba beat Pops hollow in The Knowledge of All

Matters Of A Sexual Nature. I told Pops I'd actually been hoping for something a little more practical. Didn't he have a couple of hands-on tips for me, as it were?

Pops said that his advice to me on life stood and I must take it or leave it: 'Beware of women with red hair who wear black underwear.' He'd said this to me a lot of times since Regina had appeared on the scene but he still wouldn't be drawn as to why or what it all meant.

I asked Pops what had been plaguing me for the past couple of sleepless nights. How should I ask Regina to become my girlfriend.

Pops sniffed and said in his day you asked a girl to go out with you. It couldn't be clearer than that. It sounded pretty lame but I nodded and thanked him all the same.

Pops didn't eat much of the chocolate cake so I helped him out – it was clear that nothing I'd avoided eating had made any difference to my skin anyway. Then the bill came and Pops spent like an hour trying to read it. The numbers just didn't add up. He called the waitress over and asked her how she could expect anyone to read her terrible handwriting? She got cross and said it wasn't her handwriting, it was his eyes. 'Can't you see that it's a computer-generated bill?' she grumbled.

When we finally got home (Pops was still taking it slow) I rushed through Brutus and JR and Princess and Friday (indeterminate breed). Friday was my most recent client. I had been resolved that I couldn't and just wouldn't take on another. But Friday was evidently going through an identity crisis and I just couldn't let him down.

After dropping off Friday and playing a quick game of darts with Friday's owner (Mrs Florence Guthrie), I began my preparations for the big night. The first big issue was my skin. I had decided to follow Buster's advice, which involved a radical zit-blaster technique that he swore by. It was simple, but effective. That's what Buster said.

I took a couple of small glass bottles (ones that had held capers and anchovies) and I filled them with steam by holding them over a boiling kettle. When the bottles were all cloudy with steam, I attached them to my face. They stayed there, clinging like leeches, drawing away at the poisons on my skin.

I did this for a couple of hours and I thought there was a small improvement. But my face was also covered in red circles from the bottles as though some kid had been stamping me with potato cut-outs.

To take the edge off I went for the cooling face mask of pulped cucumber (Mrs Smythe's recipe) as opposed to the moisturizing egg and milk mix (Felicity Foxcroft). I then tried the eggy mixture for in case.

Pops came in all dressed up in his penguin suit and gave me a red handkerchief to put in my top pocket and some of his aftershave (to put on my poor face). He said the suit looked great, although we should've got the tailor to take the hems up a bit. But if I pulled the trousers up high, no one would notice they were a bit long.

Then Regina arrived. She looked like a trillion dollars. She wore low-cut black denims and a black T-shirt that said *Everything I need to know about life I got from killing smart*

people and eating their brains. She went pink when she saw
me. 'Ag, no man, Red,' she said. 'You never said it was a ball
dance. I'm not dressed.'

I told her she looked wonderful and I wished that I could
change into my real clothes but Pops was staring at me and
I didn't want to disappoint him.

We picked up Grace Foxcroft and Mrs Smythe on the way
to the Entertainment Hall. Pops said he had two of the most
beautiful women in the world on his arms, and Grace looked
at Mrs Smythe and Mrs Smythe looked at Grace and I could
see that they were wondering which of them Pops thought
was the most beautiful.

Mr Groenewald had hired the local band (The Screaming
Peanuts). The whole of Port Elizabeth used them for
weddings and funerals and practically anything that needed
loud music, but they weren't a big hit until Mr Groenewald
told them to lay off on the thump-thump stuff they played at
bar mitzvahs and give us some real tunes.

Five minutes later the Hall was rocking around the clock
and me and Regina hit the dance floor. I had the best time of
my life. The thing about Regina is that she is a single-minded
kind of a girl. Like I would be dancing with her and I would
know that she was dancing with me. She wasn't looking at
anyone else or wondering whether people were looking at
her. She Was Dancing With Me. Full Stop.

It was the same when we were taking a break and having
a conversation about the latest talking point. I would say
something and she would say something back and I could
see that she was listening to what I was saying and wasn't

thinking about what she was going to say back to me before I was finished talking. She was a very focused kind of girl.

I got me up some courage and while we were slow-dancing I whispered Pops' line in her ear: 'Do you want to go out with me?'

'What?' Regina asked. She couldn't hear me.

'Will you go out with me?' I croaked a little more loudly in her ear.

Regina stopped dancing.

'Sure,' she said, in that focussed unblinking way of hers. And she walked across the dance floor to the exit.

When we got outside I was also a bit focused. It was on this amazing blue vein on the side of her amazing white neck that I had been wanting to touch all evening. I had so much spit in my mouth because I couldn't swallow (I was so full of nerves).

When I did finally touch her neck very softly with my finger, she kept quite still and she didn't say anything. She let me touch the amazing blue vein on her amazing neck until I was quite done, although as soon as I took my hand away it wanted to be on her neck again. She didn't say anything at all. She just smiled at me. So I swallowed and it made a funny burp noise and she smiled again.

When we went back into the Hall I saw that someone needed to make a serious intervention into the evening's proceedings. Some of the ladies (Sad Singles) were sitting on the chairs on the side of the Hall. They were eyeing the Lucky Ones (the couples) dancing away and were pretending not to look at the Desirables (the single old men) who were hiding out at the drinks table.

The thing about Regina is that as soon as she saw me ask Marjorie to come and shake a leg to 'Surfin' USA' by the Beach Boys, she got it. We worked as a team. So there I was dancing away with Marjorie and all the ladies and Regina was doing her bit with the old guys, who didn't need a lot of encouragement and were behaving like a swarm of bedbugs on a mattress.

The one thing I learned about my girl that night was that she could sweat. Not perspire, not glow, my Regina sweated. When she took a break I handed her my red handkerchief and watched as she pressed it to her face.

When she handed it back to me I could not fail to observe the sweaty imprint that she had left behind. I felt like I had been given my own personal Shroud of Turin. I carefully folded this artefact and put it in my pocket.

The Screaming Peanuts assessed the exhausted state of the room and played 'Candle in the Wind' by Elton John – a man who has skin the colour of a mushroom.[11] This made the oldies all maudlin, so to cheer the hall up, Pops got this YMCA thing going to the Village People, and it wasn't long before he had everyone doing the movements and singing 'It's fun to stay at the NMGV!' (Nelson Mandela Gardens Village). It was a complete riot!

I looked at Pops and I saw him happy and alive and having a blast. The Pops I knew. Not the old man with the

---

[11] He also once owned a 1978 Aston Martin V8 Vantage Coupé, known as The Beast, which he sold for eighty thousand pounds. He's a cool guy for having red hair and being born with a name like Reginald Kenneth Dwight.

headaches and bad moods and strange behaviour. I watched Pops laughing and dancing and then a very weird expression came over his face. Suddenly he started ripping off his bow tie and dress shirt and then he was at his trousers and then he was flinging his clothes around until he was down to his boxers. The silky ones with the red-and-purple hearts.

And as everyone was chanting, 'NMGV, NMGV, NMGV,' making the letter shapes with their bodies and arms, Pops pulled down his shorts and flashed his butterfly tattoo at the residents of the Nelson Mandela Gardens Retirement Village.

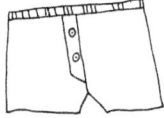

Things I Know:

Old blokes should
never wear Speedos

12

the RIVAL

Pops spent the morning after the Summer Ball lying on the couch, suffering from a bad bout of tattoo remorse – and fielding at least half a dozen calls – a couple from ladies in the Village (offering to show him their tattoos) and the rest from old blokes (ripping him something wicked). I was worried about him, but I was also very busy calling Regina. I called her at least a hundred times that day just to hear her breathe, until her mother put her foot down and said I had to be restricted to three calls a day.

While I felt a bit grumpy about not being able to call Regina, it was actually a good thing because as the excitement about Pops flashing his tattoo fizzled out, I suddenly found myself busy with something else – a craze.

It's a funny thing – crazes. One never knows quite how they start, but all of a sudden everybody's doing it.

Like at school you'll see blokes walking around with bags of marbles, then the next month it's cricket cards, and then that's old potatoes and everyone's swapping pictures of Cameron Diaz (not as hot as Halle but still the coolest of the Angels). And before you know it, if you aren't on top of your game, you're the guy that gets stuck with all the marbles and the cricket cards at the back of the pack, sucking hind tit on Cameron Diaz, so to speak.

It wasn't like the guys in the Village were betting goenies and taking cards off each other and stuff like that. Oh, no, they had been swept away by the model craze. And it wasn't Kate Moss or Naomi Campbell.

The model craze came to my attention while I was busy with my dog-walking duties. I had to be quite disciplined otherwise I just couldn't fit in all my clients. Eight clients. I'm not sure how it had happened, just call me soft. Those canines really seemed to need me.

I usually started with Mrs Rosemary Dearden's bulldog at Number 29 and ended with Brutus. I liked to spend a bit of quality time with my godson at the end of the day, so he got an extra five minutes on the standard fifteen minute walk. The whole routine should have taken just over two hours, but ten to one it took twice as long because there was always something happening when I got back from a walk. Take Mrs Dearden (the first client of the morning), for instance. She was a complete smoothie freak. Every morning, without fail, she'd be whipping up a smoothie when I arrived back after walking her bulldog – Beefie. Strawberry, chocolate, berry, banana – you name it, Mrs Dearden would be at it. Not that she ever touched the things herself (lactose intolerant), but she said she knew how essential they were for growing bones (though it beats me what she did with the things the mornings I wasn't around to drink them).

Only after a couple of smoothies and a bit of a chat about things like the weather and if I liked the fat-free or double-thick yoghurt smoothies best (double-thick, of course) would I be able to get away. And the other clients were just as bad: 'Randolph dear, would you stand still for a minute and let me measure your shoulders, I'm making a cricket jersey for a chap your size and want to get it just right.' (Client Number Two), 'Randolph, my dear, if you would just thread this needle for me while I cut you a piece of carrot cake – iced or plain?' (Client Number Seven). To be honest it was a good thing I had the walks in between because what with all the breakfasts and snacks I was getting on my rounds I really had started packing on the pounds.

Then on Monday morning, two days after the Summer Ball to be precise, after returning JR – Mrs Jacobson's Jack Russell (Client Number Five: eggs Benedict and freshly squeezed orange juice) – I heard a mixture of a sharp whistle and a hiss from the house next door. 'RRRrrr … Randolph. Hey, hey, hey, RRRRrrr … Randolph, lalalalad. Come see what I've go gogogogot for you …'

It was Mr Bradley Stutford – not one of my clients but a

chap I knew by sight. Mrs Smythe had pointed him out to me one day: 'Old Stutters,' she'd said. According to Mrs Smythe, Old Stutters was the only son of two very progressive and indulgent parents. Mrs and Mr Stutford Senior did not believe in disciplining their son too strictly, so unlike their neighbours, who used to thrash their kids regularly before supper with a sjambok, the socially aware Stutfords used to tap their son Bradley (Old Stutters) grimly, but lightly on the top of his knuckles when he erred.

As Old Stutters was a bloody naughty kid in those days, Mr and Mrs Stutford tapped their son's knuckles in their grim, firm and restrained way like thirty times a day. They only stopped this practice when groundbreaking research by a bunch of child psychologists from a British University was released which said that tapping the metacarpal bones of a developing person caused speech impediments. But by then Old Stutters was like forty years old and it was way, way too late.

So when Old Stutters called to me that day I was curious enough to follow him into his one-bedroomed home. And there on the dining room table was a model aeroplane. 'This beauty used to bomb the snot out of Herman the German in the good old days. Just look at her,' Old Stutters said. He stuttered all the way through, and it did really take like five minutes for him to say all this, but he was right; she really was a beauty.

Old Stutters said that if I would just help him assemble the wings and do some of the finer paintwork on the body of the plane, she would be almost ready to take to the skies.

So I blew off my last three clients and spent the rest of the afternoon working on the 250X3 bomber model aeroplane.

It wasn't at all like the mornings I'd spent with Mrs Smythe and the other old girls. Me and Old Stutters didn't chatter very much (a bit of a relief that), but Old Stutters did mention a couple of times that I had the most marvellous hands. 'Fafafafafa fine long fafafafafa fingers,' he said (but somehow he said it in a blokey way, which made it okay).

I wish I could have returned the compliment but to be honest his hands were covered in blue knotted rope – they really had taken a bit of a beating.

The model aeroplane craze swept the Village like a South Easter blowing off the sea in November. Before I knew it, I was aligning wings and fixing propellers and doing touch-ups and fine brushwork and it just never stopped. The old guys in the Village were completely carried away by it all – but, between ourselves, they were also fairly useless at assembling some of the fiddlier bits (and being a bit of an expert, so to speak, I was quite in demand).

The craze kept me busy in the days after Regina's mother really put her foot down and said that not only was I restricted to three calls a day but that Regina was grounded until the weekend – she had to clean her room and study for her exams which were just around the corner. My teeth ached with longing.

In the meantime, Old Stutters hosted a fine Wednesday afternoon's shindig by his koi pond, where a whole bunch of us guys paddled in our Speedos (no comment necessary) and launched our aeroplanes into the heavens. Afterwards, we drank beers and ate hotdogs and hamburgers. It was a total blast and they (the old guys) kept on saying things like, 'So, Randolph, lad, this has got to be better than all that crud the old bags have been feeding you?' and 'So, Randolph, you've got to admit it, us guys really know how to throw a party, hey? This is the real palooka, hey, chap?'. Like there was some kind of competition going on between the Sad Singles and the Desirables for my company. Really weird.

After the aeroplane craze ended, all eyes were turned to Old Stutters, but he kept his cards close to his chest. Then, one morning, he ambushed me on my way to walk JR. 'Pa-papa Piss Stttt Tittt,' Old Stutters stuttered (he meant 'Psst'), beckoning me from behind his net curtain.

He kept his eyes glued to my face when I opened the box and clapped his knotted hands together with excitement when I drew out the prize. It was a beauty. A deep red and purple triangular kite with the face of the fiercest dragon to come out of the People's Republic of China and red and purple ribbons for a tail. Old Stutters said that he and I were going to launch this beauty into the Port Elizabeth skies as soon as that South Easter took it into her head to whip us up a bit of air.

I told Old Stutters that me and Pops would stop by his house the next windy afternoon and Old Stutters said the more the merrier, although he didn't look very merry about me bringing company along. So I said, in that case, I would bring Regina as well and Old Stutters said that was totally fine (Tttttit … tit … toe … toe … tat … tat … ally), but perhaps we should stop at four people as there wasn't much more room in his beach buggy.

Old Stutters was sort of okay for a stuttering guy with buggered hands. Well, in my book a beach buggy is way cool. And even Buster would concede that it ranks way up there with the Aston Martin in *Casino Royale*.

It was a day later when the South Easter hit us. The funny thing with South Easters is that you'll be sitting out on the stoep – maybe sampling Mrs Smythe's new rusk recipe (sunflower seeds) – and all of a sudden the South Easter just sweeps down. *Whoosh!* Just like that. And then it blows for a couple of days until it gets whatever it is out of its system and then it's all still again. That's how the South Easter behaves.

It kept blowing until Sunday, so I made a date with Regina (at last) and dragged Pops off his sleeper couch, where he was having a zizz, telling him that I had a fantastic surprise for him. He looked a bit groggy but he allowed himself to be blown down the path to Old Stutters' place, where the man himself had the beach buggy all revved up and ready to go.

We hauled in Regina a short distance from the entrance gate – where she was being buffeted by the wind – and made tracks to Kammies Beach (Kakamakers Kop – but Old Stutters used the short version for obvious reasons).

Throughout the journey I couldn't take my eyes off Regina. The wind whipped her cheeks pink and I watched as she held her glasses to her face with one hand while the other hovered just above my knee. I prayed like hell Old Stutters would do me a favour and take a corner too fast or see a stop sign too late, but my luck was out and her hand just hovered above my poor sad knee until we got to the beach.

Pops had been on at me the whole trip: What was it? What was the big surprise? It surely wasn't a hell trip in some clapped out old chorrie to the beach on a day when normal people were safe and sound inside out of the wind?

But sure enough when Old Stutters took the kite out of the boot, Pops' eyes lit up like the lights on a Christmas tree. I could see he was itching to hold it, but like the gentleman he was he let Old Stutters have the first go – it was his kite after all.

Old Stutters launched the kite into the skies. It shot right up there and before we knew it, it was way down the length of the beach and Old Stutters was hanging on to the line for dear life. I grabbed Old Stutters around the waist and, God bless Old Stutters and his beautiful kite, Regina grabbed me around the waist and together we managed to anchor the beauty in the heavens.

'Fantastic! Brilliant! Wonderful! Yeehah!' Old Stutters yelled.

If I'd been able to think about it I would have realised that Old Stutters wasn't stuttering any more, but I was too busy thinking about Regina's arms around my waist. 'Isn't she beautiful, the most beautiful thing you have ever seen?' I said, and I was sort of thinking of Regina as well as the kite when I said it.

Then it was Pops' turn. Old Stutters showed him how to work the fishing-reel contraption that held the line that linked us to the kite – just a gentle touch to the reel and the kite would be off and a twitch of the wrist would pull it back.

Pops held the reel and twitched his wrist back and forth

just to get the hang of it. His hands were shaking and I wanted to yell, 'Just give it to me, let me do it!', thinking of how Regina would hold me around the waist as the wind pulled me, her and the beautiful kite along the sandy shoreline.

Then the South Easter swooped, dragging Pops and the kite down the beach after the silly seagulls. 'Pull it in! Pull it in!' I shouted to Pops, but he didn't seem to hear me, or if he did those hands of his were playing silly buggers with the reel.

I watched Pop fall on the sand as the kite took off with the South Easter. We screamed and yelled for it to come back, but it shot off across the sea and blew all the way home to China.

Me and Regina were gutted, but we tried to put a brave face on it all, because when we got to him Pops' face said everything we were feeling. I told Pops that some child in China would probably find the kite, so it would have a happy home. And Regina said that's probably what would happen – so Pops should be glad about making some Chinese boy happy. Poor old Stutters, though, just looked like someone had slammed his fingers in a door.

Pops was very quiet all the way home and went straight for his sleeper couch on the stoep when Old Stutters dropped us off.

By the end of the day the South Easter had settled herself down into a hoarse whisper and I walked Regina to the entrance gates of the Village. She was being picked up by her cousin, who she said had recently finished writing his Matric and had got his driver's licence.

As we got close to the gates I saw a bloke in a red Mini Cooper waiting outside. He leapt out as soon as he saw us and opened the car door for my Regina, putting his hand on the back of her neck as she got in. He then took my hand and pulped it into a tiny sack of bones, saying that his name was Peter, Peter Ranger. And with a name like that I just knew that he was captain of the rugby team, an academic honours student and that he only tanned deep bronze in the sun.

Buster would have said that he was a dead ringer for Roger Moore in the early days, before he got the long gums and went crusty. Themba would have said that he looked like one of those Y-front models they have on the billboards on the way to the airport, except I could guess that Peter Ranger wouldn't be stuffing his jocks with girls' hygiene products.

I looked at Peter Ranger and his hard sculpted jaw with its five o'clock shadow and his black hair and his eyes like blue bottle-glass that had been washed smooth by a million waves. He was a Greek god. Nothing less.

I watched them drive off and I thought back to the dance floor a week earlier when I had asked Regina to go out with me. What part of 'Will you go out with me?' did she not understand? Surely it was as simple as flying a kite. She was supposed to be mine. And then I kind of knew how Pops had felt when he saw Old Stutters' beautiful kite fly away from him: a mixture of confusion and miserable despair.

Things I Know:

Green Wine gums
leave a bitter taste

13

the MOVIE DATE

I was awoken at midnight by a volley of bleeps on my cellphone. I assumed it was my mother – she sends out a plague of text messages to a bunch of clients at certain times of the month (certain times which have nothing to do with that time of the month, as it were, but have everything to do with the usual crises facing the thirty-odd companies my mother is helping to run).

It seems that I am grouped with several clients who always need my mother's special support towards the middle of the month when they're not making ends meet – those nail-biting times when CEOs suddenly realise that the money is pouring out faster than it is trickling in and they don't have anything under the mattress for a rainy day.

My mother always tells us to: identify our star performers and retrench the bottom thirty percent of underachievers. And to cut costs. That is, to pull back on first-class travel and long lunches, cut middle-level management bonuses, do an audit on stationery and monitor and restrict coffee and sugar usage in the tea rooms. Then, apart from the belt-tightening measures, there are a couple of tips on breathing, remaining positive and projecting confidence. It's stuff like that.

I have always found my mother's mid-monthly tips kind of useful. It's the sort of stuff you can apply to your own life as well as to a huge corporation. With her guidance I've managed to stretch my pocket money a little further, remembered to wear clean underwear in the mornings and taken ten minute power naps after lunch. This time, however, I turned over in my bed, making a note to tell my mother about the time difference between South Africa and Thailand. But seconds later my cellphone started bleeping again. Grabbing the phone I saw that I had fifteen messages. All from Buster. The messages went something like this:

Am first in the ticket queue. ☺

Got a seat right in the front on the aisle. ☺ ☺

Have stocked up with popcorn and slush, grape.

Ten minutes to go. Can't wait.

Bought more popcorn. ☺

Buster had sent me a detailed countdown to the start of Nairobi's midnight premier of *Quantum of Solace* – the twenty-second Bond movie and the eagerly awaited sequel to *Casino Royale*. Buster's fifteenth message said the adverts were about to start, but he would give me updates throughout the movie – it would be like I was there with him. Me and him, among the few lucky ones to see the first showing of the new Bond movie on the African continent. It didn't get any better than this, Buster said.

I texted him back that I was with him all the way, switched off my phone and went back to sleep.

As I slept I dreamed I was running down the beach after Regina Versagel. The sand was soft and my feet were sucked down, making each step more difficult than the last. I finally caught up with her and she turned around. But it wasn't my Regina, it was Peter Ranger. He grabbed my head and gave me a vicious noogie and threw me on the ground. As I struggled with Peter Ranger, I saw Regina flying out to sea at the end of the beautiful kite. Come back, don't go too far away, I wanted to yell, but it was too late.

The next morning, after I had read and cleared Buster's two hundred messages from my Inbox, I was hit by a brainwave. I would ask Regina out on a movie date.

I'd been a bit under the weather since I had learned of the existence of Peter Ranger. I had called Regina three times every hour since our kite expedition but before she could answer I'd put down the phone. I didn't know what to say to her except: Who the hell is Peter Ranger? Do you like him more than me?

A movie date was the answer. She and I, alone with a cinema full of strangers, in the dark, far away from Peter Ranger, experiencing joy, fear and excitement that would require me to hold her hand, for her to bury her head in my chest . . .

I lay in bed for an hour, imagining the various groin-aching scenarios, until Pops opened the door and asked me what I was doing lazing about in bed and was I ill because I had a very strange expression on my face.

Daniel Craig (aka James Bond) and I were in the middle of a car chase and Regina was straddling my lap, biting the lobe of my ear as we sped into a dark tunnel. I croaked to Pops that I wanted to go and see *Quantum of Solace* and he replied that he thought it was a good idea and he would rustle up the usual suspects and see if we could go one afternoon during the week. But maybe I should ask Regina. He was sure she might like to see it?

I didn't have the heart to tell Pops to get a life and his own movie date. He'd been a bit down in the dumps since the kite incident.

Movies are a big deal between a guy and a girl. Themba always says girls know exactly what the score is when they get invited on a movie date. It's a code for doing it. No one ever goes to actually see the movie.

I spent most of the morning practicing what I would say to Regina when I called her after school in the afternoon:

'Hey, Regina, do you like Peter Ranger better than me?' No, that wasn't what I wanted to say. 'Hey, Reg, wanna do it ...?' No. 'Regina, hello, I was just wondering if you were doing anything ...?', 'Regina, Red here, so glad I caught you, I was just thinking ...'

Themba always says, 'No risk it, no biscuit!', so I watched the clock until I knew Regina would be home from school and then I locked myself in the loo for some privacy and made the call.

My heart shuddered in my chest as the phone rang. But when a male voice answered I quickly disconnected. I hate it when I get the wrong number. I dialled more carefully and got the same voice. Third time lucky – or not as it turned out. The male voice belonged to Peter Ranger. He was taking Regina's calls because she was 'in the middle of something'. There was the sound of giggles and scuffling and cries of 'Give me! Give me!' and Regina's voice came on the line. Panting.

She and Peter Ranger were doing a private kick-boxing class together but she would love to see *Quantum of Solace* and, oh, so would Peter Ranger, and wouldn't it be fun if we could all see it together. I said fantastic, absolutely bloody brilliant, as I bit my tongue and sweat poured from my armpits.

It's hard to keep a secret in a place like Nelson Mandela Gardens. Before I could say block booking, Mr Groenewald had negotiated a special pensioners' screening with the cinema and had organised two buses to take eighty-one of us down town. In preparation for the big day, the Entertainment Committee held DVD viewings of *Casino Royale* for all of those who hadn't seen it and needed to be brought up to speed for the sequel (Grace Foxcroft saw it seven times – or was it nine, she couldn't remember).

Finally the big day arrived. I'd arranged to meet Regina (and Peter Ranger) at the movie house ten minutes before the show started. I was dying of nerves. I wanted our date to be a big hit because although I might have been imagining it (I spent most nights imagining it) I'd been feeling a chilly distance between Regina and I since Peter Ranger had arrived on the scene.

We – the bus contingent – arrived at the cinema two hours before the start of the show. Getting old people organised is on par with getting kids in a Christmas play at a crèche organised. There was the toilet drill – the first hour (enough said) – and then getting the tickets and the popcorn.

Mr Groenewald had pre-booked the seats, but all the pensioners were supposed to show their pensioner cards to prove they qualified for the cheap ticket. More than half the party had forgotten their cards back at the Village, including, of course, Grace.[12]

To begin with the cinema manager proved himself to be a stickler for the rules, but after realising he was on a hiding to nothing, he became helluva understanding about bending

---

[12] Felicity Foxcroft only pretended to forget hers when she saw how much fuss it caused. Always wanting her kicks, that was Felicity.

them and let everyone through on the pensioner rating, except for Grace, who he said didn't look a day over fifty.

This made blood pour out of Mrs Smythe's ears and she pretended she'd forgotten her pensioner card as well, telling the manager that she'd have her day in court unless he allowed her the pensioner rate. The manager said a fight was not going to be necessary, he could see as plain as the wrinkles on her face that she was nearly eighty and he hustled her, hissing like a faulty hot-water bottle, into the cinema.

Getting everyone snacked up created another challenge (my mother calls them challenges, not problems). Most of the old folk had brought lunch boxes full of goodies (leftovers from supper, home-made popcorn, wine gums) and cooldrink bottles of juice, or in Felicity's case, gin. There was no way they were going to abide by the movie house rules, surrender their snacks and pay the cinema prices for popcorn and a drink.

The deadlock was only broken after Mr Groenewald brokered a sort of corkage kind of a deal on the goodies with the manager – not on Felicity's gin though (there were limits, Mr Groenewald said).

At long last, Regina (and Peter Ranger) arrived. After a lengthy verbal battle I managed to win the privilege of buying Regina her popcorn while Peter Ranger got to buy the slush, though I slipped some Smarties and wine gums past him when he was distracted by Felicity arm-wrestling the manager for her bottle of gin.

Felicity's eyes lit up at the sight of Regina but turned hard and slitty when she saw Peter Ranger. I saw her take in Peter Ranger's hard jaw (complete with five o'clock shadow) and his piercing blue eyes. Then she turned her eyes on me, an expression of pity on her face. 'What's he doing here?' she said, using the same tone of voice she reserved for referring to adult nappies.

It must have been the expression of misery and defeat that slunk across my face that decided Pops. He strode across the cinema floor and grabbed Peter Ranger's hand. 'We all know Reg, she's like one of the family,' he said, winking at Regina, 'but everyone is dying to meet you.'

Pops dragged Peter Ranger off to meet the oldies, who mobbed him like they were at a Woolworths sale – he didn't stand a chance against the combined forces of Nelson Mandela Gardens' finest.

Mr Groenewald got the cinema manager to allocate Regina and I two seats – A1 and A2 – way at the very back of the movie house, away from the rest of the party ('So sorry about this Red, I messed up the booking!'), while Peter Ranger found himself held hostage in the middle of a row, wedged tightly between Felicity and Old Stutters.

Poor Peter Ranger had a hard time choosing between cha … cha … cha … chatting to Old Stutters or risking the boozy attentions of Felicity, so he just hunched down in his seat and succumbed to Stockholme syndrome, allowing Old Stutters to rest his head on his shoulder and Felicity to pep up his slush with a couple of tots of the best Gilbey's.

Me and my girl hardly noticed all the goings on in the rows in front of us. We were oblivious to Old Stutters' howls of outrage as Bond buggered up the beautiful Aston Martin in the car chase ('C … c … criminal way to treat a b … b … beautiful car!') and Mrs Smythe's loud complaints about Grace occupying *her* seat next to Pops. Even the constant to and froing along the rows to the toilets (enough said) and the loud sobbing (Mr Groenewald) and shrill cackling (Felicity) when lovely Strawberry Fields got oil-slicked to death by Mr Greene didn't disturb us.

Me and my girl sat cocooned and content at the back of the cinema. I was blown away by how similar our movie habits were. Regina salted her popcorn with all the flavours (salt and vinegar, sour cream and chives, barbecue) – 'It's impossible to choose, isn't it, Red?' Regina disliked the green wine gums as I much as I did – 'They leave a horrible aftertaste, don't they?' And she liked to leave the brown Smarties for last – 'No reason, but I just feel sorry for them, being so dull …'

But there was more. Towards the end of the movie, when Bond tells M that she was right about Vesper, Regina grabbed my hand and whispered, 'I knew it, I knew it. She loved him. How could he have doubted her?'

I could see that Regina was deeply affected by this and I put my arm around her and drew her head to my chest, hoping she wouldn't mind the soaking she was getting as the tears poured down my face into her hair. How *could* he have doubted her?

I could have sat like that for hours and hours, but the credits were scrolling down the screen and eighty-one heads were turning to peer at the back of the cinema, eighty-one

sets of eyes fixing themselves like denture glue to seats A1
and A2. No, only eighty sets of eyes. Pops' were not among
them.

I scanned the rows in front of me and found Grace and
Mrs Smythe. But no Pops. Grace winked at me but before I
could wink back screams came from a few rows in front of
them and some of the patrons began pushing and shoving
each other and jumping on their seats.

Then a head emerged at the end of one row of seats and
before I could say what the heck are you doing crawling
around on the ground, Pops scuttled away on all fours
towards the exit, shouting for everyone to keep their heads
down and hit the floor.

I allowed my lips to briefly graze the top of Regina's head
and sped after Pops, who leapt up, threw himself against the
exit door and ran for the toilets.

We spent the next half an hour trying to get Pops to open
the door and come out. Me and the theatre manager and
Mr Groenewald and thirty other blokes who needed to take
a leak and didn't think they could hold on until they got back
to the Village.

Pops only agreed to come out when Mr Groenewald
assured him that he would get Inspector Tollie Prinsloo from
the Summerstrand Police station to investigate his claims:
That he'd seen Mr Greene in the movie house. That no one
in the Village was safe. That Mr Greene was going to poison
the Village's water supply. That Mr Greene and the CIA and
the rogues in the British government ...

As soon as Pops opened the door I stopped listening, left

him with Mr Groenewald and went in search of Regina. There was no sign of her and Felicity said she'd seen her leave with Peter Ranger. She spat out his name like it was a green wine gum and handed me a note from Regina which said *PRIVATE AND CONFIDENTIAL*, but the creases were all in the wrong places, so I knew that Felicity had stuck her nose where it didn't belong.

What was written in the note made me forget about Pops' weird behaviour. It made me oblivious to the way he stumbled onto the bus, his eyes filled with suspicion and fear.

I read that note over and over again on the way back to Nelson Mandela Gardens: *Hey, Red. Sorry I had to run. Peter Ranger wanted to take me for a milkshake on the beach. Thanks for the movie. Love, Reg.*

My mother always tells me and the other CEOs in her mid-monthly texts that we need to stay positive, that every dog will have his day and that things will be better in the morning. I kept my eyes focused on the one word at the end of Regina's note. Love. Love. Love. And it was in this word that I found my quantum of solace.

Things I Know:

Old People eat a lot
of beans in lean times

14

the MIDNIGHT NIGHTMARE

Pops had this bottle on the kitchen shelf that was filled with battered old coins that he'd found on his walks. Like if you were wandering around with Pops and he spotted a coin, no matter what he had in his hands or how fast he was walking, he'd stop and bend down – or even go back – for that five cents. He said picking up coins brought you good luck.

He kept the bottle of coins where he could see them so that every day he would remember how lucky he was. Apart from all the good health luck and the amazing grandson called Randolph luck, what Pops meant by this was that he'd been very lucky with money.

Before he retired Pops used to build roads and bridges.

Not personally, but he did the drawings and ordered the materials and stuff that you need. And he used to make sure that the chaps who built the bridges didn't make them fall down too often.

Then, when he quit working, he'd taken his pension in one big lump sum and invested it in some shares. Pops said it wasn't rocket science, this investing thing, any baboon could do it. They'd proved it. Some scientists gave a bunch of baboons some darts and allowed them to pick out shares on a big dart board. And the performance of their portfolios was pretty sweet.

So that's what Pops did. He took the share page from the daily business newspaper and a red pen and stabbed the page twenty times with his eyes closed. And just to make sure that he was being entirely random he turned the page around about ten times first, so he wouldn't know if it was sideways or upside down or whatever. Then he bought those shares which had been marked with the red pen.

Pops said that just like the baboons', his portfolio had been a stunning success and he lived off his dividends, even though he was no expert on the stock exchange and investing money and stuff.[13]

One of the things that I learned about old people at Nelson Mandela Gardens was that money was a big thing, almost as big as the weather, especially for those folk who didn't have too much of it. And some of the old folk had not

---

[13] Pops always said that his real expertise was in the meaning of life, and that he learned something new every day, which really was what life was all about.

been as lucky as Pops.

There was this one couple at Number 56, the Robertsons, who lived on a sniff of boiled cabbage and a prayer, Pops said. Mr Mark Robertson had been hoping to get his pension from the government in Zimbabwe, but things had gone a bit AWOL and his cash got nicked by a crook Pops called Mad Bob. So the Robertsons had to rely on Mrs Enid Robertson's pension, from when she was a secretary, which was a little thin on cream.

You could always tell the lucky ones from those who were scraping by, hoping that they wouldn't live past seventy-five, because if they did there wouldn't be any money left. The rich ones brought steak and lamb chops to the braai and the poor ones brought small pieces of boerewors which they ate on a couple of rolls. The rich ones went away twice or three times a year to timeshare places along the coast or to see their children in other cities while the poor ones had to stay put and hope that their kids would come and see them. Which more often than not they didn't, because let's face it, the kids were more than likely paying the rent at the Village and that should have been that. Right?

My mother tells me that economists use something called the lipstick index to measure a country's economic health. It is a term coined by a bloke called Leonard Lauder, who runs a cosmetics shop. He claims that women spend loads of cash on lipstick in tough times instead of buying expensive dresses and jewellery. But there wasn't a lot of lipstick being bought in the Village so I employed the baked bean index as my guide. When cash was short, the Village bought cans and cans of the stuff instead of chicken or beef – or, heaven forbid, cheese (which was more dear than beef). During those lean days in the village, it was quite a gas.

There was this rich couple that lived right on the other side of Pops called the Blackmans. Lawrence and Helen Blackman. If there had been a Village Rich List, the Blackmans would probably have come top. But apart from being the moguls of the Village, the Blackmans were really nice people and they tried hard not to shove their wealth in everyone's faces.

There was this one time that Mr Blackman wanted to buy his wife a new car for her seventieth birthday. And Mrs Blackman asked for exactly the same make, model and colour as the car that she already had, just so no one would notice. But of course everybody did, because the number plate was different, and in addition, nothing got past anyone at the Village.

The Blackmans also tried to pass their cash around a little, but in ways that weren't too obvious. Mrs Blackman bought like ten books a week which she read, or she didn't, but either way she passed the books straight on to the Village library – even if she hadn't finished reading them, or not, as it were.

The Blackmans were always very sweet with each other. Like you could see that Mr Blackman was still very taken with Mrs Blackman, even though she was fat and old and not as attractive as she was when they'd got married fifty years before.

Themba says that rich old ugly blokes tend to stick with

what they have most of the time just to keep the gold-diggers away. They don't like to get caught like this bloke Themba knows of called Sir Paul Moneybags who made a stash of dosh playing in a band and married this one-legged chick thirty years younger than him (Paul – not Themba). And now she's cleaned him out and he's so, so surprised. Like what did he think – that she was in love with his skinny knees and baggy buns and turkey neck? You've got to feel for him though, being short-changed like that when he could have shopped around and bought himself one with two legs. That's what Themba says.

Pops was quite friendly with the Blackmans, on account of the fact that Mrs Blackman was also on the Entertainment Committee. We used to stop by sometimes for cocktails and nibbly bits on their verandah (they said verandah, never stoep). One week I mentioned to Mrs Blackman that it would be nice to have a ping-pong table in the Entertainment Hall and Mr Blackman got one delivered a couple of days later. They were generous like that.

Having a ping-pong table was great. It was the only game I could win at. Though, let's face it, it isn't helluva hard to thrash a bunch of people with dodgy eyesight whose reflexes aren't as good as they used to be.

Felicity Foxcroft even said she wouldn't play me any more after I savaged her in seven straight games without letting her take a point. I turned her around after I told her that ping-pong had been medically proven to be even better than Sudoku or omega-3 for retarding the onset of dementia. Poor Felicity, she was terrified of becoming gaga like Grace.

The Foxcroft sisters were quite well off. But this didn't stop Felicity from pretending otherwise. She had a 'no note, no plastic' rule and so refused to use credit cards or paper money. Instead, she collected all her coins in an enormous gold velvet clutch purse and used them whenever she paid for groceries.

I watched her once. She had obviously set herself a challenge, like twenty coppers and thirteen silvers, and she made sure she paid using exactly those coins. It took forever while she searched for them in her purse, and it drove the people in the queue behind her crazy, especially when she dropped some of the coins and had to scrabble around on the floor for them. Felicity was like that, always looking for some nastiness to give an edge to her life.

Pops would have come somewhere on the Rich List, but he wasn't in the Foxcroft or Blackman league. His attitude to cash was that he'd spend it on things that added meaning to his life – and to the lives of other people he thought were okay – and when it was gone, it was gone. And a good time would have been had by all.

I'd never really thought about money before I spent those few months with Pops. I expect it was because my parents always seemed to have enough of the stuff; although they never chucked it around unless they wanted to give me a break from them by packing me off to the mall for the weekend.

But when I did start to think about it I concluded that Pops had it just about right, and I decided I would use some of mine to buy Regina Vesagel a little gift as a token of our oneness. Perhaps that's what a girl wanted from a boyfriend. Maybe Regina thought I was too cheap? But surely, surely she wasn't the kind of girl to be won over by a spin in a red Mini Cooper and a ten buck milkshake?

I agonised over a choice of gift. Over supper I asked Pops what sort of gifts he had given my grandmother when they were first courting. Pops looked at me as if I was a nutter. 'Flowers, of course,' he said. 'And pass the salt.'

I felt a surge of relief. Pops could be cranky and weird sometimes, but he knew how to get a girl. I would buy Regina the biggest bunch of flowers money could buy. But there was one thing money couldn't buy: Courage. And I needed to get me some of that. Perhaps it was too late and Peter Ranger had got there before me? Just the thought of Regina accepting flowers from Peter Ranger made me sweaty with jealousy. Surely she wouldn't do that to me?

At any rate, that night – it was the Friday after my movie date with Regina (and Peter Ranger) – I awoke with quite a fright after a terrible dream: Peter Ranger had me gripped by my scabby, sunburned ears and was lifting me high in the air to see the view from Port Elizabeth to East London. As I screamed soundlessly in pain and the water poured from my eyes, I saw Regina running through a field of flowers. Stop, I wanted to yell, don't run that way, but the sound was stuck in my throat.

I woke up drenched in sweat, my chest in a vice grip. The bedroom lights were on and there was this crazy man ransacking Pops' metal filing cabinet, which was in the corner of the bedroom next to the desk. It was the place where Pops kept all the documentation relating to his finances, taxes and car licenses – boring stuff like that.

I was so completely groggy I felt like I was trapped in a crime story from one of the newspapers, but then the crazy man turned around and I saw that he was Pops. He didn't look like Pops at all. His eyes behind his round spectacles – the ones he'd owned since his university days – were wide and frightened. His hair, what he had left of it, was standing up like a baby pigeon's and he was stark naked.

Pops was shouting and raving at the filing cabinet as he flung papers out of files. Then he sat down and put his arms around his skinny legs and started sobbing. It was such a performance I thought something terrible must have happened. And it had. 'I'm bankrupt,' Pops said, staring up at me with that frightened look in his eyes that I'd never seen before. 'All my money's gone. I'm ruined.'

I got out of bed and sat down with Pops on the floor. Maybe someone else would have held him, but hell, he was naked and I'm not one of those guys who really likes hugging other guys, even if he is my grandfather. So I just patted his shoulder and said, 'It's okay, Pops. Everything's going to be okay.'

But it was really not okay. I tried to get him to stand up and go and get some clothes on, but he wouldn't move and he didn't stop whimpering.

I panicked. It's at moments like these when you want to be able to call your parents – they would have known what to do. But they were never there, and Mrs Kibaki (my old housekeeper) was ten thousand miles away in Nairobi and anyway she slept like a dead elephant's foot.

I panicked some more. I couldn't just call anybody. I didn't want people out there talking about how Pops was going stark raving mad. Mr Groenewald would get Pops locked up in Malkoppies sooner than I could say my grandfather's not a nutter.

I held my hands over my face, blocking out the sight of Pops sitting starkers on my bedroom floor sobbing like a small boy. Then I thought of Grace. Fat, cankled, gouty, gaga Grace who had a soft touch and who never yelled when I put my feet on the couch. I could trust Grace.

I also knew that she would be the first person Pops would turn to in a crisis. I figured this from something he'd said one Thursday after our Scrabble game. He'd said he thought that Grace was possibly the most honest person he had ever met. And he'd said that he could tell because he'd had the same conversations with her over and over again and she never wavered in her attitudes and views. She was always constant, no matter what mood she was in or how she was provoked to behave otherwise. 'A woman of frightening integrity,' was the way Pops had put it.

I hoped Grace was up to helping me with Pops and then forgetting about it all the next day. I didn't want word getting out that my Pops was a frenzied cuckoo-loon.

I called Grace and she was around in two ticks. She took one look at Pops and took charge – putting him into some pyjamas, the brushed cotton ones he wore when he said he felt a bit of a chill coming on, and tucking him into his sleeper couch on the stoep.

Then her eyes went a bit vague and she said, 'I can't imagine why I agreed to give you a Scrabble lesson at this time of night, Randolph, but I couldn't sleep either.'

So me and Grace played a game of Scrabble cross-legged on my bed. I made words like HEART, LOVE and KISS. And in the quietness of the early morning, I told Grace about Peter Ranger. I told her about his hard jaw and his hard thighs and that I didn't understand what was happening with me and Regina. I had asked her to go out with me at the Summer Ball. She and I were supposed to be soul mates. And if I could just muster the courage to send her some flowers, I knew she would understand that we were one.

Grace made me tell her everything. Then she made me tell her everything again. And then she asked to hear it all for a third time. I knew it wasn't because she'd forgotten; it was because she wanted to hear it again and again. She breathed in my words like a fish starved of oxygen.

At the end of the sixth telling and when she'd completely whipped me (with words like HEARTBROKEN, LOVESICK and SUNKISSED) and ground my nose into my defeat, she got up and said, 'Don't tell your grandfather I was around so late tonight. I've got my reputation to think of.' And then she winked at me.

I got the impression that Grace sometimes remembered more than she let on. But I was happy to pretend with her that what had happened was just a midnight Scrabble lesson. And that there wasn't a crazy, terrified man lying on the sleeper couch on the stoep battling his nightmares.

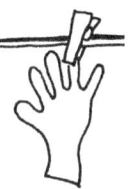

Things I Know:

The Village library
has a sloppy lending
system

15

the KNOWLEDGE OF BOOKS

My mother says that when life hands you a lemon, make lemonade. She also says things like: the tests of life are not meant to break you, but to make you. Her favourite is: never talk defeat, use words like hope, belief, faith, victory.

She gets these inspirational words from an American bloke called Norman Peale who wrote a book called *The Power of Positive Thinking*. She gave me a copy of the book on my seventh birthday and said that it would help me stop being such a negative worry-boots all the time.

I read a couple of pages from Chapter Six: Stop Fuming and Fretting after I woke up and put on my jeans and found they were sopping wet from my glass of bedside water – which Pops had knocked over while he was chucking the contents of his filing cabinet around my/his room. The soggy jeans weren't the catalyst for my bout of fretting and fuming. It was the note Regina had written me after our movie date which I discovered smudged and dripping in the back pocket that did it. And it didn't help that I'd been up all night playing Scrabble with Grace Foxcroft and then worrying about why Pops was behaving like a nutter. Because if there was one thing I knew for certain it was that Pops was definitely not bankrupt and that made his behaviour in the early hours of the morning totally dubious stuff.

Pops was having a lie-in that morning. It was unusual for him not to be up and about before everyone else in the Village. He always said that there was plenty of time to sleep when you were dead and that life was too short to waste it lolling about in bed, but I supposed he was feeling as tired as I was.

I made him a cup of tea and then went back to his/my room and stuffed all the papers back in the files as best I could before heading off to the library. My mission: research. After tossing and turning all night I had come up with a couple of theories as to what had caused Pops' weirdness. Now I needed to check them out and there was only one place in Nelson Mandela Gardens that I could do that – the Library.[14]

The Library was next to the Entertainment Hall. It was

---

[14] The Internet cafe was closed for a few days after some clown infected all the computers with a super-toxic virus.

only open for a couple of hours in the mornings as it was staffed by the residents – a handful of whom took it in turns to check the books in and out.

That's another thing I learned about old people. They take their obligations really seriously. If they say they'll do something, they'll do it. For example, I was taking the garbage out one Friday morning and I overheard these two oldies talking about what they were doing for the day (watching the weather, fetching the post – to mention a few of the highlights) and the one asked the other if she wanted to make a fourth in a game of bridge. And the other said no – on account of the fact that she had her library duty. She said it with a long sigh, like she was really sad to miss out on the game and that library duty was a big drag. But I could also hear that she wanted the other oldie to know that she had really important things to do, stuff that people would notice if she didn't do it. Like she was indispensable or something, and if she fell down dead one day and didn't pitch for library duty it would be a really big deal for everyone.

As soon as I stepped into the library I saw that there was a table at the front of the room which had a sign that said *New Releases* stapled to it. It was obviously for all of Mrs Blackman's books and as there was heavy demand for them I wasn't surprised to see that the table was empty.

Behind the table was a desk and behind the desk that day was Mr Andrew Cuthbert. Not one of my favourite residents, if the truth be told. He always looked at me with an attitude. A bad attitude. I hadn't a clue what I'd done to get his back up, but I could tell that he really didn't like me. He always wrinkled his nose when he talked to me, like he didn't like my smell.

At any rate, I wasn't looking forward to wrestling the whereabouts of the kind of book I needed from Mr Cuthbert, so I walked around the shelves, trying to find it on my own. But the old fart wouldn't let me. He followed me around like a stray dog, like I was about to steal or deface one of his precious books. 'Can I give you a hand there, Randy?' he finally asked, in a tone of voice that said he knew how much the 'hand' and 'Randy' combo would get to me – and that he knew that I knew that he did it because he couldn't stand my guts.

There were two ways I could have dealt with Mr Cuthbert. There was the Randolph St John Goodenough Junior way, which was where I went into a rage-sulk or lost my cool so that he got off big time knowing how he'd got to me. Then there was Pops' way. Pops always said that no one got hurt if you just treated everyone right. You didn't get hurt and they didn't get hurt and that was the way that life should be. People not hurting each other, because let's face it, we were all people. So I turned to Mr Cuthbert with my goofiest gee-whiz smile and said very loudly and very slowly, 'Gee, thank you, Mr Cuthbert. I'm looking for a medical reference book. Would you find one for me?'

And while I knew that in principle I had stuck to the rules of engagement à la Pops, I also knew that Mr Cuthbert knew that I had wanted to jerk his chain by speaking like I did – and that he knew that I did it because I couldn't stand his guts.

'Soap and water three times a day,' he snarled at me. 'That's the only way to deal with chronic acne, boyo. You don't need a medical reference book to tell you that.'

He said it really loudly so that everyone in the library turned around to look at the red-haired boy with terrible acne, alias me.

Just before I bludgeoned Mr Cuthbert unconscious with the nearest dictionary, Mr Trevor van Rooyen, from Number 17, asked Mr Cuthbert where all Mrs Blackman's 'new release' books had got to. And it wasn't just Mr van Rooyen who wanted to know; there was a queue of other residents waiting to ask the same question.

It transpired that the ten 'new release' books were in the custody of Mrs Frida Hackering (at Number 83) along with one hundred and nineteen other books she still hadn't returned from the beginning of the month. Somebody had to go and get them back from her before there was a riot. But everyone at the library appeared to be suffering from a violent attack of selective fatigue syndrome:

'I can't do it, you go.'

'No, you.'

'I can't, she won't give them to me.'

'But it's your turn!'

Things were getting a bit unruly, until, suddenly, all eyes turned to me. I could see from the way Mr Cuthbert was smiling at me (one notch away from a sneer) that there was something very dodge about the task I was about to be asked to perform, so I muttered something about having to meet Pops in five minutes (white lie).

But Mr Cuthbert said what a pity, because he knew that Pops himself had been very keen to read the latest John le Carré and Dennis Lehane – two books which were being held hostage by Mrs Hackering. Pops would be very disappointed – very, Mr Cuthbert said and gave me a look which said he thought I was the crappest grandson a grandfather could possibly have. It was that look that did it. I said I'd go. I wasn't going to have Mr Cuthbert telling everyone in the Village what a pathetic excuse for a grandson I was.

On my way out, Mr Cuthbert handed me a medical journal. I barely glanced at it. Instead, I slipped another book I fancied into the top of my jeans and met his sneer with a greased-up grin. My book was called: *The Girls' Guide to Guys: Straight Talk for Teens on Flirting, Dating, Breaking Up, Making Up & Finding True Love* by a lady called Ms Julie Taylor. It would have been good to have found the equivalent book for guys, but maybe, I thought, it would be to my advantage to learn something about the opposition's perspective, as it were.

Since our movie date I had been too nervous to phone Regina. I couldn't bear to find her sitting on the beach sipping milkshakes with Peter Ranger, or sweating through another kick-boxing class, or out seeing a movie and about to share a box of popcorn – which she liked plain, not salted after all, just like Peter Ranger.

When I knocked on Number 83, Mrs Hackering opened her door to me and said, 'Why, Mr Dawson, do come in.'

I realised instantly that she'd mistaken me for the vertically challenged redhead from Number 73, so I put her straight and she said, just as pleasantly, 'Oh, sorry, Randolph dear, do come in.'

Her house, to put it bluntly, was a tip. Spiders were doing a trapeze act across her lounge ceiling and cockroaches were juggling ants in her kitchen. I'm exaggerating, but the house was pretty filthy. Not only was Mrs Hackering a selfish book-hoarder, I decided, she was also a slob. However, she was jolly nice too, and she sat me down and fed me tea and toast with last century's anchovy spread on it.

I'd been brought up to be polite, so I swallowed down the tea and did my best with the toast. Finally, I tackled her on the issue I'd been sent to deal with and asked her about the books she'd been hoarding. 'Mrs Hackering,' I said, 'Mrs Hackering, I wonder if I could retrieve some of those books you've taken from the library. The other residents are going crazy for the new Dan Brown and John Grisham.' (These were authors who brought out books every year, year after year after year, even when they were what Pops called Ess Aitch One Tee.)

'Randolph, books are my life,' Mrs Hackering said, addressing me though her eyes were looking at a spot somewhere around my left armpit. 'They are my passion. As a former professor of English literature I expect the library to grant me some leeway in the study of the latest fiction releases.' She held up the latest John Grisham, like she would a precious antique, and said, peering at the book, 'Take, for instance, this new release from PD James, the mistress of crime fiction, I need at least a month to study each criminal nuance.' And then she gave me a look that told me that if I even thought about touching one of the books in her house she'd carve my arm off at the elbow.

I could see why I'd been given the pleasant task of dealing with Mrs Hackering. I had more chance of pummelling Peter Ranger to death in a round of kick-boxing than getting her to surrender even one of her precious books. She was totally gaga. Not eccentric, not charmingly different or unconventional, but downright bats.

I took my leave from Mrs Hackering and decided in the interest of self preservation to go straight home. I didn't think I would survive the wrath and disappointment of the waiting bibliophiles at the library.

When I got home Pops practically ripped my ear off, he was so mad. 'What's all this mess? Who's been pulling papers out of my filing cabinet?' he said, waving his arms around the room and pointing at some of the bits and pieces I'd missed when I'd been shoving everything back in the cabinet.

I actually didn't know what to say to Pops because there was only one answer: 'You'. But he didn't look like he was in the mood for that answer. Maybe Pops had been sleepwalking, so he didn't remember? It was a very confusing situation.

So I told him I'd been looking for my passport, just to check that everything was in order. It was lame, but Pops must have believed it. It didn't stop him being cross though. 'Well clean up after yourself when you mess with other people's stuff,' he grumbled.

When I look back on that day I know I should have paid more attention to what Mrs Hackering had unwittingly displayed for me. That going blind and not being able to read her beloved books had pushed her around the bend. But I was too keen to get into my bedroom to read what Ms Julie Taylor could tell me about how to isolate Peter Ranger and divine the mystery behind Regina's flirting techniques.

As for the medical journal – even if I hadn't left it under the couch at Mrs Hackering's house, I don't think the *Colour Atlas on Skin Diseases*, which Mr Cuthbert had so gleefully shoved into my hands, would have given me any answers about Pops.

Things I Know:

Ouma Doreen does
not belong to a Village
newspaper syndicate

16

NOTICES FOR THE DEAD

Mrs Doreen Cupido was one of the nicest old ladies in the Village. In fact, if they had given out awards for nice people, she would have won first prize along with Grace Foxcroft and Mrs Collins.

Between ourselves, I'm actually going to put Mrs Cupido at the front of the queue for niceness – at the risk of being disloyal to Grace, who was my most favourite person in the Village (apart from Pops) – because Mrs Cupido was even nice to people who hadn't a clue that she was being nice to them – because they were all dead. So she must have known that she wasn't going to get anything back from them because they couldn't do her any favours. Not like Mrs Smythe, who kept track of all the times people borrowed sugar off her and who sent her Christmas cards and stuff like that. Keeping score, she called it.

I know all about the nice doings of Ouma Doreen – she told me that I must call her this (which was fine by me because she seemed to like it a lot) – because of her scrapbook. She showed it to me when I was passing by after walking Mrs Veronica Franklin's basset (Client Number Four).

'Rrrrrrandolph,' Ouma Doreen called out to me, beckoning to me with a long finger from the doorway, 'let me show you my secRrrrret.'

Ouma Doreen rolled her Rs like a drunk German on account of the fact that she came from a place called Malmesbury (somewhere near Cape Town) and helped along by her falsies, which she'd had since she was twenty years old because she never flossed when she was a kid.

I was game for any kind of secret. Particularly the secret of how to sprout thick black hair, get a six-pack, grow a couple of meters, iron out the cracks in my voice, get rid of my zits, gain the perfect tan, change my name to Peter Ranger and turn the real Peter Ranger into a loser called Randolph Goodenough (just minor voodoo stuff like that).

But Ouma Doreen's secret wasn't going to get me closer to Regina. In fact, it was one of those weird things that would keep most girls at a distance.

Ouma Doreen kept a scrapbook full of the names of all the people over the age of fifty who'd died in Port Elizabeth. She got all her Intel from the classified section of *The Herald* newspaper. She cut out the obits and pasted them into her scrapbook – something she'd been doing since she and her hubby Basil (I must call him Oupa Bas) moved from the Cape to the Village four years earlier.

If I had been a detective, I would have been able to deduce one important thing about Ouma Doreen and Oupa Bas, and that was that they didn't belong to one of the newspaper syndicates in the Village. The other oldies would have killed her for chopping bits out of the newspaper. Destroying parts of the daily rag before all your syndicate members had had a chance to read it was right up there with not scooping your dog's poop or biting the ends of the pencils in the Pictionary set.

'I think of it like this, Randolph,' Ouma Doreen told me, 'a deceased person is alive for as long as he or she is remembered. As soon as the person is forgotten by the living, he or she will no longer be.'

So she remembered them. Every day she paged through her scrapbook, chatting to this one and that one. Not that they could hear her, or even answer her back, but Ouma Doreen told me that by talking to them she was remembering them. When it was this one's birthday she'd bake a cake, when it was a wedding anniversary she'd make a card and when it was D-Day she'd light a candle.

Ouma Doreen was one of the few people in the Village who didn't flinch at the D word. Dead, deceased, departed, done with, she said these words loudly and without fear. She was ready and she knew where she was going when she died, she said.

Ouma Doreen's secret kept her really busy. Apart from carving up the newspaper every day and pasting in her new dead people, and marking some of the important milestones, she also tracked them down in Matthew Goniwe Cemetery and visited them on occasion. And she never went empty-handed. There was always a posy of flowers, or a card, or something pretty she'd found, like a weaver's egg or a feather. Something she could leave behind on the grave that would make people feel that they were being remembered and were still part of the world.

When I got home after visiting Ouma Doreen that Monday I found Pops pacing the carpet, wearing it out as it were. Up and down, up and down. 'Wassup, Pops?' I asked.

Pops stopped and looked at me. Then he looked at his watch. 'It's nearly six o'clock,' he said and glared at me.

I shrugged. And so?

Pops tapped his watch. 'She's never home this late. Something must be wrong.'

I didn't have a clue what Pops was talking about, but I could see that he was fretting. 'Who's never late?' I asked. 'Are we having guests?'

Pops sighed. 'Of course not, I'm talking about your grandmother. Where can she be?'

One of the more honest answers to this would have been: six feet under in Matthew Goniwe Cemetery. But I'm not one of those people who think honesty is always the best policy, especially with the way Pops was looking at me right then.

I told Pops that he shouldn't worry and I ducked into

my/his bedroom for a bit of a think. The thing was, my grandmother had been dead for seventeen years. She had just made it past midway to a century (so she would have been old enough to crack a spot in Ouma Doreen's scrapbook) when she took off into the good night.

When I think of my grandmother, she's right up there with John Lennon and John F Kennedy and Martin Luther King and Chris Hani and Mahatma Ghandi. This is not to say that my grandmother was assassinated by some lunatic. No. She's just one of those people who I really wished I'd met. Because she was so extraordinary.

Pops doesn't talk about my grandmother much – he says it feels like his heart is being squeezed to death by one of Mrs Blackman's compression stockings (that she wears to keep her varicose veins under control). But when he does, usually after he's seen a brilliant sunset, or when the waves on Summerstrand beach are gigantic and wild, his eyes light up and he flaps his hands about and he says 'fierce and extraordinary' about a million times.

I'm sorry I never met my grandmother or kept her company during the bad old days as she sat inside those police stations, knit-knit-knitting, day after day, night after night, refusing to go home until a doctor or a lawyer or Bishop Tutu arrived to help the people detained inside.

I wish I'd stood with her outside parliament, every year, year after year, wearing a black sash across my chest, holding that placard high, silently protesting against things Pops said I could never understand because I was lucky enough to be born free. 'She gave those fascists hell!' Pops would say. 'She drove them crazy, she never kept her mouth shut, she fought them every day of her life. That was your grandmother. My Boadicia. She never stopped fighting.' But then his face, shiny and bright with memories, would sag in the middle like one of Mrs Smythe's cakes. Because both of us knew that at the very end, when there was no breath left, she gave up the fight and left us forever.

I was thinking about these things when Pops put his head around the bedroom door. He was going to have a word with Mr Groenewald. Something had happened to my grandmother. Mr Groenewald could perhaps have a word with Inspector Prinsloo. They could start a search party.

I did some quick scenario planning and concluded three things: that Pops was in a bad way, that involving Mr Groenewald would only make things worse and that I needed to do something about it. So I crossed my fingers and lied.

I looked up from my pillow and told Pops that my grandmother had phoned to say that she'd been held up, that she'd be home really late and that he shouldn't wait up for her.

Pops shook his head. 'That woman!' he said. 'Doesn't she know she has a husband to take care of?' But he looked proud. And relieved too, because he knew exactly where she was – looking after a whole bunch of other people she thought needed her more than he did.

The next morning me and Regina were dancing at the front of the barricades. Regina's wild red hair was blowing free of her paisley bandanna as the tear gas canisters exploded at her sandalled feet. I picked her up in my arms and was about to carry her out of the way of the rubber bullets and the mounted policeman who looked like Peter Ranger when Pops put his head around my bedroom door.

Pops was fretting again. My grandmother wasn't home from the shops. She always took a walk every morning to get fresh rolls and croissants from the bakery, but it had been two hours and she wasn't back. Something had happened, he was sure of it.

I knew then that another lie wasn't going to make things better. I could see from the look on Pops' face (like he had just eaten a slice of one of Mrs Smythe's collapsed-in-the-middle cakes) that this new weirdness of his was going to carry on for days and days unless I took decisive action.

I left Pops pacing the kitchen floor and told him I would be back in ten. Then I hotfooted it to Number 90, the house where the Cupidos lived at the end of the Village.

Oupa Bas and Ouma Doreen were over the moon to see me. They loved guests for breakfast, they said. It was always the best way to start a day, in the company of friends. So I took a seat and allowed Ouma Doreen to make me a cheddar cheese and apricot jam sandwich and some tea sweetened with condensed milk.

One of the nicest things about Ouma Doreen was that she was so easy to talk to. She was one of those people who allow you to speak without interrupting and saying things like 'I know what you mean …' and 'that happened to me …' and then going on to tell you their own boring story. Ouma Doreen just allowed me to talk, her calm brown eyes resting on me, drawing out every troubled word like tea tree oil on an itchy bite.

After I had spilled the beans about Pops' weird behaviour, she poured me some more condensed milk with a drop of tea, patted her doek full of curlers and said I should drink up while she got ready.

On our way back to Pops' place we passed Mrs Smythe who was mulching her bonsais on the stoep with her morning tea bag. She waved at me while pretending not to see Ouma Doreen. I knew why – because Mrs Smyth didn't like people who weren't, according to classification criteria she couldn't stop using, white. I was sort of glad for Mrs Smythe's sake that my grandmother wasn't there to see this behaviour because I am sure that it would have made her get very fierce.

We found Pops on the telephone, kicking his heels against the wall as he held on for the superintendent at the Chris Hani General Hospital. If my grandmother had been hurt and was lying in some hospital bed, Pops wanted to hear about it from the chap at the top.

Pops put the phone down when he saw Ouma Doreen at my side. 'Have you found her?' he asked. 'Is she all right?'

Ouma Doreen told him the two of them were going for a little walk, just a few blocks up the road from the Village. And that he was to stop worrying. 'I know just where she is,' she said. 'She's fine.'

Pops grabbed his hat and walking stick (a new one he had taken to using in the days after the filing cabinet incident) and the two of them went off down the pathway.

I knew where they were going without Ouma Doreen

having to tell me. In her large bag slung across her shoulder I could see the bulge of her scrapbook. And she was carrying one of the special arrangements of flowers she usually saved for those heart-wrenching D-Day anniversaries: love-in-a-mist, a spray of baby's breath and forget-me-nots.

When they returned from Matthew Goniwe Cemetery, where Pops had placed the flowers on my grandmother's grave, he searched through his photograph album and gave Ouma Doreen a snap of my grandmother for her scrapbook. Then he looked at me all red-eyed and apologetic and said that of course he knew my grandmother was gone. He wasn't off his head. It was just that some times he had a hard time believing it. Then he said that he really wanted to be alone and took himself off to his/my bedroom.

Ouma Doreen took the photo of my grandmother, tucked it between the pages of her scrapbook and said that she'd be honoured to remember such a fierce and extraordinary lady. Before she left, she fixed her eyes on mine and said that I shouldn't worry my head about Pops' behaviour. I really shouldn't worry at all. These things happened.

But her brown eyes dropped away from mine a little too quickly. And I could see that Ouma Doreen was just being nice and that it really should not have happened at all.

Things I Know:

Some Old People
don't deserve the
children they get

17

the MEMORY BOXES

I had been at Nelson Mandela Gardens for nearly seven weeks when a parcel of school books arrived for me in the post. It was accompanied by a typed letter. From my mother.

She and my father had been busy, busy, busy in the capital of Thailand. They had found themselves an apartment, a driver, a cook and a housekeeper. The city was also very busy – full of people who didn't have any water (who my father was dealing with) – and full of interesting smells – which my mother was not dealing with.

It wasn't a very long letter, but she did mention that she'd received a postcard from Pops with a picture of a cow wearing sunglasses suntanning on the beach. Was Pops all right? She couldn't read his handwriting. He seemed to be writing backwards, like kids do when they hold a mirror up to a piece of paper. Was it some kind of game Pops and I were playing?

There was a note at the bottom of the letter from my father. It was in point form:

1. Hear Joe Slovo Dam only 40% full. No more showers. Share bath with grandfather.

2. Use bathwater for garden, flushing toilets, washing clothes.

Point Number Three was all scrunched up at the end. It could have said: *Only flush when necessary – like after making a Number Two.* Or: *I'm missing you and wish you were here.* My father's handwriting is pretty ghastly, it must be said, so I couldn't be one hundred per cent sure either way.

My father has been going on at me about Water Conservation from the moment I could understand English. When I was four years old I remember asking my father to sing me a nursery rhyme. Instead, he showed me how to purify a glass of smelly water using one of his old socks. 'Far more useful than "Twinkle, Twinkle little star", Randolph,' he'd said. It's one of my earliest childhood memories. Sort of special really.

I showed the letter to Pops and he said that families were funny things. You just had to love them. Here was a woman who couldn't read her own father's handwriting and a man who wanted his son to swill around in confined aquatic spaces with his father-in-law.

The letter got me thinking about family and relatives (cousin-relatives in particular) and the rules of engagement, as it were. To be honest, I'd been thinking about nothing else since meeting Peter Ranger. The nothing else being whether Peter Ranger and Regina Versagel (cousins) could ever get married.

Themba says there are these tribes in the rainforests of South America with very kinky customs. Like the fathers marry the daughters and the sons marry the daughters and at the end of the day everybody is married to everybody else and it's a huge happy free for all and everybody has a jolly good time. Themba says it's a bit like Hef and his three babes Holly, Kendra and Bridget at the Playboy Mansion but like on a bigger scale.

I wasn't too worried by this because Port Elizabeth was getting very little rain and so it couldn't be classified as a rainforest. And anyway, Regina and Peter Ranger were of the Christian persuasion and weren't into Amazonian cult stuff. But I needed to get to the bottom of things, so to speak, so I went to consult Mrs Collins on the Anglican way.

Mrs Collins said it was very sweet the way I was taking my duties as Brutus' moral guardian so seriously, but to be honest he was way past getting busy with that sort of thing and had been fixed several years ago. But for future reference, it went like this: a person was not allowed to have relations with the progeny of his mother or father (or their progeny's progeny).

I wasn't clear from what Regina had told me where Peter

Ranger fitted in on the progeny stakes. I wondered how I could raise this delicate question with her (if I ever got the guts to pick up the phone again) as I made my way over to Mrs Amanda Griesell's place.

It had become a bit of a thing, my visits to Mrs Griesell. Ever since she'd called me over while I was delivering a newspaper to Number 39 a couple of weeks earlier: Could I, would I be a dear and go and pay her telephone account? She was not able to get out any more and she couldn't risk having her telephone cut off – one of her sons might phone.

Mrs Griesell had seen better days. Now she was seeing the worst of the last of them. Mrs Smythe had told me that it had all happened very quickly: one day Mrs Griesell was at the doctors with an itchy mole on the side of her neck and the next they opened her up and closed her up even faster. There was nothing to be done except to hope it came quickly. It would be a merciful release, Mrs Smythe had said. Then there would be a vacancy and someone on the Village's waiting list would get lucky. There was nothing likeable about Mrs Smythe when she said stuff like this and I was glad I wasn't related to her and wasn't therefore obliged to love her.

While Mrs Griesell waited for the end she was putting her things in order. And I was helping her. Apart from the funeral arrangements (cremation after a laying out at Doves Funeral Parlour) and the will (everything split between her two sons apart from a little something for the maid, who had been with her for ten years), there was the disposing of personal effects. And that's where I came in.

Mrs Griesell was making up special memory boxes for

her sons Lars and Ernst, the progeny from her marriage to a Swede called Mr Hors Griesell, who had passed on nine years earlier. The memory boxes contained all the things that she had treasured from her sons' childhoods and that she now wanted them to have.

There was a whole lot of stuff going into these boxes: Lars's baby teeth, a letter to Father Christmas (*Dere Santa, yore bered is fake and you smel like vodca*) and an X-ray from the time Ernst broke his arm when Lars had pushed him off the garage roof. The kind of stuff that blokes hate their mothers for keeping.

While I was assigning all this junk to the two boxes, I kind of got to know Lars and Ernst quite well. I could tell that Ernst was the nice guy. He had a whole lot of certificates from school for being nurturing and caring to the kids in the junior grades (and he had done a first aid course and was a Scout). A bit of a loser, but the kind of guy mothers like to have around. Except that neither Ernst or Lars had been around for a while – like twenty years. Lars was in Canada and Ernst was in Australia. It was as though they had gone to the opposite sides of the world just to avoid bumping into each other or something.

Mrs Griesell told me that they were coming home as fast as they could but it was taking a while because Canada and Australia were far away and her sons had demanding jobs. But they would get there before the end.

That afternoon, it was the third Friday in November, the memory boxes were finally done and I could see that Mrs Griesell was also nearly done because the social worker was around, making noises about her being moved to the Village's Frail Care Unit for 'the next couple of days'.

What she really meant was 'the last couple of days' because everybody knew that there was only one way out of the Frail Care Unit (in a box – one that looked like a coffin and not a memory box). It was such a depressing place, those that went in called it quits as fast as possible.

But Mrs Griesell was determined to hang on for as long as it took Lars and Ernst to arrive and she was going to hang on in her own home. That's what she told the social worker.

I threw myself around my bed that night, thinking about Peter Ranger and Regina, but shortly before dawn the emergency siren went off, making its *eyawa-eyawa-eyawa* noise. It didn't wake me, because I hadn't slept a wink, and it didn't wake Mrs Griesell either – because she had pressed the emergency button and then stopped hanging on waiting and just let go.

I knew I should call Regina the moment it was confirmed by Mr Groenewald. Mrs Griesell had been one of the residents Regina had popped in to see in between her card-playing marathons with Felicity Foxcroft and she would have wanted to know.

I hadn't spoken to her for more than a week – not since our movie date – and my fingers trembled as I scrolled down to the familiar number in my phonebook.

Her voice sounded cold and distant in my ear. 'Long time, stranger,' she said in a sort of snarky voice.

I knew I owed her some sort of explanation, but she owed me one too – about Peter Ranger and why she drank milkshakes on the beach with him when she should be walking Brutus and playing ping-pong with me. But this was not the time.

I told her about Mrs Griesell and she said: 'Oh, no, Red. It was too quick.' And from the snuffling sounds she was making on the phone I could hear she was quite overwhelmed. I was making the same snuffling noises back to her and when she said, 'Hang in there, Red, just hang in there' I felt the distance between us disappear.

On the Monday of the funeral Regina took a day off school so that we could go to the Funeral Parlour to say our last goodbyes to Mrs Griesell.

Mr Groenewald had arranged a kombi to take the residents down the road to Doves and he'd even put cooler boxes filled with cans of fizzy drink on board to make it a bit of an outing for everyone. The residents seemed to be in need of cheering up. Everyone was very subdued and on their best behaviour – like they were holding their breath, determined not to draw any attention to themselves just in case the Big Guy was looking for another candidate now that Mrs Griesell was out of the game.

Me, Regina, Pops and the Foxcrofts were part of the first contingent to make the trip down the hill to the Funeral Parlour. Regina and I hung around outside the front while the others went in.

Grace was the first to emerge. 'Who is that?' she asked

– which I thought was a little insensitive even for someone as gaga as Grace, especially seeing as Mrs Griesell had only been gone a couple of days.

But it was when Felicity emerged that I knew there was a problem. 'I wasn't told it was fancy dress – which of the Musketeers is she pretending to be?' she said, clutching herself with excitement.

Regina and me made it into the room fast and peered into the casket. Mrs Griesell lay dressed in a lilac suit, sporting one of the most luxuriant black moustaches I had ever seen. I looked at Regina. 'That's not her, is it?'

Regina shook her head. 'No, it's not, Red. It really isn't. Not even close.'

The director at the Funeral Parlour was all apologies and said he would set things right in a couple of ticks. He removed the casket with the bloke in it and put Mrs Griesell on show.

The rest of Mrs Griesell's funeral went off with only minor hitches. Lars and Ernst didn't make it in time for the commemorative tea, but Mr Groenewald read out a dedication which Ernst had faxed over. 'She suckled me at her breast, she wiped my tears when I fell, she paddled my bottom when I was naughty and gave me the best love a woman has to offer,' Mr Groenewald read.

The speech caused quite a stir. 'I had no idea it was *that way* between Mr Groenewald and Mrs Griesell!' Mrs Smythe hissed, and Mr Groenewald's face got redder and redder as Felicity heaved and snorted with glee.

I glanced at Regina. Her glasses were misted over and

her chin wobbled like she was trying to stop herself from howling. I reached over to take one of her hands but she'd tucked them between her knees and I didn't want it to seem like I was grabbing her between her legs and stuff.

After the tea, me and Regina took my godson Brutus for a walk. We stopped by Mrs Griesell's house, where a bunch of guys from Elliott were packing all her possessions into a van. A big, middle-aged bloke was giving the removal guys instructions.

Brutus went straight for the guy's crotch and when he got told to 'Bugger off, Sheila!' in a nurturing, caring sort of way, I knew at once this was Ernst, the nice son from Australia.

Brutus then made a beeline for the overflowing garbage bins by the side of the truck and started scratching around in the green double-strength bags. He got covered in some really sick-smelling stuff and dragged away a box that only I would have recognised (oh and Mrs Griesell if she was looking on). It was the Ernst Griesell Memory Box and it had been crushed into that heavy duty garbage bag along with all the old newspapers and crap that Ernst had told the guys from Elliott not to bother moving.

I wanted to scream at Ernst, to tell him to stop, but my voice was locked in a sore space in my chest.

As I watched Brutus trash Mrs Griesell's precious memory box, I mentioned the progeny question to Regina. To be honest it came out all choked and jumbled, but Regina assured me that she wasn't related to Brutus or Ernst and certainly not to Peter Ranger. 'I call him my cousin because our families are very close,' she said. 'Peter and I are more like brother and sister. But we're not blood relatives at all, you know, Red.'

The story was that Mrs Versagel (who was not Mrs Versagel then) and Mrs Ranger (ditto) had been born in the same hospital forty years earlier. They were best friends for life and went to the same school and ... But I wasn't hearing anything Regina was saying any more because all I could see was Peter Ranger and Regina and Hef and his babes (Kendra, Holly and Bridget) and Lars and Ernst and Brutus doing stuff to each other I'd always been told families never did – well not the kind of families I knew.

Regina stopped talking when she saw my face and she asked me if I was feeling all right. I said I wasn't and that I was going to lie down, would she mind taking Brutus back to the Collins' residence? She put her hand on my arm but I pushed it off and turned my back on her.

As I walked away Regina called out to me that after dropping off Brutus she would go and visit Felicity, but could she stop by afterwards to see how I was feeling? I could hear by the tone of her voice that she wasn't sure what was going on and that my behaviour had upset her but I still didn't answer her. In a mean sort of way, I was glad.

I got home and went straight for the box under my bed where I kept my special memories. There were the photos of my housekeepers, my baby teeth and a birthday card from my mother she'd sent me from Mauritius on my fifth birthday. *You're old enough to make your own bed now*, she had written.

The letter from my parents that I'd received earlier on

in the week was lying next to my bed. I gave it a vicious crumple and took a very long, very hot shower. Then I put on the sprinkler full blast and turned on the washing machine and flushed the loo five times. And then I flushed it one more time – just for my mother and father and Mrs Griesell's memory boxes.

When I was done, I walked down to the entrance gates of the Village where Regina always caught her lift home at five o'clock sharp. The red Mini Cooper was idling outside the gate and I saw the black curls and the iron jaw and the vice-like hands on the steering wheel.

Regina saw me as she came up the path from Felicity's. She waved and came over to ask how I was feeling and to say goodbye. Then she saw the car. 'Oh, good, it's Peter Ranger,' Regina said, smiling for the first time that day. 'He's come to take me home.'

She turned to me and I could see she wanted to give me a hug, to say she was sorry about Mrs Griesell, but I put my hands out to keep her away. Back off, my face said. Don't touch me.

Regina stumbled off as though I'd struck her and got into the car. Before she buckled up, she threw herself into Peter Ranger's arms and he stroked her around and around on her back – in what I suppose could be termed a brotherly fashion. It's something I wished I could have done. And as I watched from behind the gate I felt my face grow ugly, turning me into someone who looked like a close relative of Mrs Smythe.

As the car drove off, Regina stared back at me. She looked confused, dazed and awfully sad – a bit like the way Pops had looked when he'd come out from saying goodbye to Mrs Griesell at Doves that morning. It had been as if although he could see from looking at the strange person lying in the casket that something was terribly wrong, he just didn't know exactly what it was.

Things I Know:

Don't leave it too
long to tell people you
love them

18

the NEW RESIDENT

There was a lot of stuff that got the residents at Nelson Mandela Gardens all revved up (apart from oysters). It was as though the old folks had nothing better to do than to get uptight about things that other people wouldn't really bother about. That's how it seemed to me sometimes. But, hey, what did I know?

There was a long list that really got the bunch at the Village going. The top five were:

1. The weather (it was certain to rain) – Major Excitement
2. The failure by a resident to scoop his/her pet's poop from

the sidewalk – Major Sin

3. Hogging the latest Mrs Blackman best-seller from the library – Major Crime

4. Buggering the daily newspaper too much (if you were part of a newspaper syndicate), especially the classifieds with all the obits – Major Misdemeanour

5. Nicking the dice from the snakes and ladders set – Major Offence

But there was something that beat all this stuff in the excitement stakes and that was the Arrival Of A New Resident. This was considered a Big Deal.

The New Resident arrived five days after the passing of Mrs Griesell. Some people might say it was a bit insensitive that it all happened so fast, but let's face it, Mrs Griesell didn't need her old place any more and the waiting list at Nelson Mandela Gardens was pretty long (so long in fact that a lot of the applicants fell off the list and went on to the Big Mansion upstairs before their time for a house in the Village arrived).

The New Resident at Number 34 – right opposite Felicity Foxcroft – was a retired pilot by the name of Captain Jack Eagle. He'd spent the past forty years of his life flying 747s all over the world. Name a place, Captain Jack had flown there. He could tell you about the perilous state of the landing strip of Ottawa Airport, what the departure lounge in Brisbane looked like and the cool things you could buy from the duty-free shop in Auckland. He knew all kinds of details about the major cities of the countries where most of the residents had kids and grandchildren, so Captain Jack was an instant hit in the Village.

Captain Jack had also met the most interesting people on his travels. Not only big-shot politicians like Nelson Mandela (Business Class 1A – who had the chicken) and FW de Klerk (Seat 3B – a beef man), but all the glossy people of this world. Once he had even flown Timothy Dalton, one of the lesser known 007s (two movies), to Los Angeles. Okay, so Buster would say that old Timothy was the crappiest Bond guy on account of his sensitive hero persona, which was just a bit girlie – but I still thought that it was a bit of all right that Captain Jack had met him.

Unsurprisingly, Captain Jack was a big hit with the Sad Singles. They went wild for him. I didn't get it at first because there were a number of widowers at the Village and they hadn't captured the imagination of the ladies in the way that Captain Jack did. But our Captain Jack was a bachelor – and that made all the difference.

Themba tells me that there's a thing called the 'bachelor factor' which really turns the chicks on. Part of it is the challenge, the thrill of the chase, and then there's the mystery of the unknown which surrounds the bachelor. With bachelors you know for a fact that some woman hasn't sorted his socks or starched his collar or dealt with the toilet seat issue on a daily basis. The bachelor is untarnished by these mundane domestic intimacies. An untamed beast, as it were.

On a more important note, Themba says that everyone knows that bachelors get it more often than married blokes.

It's because, as they're constantly moving on to new terrain, the bachelor is always up – so to speak – for trying different things. So you know you'll be getting five-star room service when you do it with the bachelor, as opposed to the quick takeaway you'll get with a regular married guy.

If I considered that Captain Jack had flown to more than thirty-five countries and had been put up in swanky airport hotels with dimly lit bars full of air hostesses wanting to fiddle with all the buttons in his cockpit ... Well, my mind boggled. And it was boggling the minds of all the Sad Singles too.

I was a little in awe of Captain Jack, it must be said. He was the kind of grandfather most chaps would have given away their granny to have. And as much as I thought my Pops was the best in the world, to be honest, he'd been a bit weird and cranky of late. Captain Jack, meanwhile, was someone people trusted to take them thirty-six thousand feet into the air for twelve hours at a time. The kind of guy you would put your faith in.

I was down at Felicity's the day after Captain Jack arrived in the Village, watching the ladies from her lounge window beating a mud path to his front door in the hope that one of them might become the one to sort his socks and put the cap on his toothpaste.

Felicity had shown no interest in the New Resident. I don't think she even knew his name. She had very little time for most people and most people had very little time for her. Most people except Pops – and Regina Versagel.

I had taken to visiting Felicity at odd times that week in the hope that I might bump into Regina. I hadn't seen her

since Mrs's Griesell's funeral and I felt too messed up inside
to call her and tell her how bad I felt for behaving like such
a turd factory. Instead, I spent my time imagining the casual
encounter which would allow me to see her again – and tell
her something that would make things right between us.

But despite haunting Felicity's house at all hours of the
day and night I hadn't had a single Regina sighting. I just
couldn't figure it out. Was she sick? Had she and Felicity
fallen out as well? Would I ever see her again? Between
ourselves, my tummy ran like a soft serve ice cream machine
with the worry of it all. I was being eaten from the inside out
by visions of Peter Ranger and Regina. Not cousins, but as
close as brother and sister. Like the Greek gods: Zeus and
Hera. Brother and sister and married to boot. Those Greeks
had a lot to answer for.

I had spent an agonising couple of days pruning back all of
Felicity's lavender, mowing her lawn, taking out the garbage
and bottling seventy bottles of peach jam. And Felicity had
just started on about how she thought I might like to help
her sort through her garden magazine collection (spanning
thirty years) when it came out. I just couldn't stand it any
more. 'Where is she?' I snapped. 'Why isn't she here? What
have you done with her?'

It must be said that I wouldn't have put it past Felicity to
hide Regina away when she saw me coming. She would have
got a kick out of that, I know.

Felicity fixed her hard grey eyes on my face. 'Oh,
Randolph! And here I was thinking all this time that you'd
come to see me,' she said. 'I would have mentioned it earlier

if I'd known: Regina is studying for exams, she'll come around tomorrow.'

But the way she said it, in that smug way of hers, I just knew that she had been onto me all along.

I said I had to be going then and I would be around tomorrow. Felicity replied that she would walk with me part of the way as she wanted to pop into Grace's. We were halfway there when I spied Mrs Smythe coming our way. She was with Captain Jack and she waved at us madly just in case we hadn't seen her. In fact, the way she was waving her arms around, it seemed she was quite determined to make sure that everyone in the Village saw she was with Captain Jack. She was out of breath from all the mad waving by the time we got to her. 'Felicity, Randolph, you just have to meet my new best friend, Captain Jack Eagle . . .'

And then Mrs Smythe stopped to have a coughing fit.

I was a bit preoccupied with the whole coughing saga, but when I took a break from thumping Mrs Smythe on the back I noticed that Felicity and Captain Jack were staring at each other in the oddest fashion. Felicity's expression was similar to the one she'd had on when she'd realised that I had put in half the quantity of sugar into her peach jam and that the whole batch was pretty much screwed (contempt/ rage). Captain Jack had the same look on his face that all the blokes in the Village got when they looked at his collection of photos of a blonde beauty queen called Anneline Kriel, whom Captain Jack had had the privilege of flying to the Bahamas one year (adoration and something else which I didn't think old blokes should really be feeling).

'Filly? Blow me down, Filly. Is that you?' Captain Jack said to Felicity.

But Felicity just hissed at him through clenched teeth and stormed off wheezing in the direction of her house.

It was all a bit strange, but to be honest, what with Pops' weirdness, I was starting to figure that all old folks had strange turns every now and then. But it all came out in the end. There was no way poor Felicity could have kept her secret, especially as Mrs Smythe had smelt the whiff of a scandal. By that evening, everyone in the Village had heard the whole story. It went like this:

Forty-five years earlier, Felicity had been dating a nice young man called David Eagle. He bought her cream sodas at the roadhouse on the beachfront, he escorted her to light comedies at the bioscope, he played long games of tennis and gin rummy with her into the late afternoons and he held her hand with gentle respect. He was a nice sort of a guy and Felicity was all set to boot his boring arse out of her life except for one thing: there were days when David Eagle behaved in ways that made all the humdrum days worthwhile. There were the wild bouts of hot ear-nibbling in the back seat of his Lancia Fulvia at the drive-in, sweaty games of strip poker into the early hours of the morning, dry martinis in the cocktail lounge at the Beach Hotel followed by breathless marathon tango dance sessions. And it was during dates like this that Felicity knew that David Eagle was The One, but she never said anything because there were too many days when she knew he couldn't be The One because he was such a bore.

Then, one day, David Eagle introduced Felicity to the

other special person in his life: his identical twin brother Jack. Except Felicity could see that they were not identical at all: Jack Eagle's pitch-black hair was glossier (more Brylcreem to tame all the unruly curls), his moustache was fuller, his sideburns were longer, the wrinkles around his devilish blue eyes were crinklier and – something Felicity cursed herself for never noticing (the big give away) – he always ate the olive in his martini.

It all went downhill after that. Felicity booted them both and David Eagle took his bruised and boring heart off to a place called Nelspruit, where he grew avocado pears and married a primary school teacher called Dot. And Felicity and Captain Jack never saw each other again – until the day their paths crossed again in Nelson Mandela Gardens.

'Filly wouldn't take my calls,' Captain Jack told me during a heart-to-heart the following day (after I'd delivered him some ice for these killer cocktails he made – a secret Maori recipe of crushed ice, rum and pineapple). 'She said she'd had a ball but it was time to move on. Oh, damn her cold, trifling heart! Just to think, all the time she had been playing with the both of us, and there I was thinking I had the upper hand. Oh, the wench! The vixen! The one . . .' And with that Captain Jack slipped into a cocktail-induced coma.

I left Captain Jack to sleep it off and went on to Felicity's. I found her drinking triple Red Bulls and vodka and smoking unfiltered cigarettes while grimly watching Captain Jack's house through a pair of binoculars. 'She'll be arriving at four,' Felicity said. 'She doesn't know you're here and I won't be around when she comes.'

Felicity said she was going over to Captain Jack's to tell him what she should have said forty-five years earlier: that he was a sonofagun for pretending to be David, and that he'd broken her heart, but that he was The One and that she wasn't too proud any more to tell him. 'And you stop messing that girl around, you silly idiot,' she growled at me. 'Sort things out. Do you hear me?'

I said I heard her loud and clear because her face was two inches from mine and she had me by my collar and was shaking me up and down like I was a cocktail shaker.

Felicity swept off across to Captain Jack's and I sat waiting for Regina while my stomach churned like Mrs Dearden's smoothie maker.

I didn't let Regina get past the doorway before I started talking and I didn't stop for like ten minutes. I told her I'd behaved like a louse because Peter Ranger didn't get blotchy in the sun and because I didn't have a driver's licence let alone know how to fly a Boeing but that one day I'd have clear skin and know how to play strip poker ...

My stomach was making the most awful sounds and I could feel a hot sweat breaking out all over my neck.

My girl stood in the doorway and shook her head: 'Don't tell me you also ate some of that peach jam of Felicity's? She called me the other day and told me that some idiot had only put in half the sugar – it's complete poison.'

I shook my head and Regina smiled. 'Oh, good, because then you'll have no excuses when I thrash you at ping-pong.'

On our walk to the Entertainment Hall I cleared my throat and whispered to Regina, 'You're the one.'

Then I wondered about all those things that were never said or things that weren't ever said clearly and were misunderstood. Things that kept people like Felicity and Captain Jack apart for forty-five years because they were too hurt and proud. And so I got me up some courage and croaked, 'Will you be my girlfriend?'

Regina smiled at me and I hoped her smile meant yes, but to be honest I wasn't sure if she'd heard me over the sound of laughter and Tango dance music coming from Captain Jack's house.

Things I Know:

Old People stick
to the rules because
they're scared

19

the DRYING HOUSE THIEF

There was this place at Nelson Mandela Gardens called the Drying House. In reality it wasn't a house at all, it was just an enclosed courtyard next to the Entertainment Hall where people could go and hang their washing in the sun. It existed because of a rule at the Village which said that a resident may not hang his/her washing on their premises so that his/her washing was visible to other residents. You could hang your washing up to dry inside your house, or on your stoep (if it was enclosed), or in your garage, or if you were lucky (like Pops) you could hang it out the back of your house on a wooden clothes horse – because it was protected from public scrutiny by a wall. This was a good spot for his washing because it got the sun and stopped him ending up like poor old Grace Foxcroft, who always smelt a bit like exhaust fumes because she had to hang her washing in the garage and it didn't get that nice sun-kissed smell.

I never got to the bottom of the public display of washing issue during my stay at the Village. I suppose the Rules Committee thought it was aesthetically unpleasing to view old people's underwear and pyjamas. Or that the visible display of old people's washing all over the Village would lower the tone of the establishment. However, whatever the objection, having the Drying House meant that all the residents' washing could be viewed en masse by everyone who hung their washing there. So instead of a few pervy individuals glancing at the odd washing line on their way to get their newspaper or while out walking their dog, the Drying House provided the ultimate visual orgy of old lady blouses and old man trousers. Go figure.

Buster said that the whole reason for the Drying House was rooted in phobia. Buster is quite the expert on phobias. For example, he told me that Roger Moore almost didn't get the part of 007 because he had a phobia of guns (not gums, that came later). This fear of guns came about after a rifle exploded in his hands when he was doing his national service in the British military. It was a pretty frightening accident and apart from making him blink every time he heard a bang, or even when he squeezed the trigger of a gun, he was also deaf for a while. Buster said it was a good thing Roger overcame his phobia because having a deaf, blinking bloke as Britain's number one spy would have been a bit of a downer for the ratings.

I wasn't sure whether Mr Groenewald had a phobia of water (hydrophobia) or of washing (ablutophobia) or even of washing lines, as Buster claimed, but he was the brains behind the Drying House, so maybe there was something in it.

The Drying House rules were very strict. Very. The use of the House was allocated to certain residents on certain days of the week – Mondays to Saturdays (no one washed on Sundays). Pops had Wednesdays with houses 31 to 45. There were fifteen washing lines and you occupied your line when it was your day (though no allowances were made to give extra washing line space to the Lucky Ones – which made the Sad Singles feel just a tiny bit better about everything).

The thing was, Pops didn't use his washing line. When he had to wash the occasional sheet or towel he used his wooden clothes horse. Not like Mrs Tracey Barber in Number 33 who washed and changed her sheets and duvet cover every week (paisley for Weeks One and Three and stripes for Weeks Two and Four). She was desperate for extra space. So Pops gave out his washing line to people like Mrs Barber and Mrs Debbie Brewer (who was allergic and so was always washing her curtains and sofa covers).

I became an expert on the ins and outs of the Drying House in the first week of December, a week that became known in the Village as the Week Of The Drying House Thief. It was a very exciting time and it kept a couple of the residents' hearts pumping faster for many a day after.

The first I heard of it was from Mrs Trudy Venables (Number 14). She was part of the Monday washing crowd and used her line mainly for teddy bears and soft toys. For many years she had been placing a large cardboard box at the checkout of the supermarket a few blocks from the Village so that people could offload their old toys. She washed them, fixed them up and then gave them to the local orphanages.

To cut a long story short, Mr Cedric Framesby's dressing gown had gone missing from the line. It was a beautiful red silk gown all the way from Hong Kong which had been given to him by his son the previous Christmas. But that wasn't all. There were several other items that had gone missing from the lines of residents with whom I wasn't acquainted: a cashmere cardigan, a red velvet cushion cover (one of a pair) and a pure wool knee blanket.

One of the things I learned at Nelson Mandela Gardens was that old people take things like rules and laws very seriously. It's as though they think that if they play by the rules they'll earn points – like Voyager Miles or airtime credits. But, if the truth be told, obeying the rules is really one of the few things left that they can actually still do, apart from knitting and playing board games and stuff like that. Mostly, I think they stick to the rules because they're scared. Not just scared of getting caught, but scared really of everything. And the residents at the Village got especially scared when life's Big Rules got broken, so when things went missing that Monday Mr Groenewald was forced by public demand to call in the cops.

It took a day for Inspector Prinsloo to make his way up the

hill to the Village – I suppose he had more pressing things on his desk than some missing washing from a retirement village – and by the time he did some thirty-four more items had gone missing. Fear and panic stalked the narrow pathways of the Village and the washing lines of the Drying House swayed in the wind forlorn and empty – the residents were playing it safe.

I was around at Mrs Smythe's place (she was using my hands to cut out the fiddly bits for her patchwork quilt) and of course she was telling me exactly what she thought about the thefts. 'It's those people from Number 90,' she said, her nose wrinkling as she mentioned Ouma Doreen and Oupa Bas. 'The couple of coloured extraction.'

When Mrs Smythe said things like this I wanted to tell her exactly what I thought of her. I wanted to tell her she was a spiteful, ugly old lady. But then when I looked at her I thought she looked bitter and twisted and recently widowed, so I told her my money was on Gregory. Monkeys loved soft, colourful things. It had to be him.

Mrs Smythe said how could I, how could I accuse that sweet, innocent little monkey?

Later I went over to Grace Foxcoft's house to see if she had any views on the latest, hottest talking point. I found her turning out her cupboards, searching for her precious shawl all the way from Kashmir (seventy per cent pashmina, thirty per cent silk). We threw things around for a while until I discovered it in her broom cupboard (where Felicity had probably hidden it). Grace was in tears: she had been certain it had been stolen.

It seemed everyone in the Village was spring-cleaning their cupboards, looking for things that they were sure had been pilfered by the Drying House Thief. The Village was in a state of siege.

I myself was feeling a little under siege – the green-eyed monster was again chewing its way through my grey matter. When I had called Regina to check how her studying was going, she'd told me that Peter Ranger was tutoring her in history. They were just about to get onto the Greeks and the Egyptians (and everyone knows the Egyptian royalty were as inappropriate in regard to filial relations as the Greeks). I implored her to skip ancient history and stick with the Crusaders, but she said she was sticking close to the curriculum with Peter Ranger and goodbye.

Later, at home, I was looking for Pops' razor (he let me use it now and then to encourage the growth of my non-existent beard) when I saw a red silk dressing gown hanging in the cupboard. And in the drawer, with his socks, was a cashmere cardigan.

I was jolly happy for Pops that he'd splurged out on some new items. In the weeks that had followed his midnight paper-throwing incident he'd been in the doldrums about his finances. He'd kept on making noises about landing up in the poor house and tightening his belt and the difficulties of making ends meet. He'd also spent a few days yelling at his bank manager on the phone about where the bank had hidden all his money. None of it had made any sense to me or the bank manager (and probably not to Pops either, if he'd stopped to think about it). So this was a good sign. Pops had been indulging in a bit of retail therapy. His paranoia and financial worries were obviously at an end. I rummaged through some more drawers, and hey, it wasn't just a bit of shopping, he'd really been burning that credit card. His cupboard was stuffed with clothes I'd never seen before.

Then I realised that most of them weren't that new-looking. It all clicked into place when I spotted a red lacy bra and matching knickers (doodle-mesh thong). This was underwear that I knew like the back of my hand. It belonged to Mrs Suzie Graham from Number 24. She had the sauciest underwear collection in the Village (courtesy of Victoria's Secret) and displayed it every Tuesday in the Drying House. Mrs Smythe said she had no shame, but the old guys loved her for it.

I looked at all the other stuff and got that feeling in my stomach that I got on Sunday nights during term time when I hadn't done my homework. It was like a prune was hurtling through my stomach to the finish line. It came to me: Pops was the Drying House Thief. It was not Ouma Doreen or Oupa Bas or even Gregory. It was Pops.

I grabbed the stuff and shoved it into a garbage bag. Then I went and confronted Pops. He was in the kitchen making curry, chucking in spoonfuls of cumin seeds and cloves and all the spices he loved. 'Hey, Pops, look what I found,' I said.

Pops wiped his hands on a cloth and looked in the bag. Then he looked at me. His eyes were bright with excitement. 'It's the stolen washing,' he said, rummaging through the stuff like he'd never seen it in his life before. 'See, it's Mrs Graham's naughty knickers. Where did you get this?' Then he paused and looked at me again, but this time the look in his eyes was different. 'You didn't …?' he finally said. 'You didn't do it, did you? For fun as it were, a little prank?' He had this half smile on his face but I could see that he hoped I hadn't done it, because stealing other people's stuff and making them sad and worried wasn't really funny.

I knew then that Pops couldn't be the Drying House Thief. Not this Pops who was standing in the kitchen looking at me with a big question mark in his eyes. Because this Pops didn't remember anything about taking Mrs Graham's underwear off the line. So I told him I found it stuffed under the hydrangea bush when I was watering the garden and that I would take it to Mr Groenewald at the office and tell him.

Pops gave me a hard stare. I could see he was struggling to believe me, so I told him again about how I found the stuff and this time I added in loads and loads of detail. Which is always a big mistake, and I could see he believed me even less. So I left him cooking and went to take the stuff to Mr Groenewald.

I told Mr Groenewald my story about the hydrangea bush and he put his hand on my knee and asked me if I wanted to tell him something. Sometimes people did some things and then they were sorry. We could sort it out.

But I stared him out until he dropped his eyes and sighed. There was no ways I'd rat on Pops.

Mr Groenewald made me go over my story at least twenty times, but even though I kept my cool and he never tripped me up, when he shook my hand at he door and thanked me for turning the stuff in, I could feel by the grip of his hand and see from the hardness in his eyes that he thought I was a good-for-nothing, trouble-causing, attention-seeking little jerk. And that he would be watching me, oh, yes, he would.

On my home I called my Regina. I wanted to tell her what had happened. I wanted her to help me figure out what the heck was going on with Pops.

Regina's mother answered the phone and sighed when she heard my voice. Regina could not and would not come to the phone. And no, she would certainly not call me back later. Her cellphone had been confiscated. She was writing an exam the next day and she was at Peter Ranger's house cramming fit to burst.

I felt fit to burst. About Peter Ranger, who looked like a Greek god, and Pops, who was the Drying House Thief. I went home and had an emotional moment in the safety of my bedroom and then lay down, covering my face with the red handkerchief that smelled of Regina's hot sweaty face. Her face on mine. It gave me a measure of comfort.

I lay there under Regina's face until Pops called me for supper. Just leftover cottage pie from the night before. Leftovers! Pops! But Pops said he wasn't in the mood for eating the curry he had made.

We sat in front of the television, watching the weather forecast eating cold mince and mash. Pops didn't eat much and wasn't excited when the weatherman said it was sure to rain. In fact, he spent most of the time watching me.

That night I wondered about the Pops who had chucked his stuff out of the filing cabinet at midnight. And the Pops who had stolen other people's clothes. And the Pops who had sulked over a card game and didn't seem to want to eat any more. And the Pops who was always grumpy with headaches and had flashed his arse at the Summer Ball. I wondered about this Pops. And I knew that Pops was wondering about me too.

Things I Know:

Small things mean
a great deal to Old
People.

20

the GARDEN INCIDENT

Everyone was behaving very strangely at the Nelson Mandela Gardens Retirement Village. Not just Pops. Everyone.

For example: I was walking my godson Brutus on Wednesday afternoon and as we passed the Blackman's house we saw a delivery vehicle around the back. This was not unusual, it must be said, as the Blackmans were always getting deliveries – stuff from caterers when they were entertaining or from the florists. They spent money like it grew on trees. Or, at least, that's what Mrs Smythe always said.

Mrs Blackman was usually very chatty and when I passed

by she would often call me inside and say things like, 'Try this, Randolph, and tell me, is the Russian better than the Iranian?'

Then she would make me eat these biscuits covered with stuff I called fish eggs and she called beluga caviar. It was sort of like a trick question, because both the Russian and the Iranian caviars come from the same species of sturgeon found in the same waters off the Caspian Sea. This is what Mrs Blackman told me. She was quite the expert on caviar.[15]

But on this particular day Mrs Blackman didn't invite me inside. Sure, she came to the front of the house and talked to me, but I could see that her heart wasn't in the conversation. She kept on turning around to look at the delivery vehicle and I could see she didn't want me to be looking where she was looking.

So, of course, when I said my goodbyes, I made like I was walking on and then I circled back to the other side of the Blackman property. The sign on the side of the delivery vehicle said *Summerstrand Nursery and Landscaping* and these two guys were taking plants out of the van and stacking them neatly into the Blackman's garage.

There were loads of plants. Old Aggie's panties (Regina always called them this – they were actually agapanthus) and butterfly plants and bloukappies. You name it, the Blackman's garage had it.

It was not all that interesting to me that the Blackmans

---

[15] Which I think on a bad day could rival the Bond Movies or All Matters Of A Sexual Nature, but on any day would definitely blow my father's area of expertise out of the water.

were stockpiling plants in their garage, so me and Brutus carried on with our walk.

I was just at the old oak tree by Number 18 (Mr Thorne's house) when Brutus stopped to do his business. Brutus was not one of the quiet ones. When he did his thing he stuck his arse right up in the air and he pushed and pushed and made these fierce grunting sounds. The expression on his face was so anguished that I, for one, was convinced he had a soul.

When Regina accompanied me on my walks with Brutus I always found this whole toilet thing a bit embarrassing, if the truth be told, but Regina didn't blink. She was like that, Regina, she took everything in her stride, as though a dog doing his business was a quite natural and normal occurrence. 'Ag, shame, poor Brutus. It's tough when you get old and things don't work as smoothly as they did when you were a puppy,' she would say to Brutus, watching quite calmly as he did a break-dance action with his bum on the grass to finish off.

I missed Regina. Another two days and then she would be finished with her exams and I could see her again. I had called her the night before and managed to catch her on the landline while her mother was washing her hair.

I hadn't wanted to disturb her concentration. I had just wanted to tell her to read the questions three times before attempting to answer them and to choose E on the multiple choice ones. And to breathe deeply. And that her hair smelled of cinnamon.

I said hello and then mentioned the cinnamon thing in my best Mrs Collins French.

'What?' Regina said.

I said it was something I was trying to tell her in French.

'Well, I'm writing Xhosa tomorrow, so that's about as useful as a third nostril!'

Then I heard Regina's mother calling her and before I could say anything else Regina had slammed down the phone.

I was bending down, cleaning up with the scooper and the plastic packet (how I missed Regina – she usually scooped while I held the packet open) when Mr Thorne looked over his Indian Hawthorne bush. 'Why are you spying on me?' he snarled.

I got quite a shock because I thought he was talking about the time I did my recce on him and Mrs Dodge. Then he said quickly, 'Oh sorry, Randolph, my boy. I thought you were someone else. Forgive me, I know your grandfather isn't entering this year.'

I told him it was quite all right, even though I hadn't a clue what he was blabbering on about.

Things became clearer when we got to Mrs Smythe's. She was wearing her gardening clothes and was up to her elbows in soil. She was also bitching like mad. 'I booked Elias three weeks ago to come and do my digging. And that Grace Foxcroft stole him. She said I'd double-booked. Ha!'

Elias was one of the three gardeners from New Brighton township employed by the Village. When he wasn't doing something for Mr Groenewald, he worked for the residents on a one-on-one basis. He was in great demand.

Mrs Smythe said she just couldn't do without her

wonderful Elias who coaxed her plants out of the soil with the language of the Xhosa gods. She loved her Elias, she just loved him.

I took this as another example of Mrs Smythe's Cognitive Dissonance but I wished Elias was around so that I too could love him when he taught me to say your hair smells like cinnamon in Xhosa (to coax my Regina into a better mood).

I didn't know why Mrs Smythe was so mad about Elias so she told me. 'I'll never be ready for the judging tomorrow. And I'm supposed to win this year.' And it was then that I heard all about the Village's annual Beautiful Summer Garden Competition.

It was a big thing in the Village and everyone took it very seriously. Mrs Smythe had come third the year before because her bed of agapanthus only opened after the judging. 'But what a glorious showing it was when they finally did open,' she said.

The following day, Mrs Smythe told me, Mr Groenewald, assisted by three members of the Port Elizabeth Garden Society, would decide who had the most beautiful garden. As a result, all the competitors were working like the blazes to try and perfect the winning entry. Each one was trying to do something unusual that would catch the judges' eye.

Mrs Smythe took me into her confidence. She had been nurturing one hundred St Joseph's lilies and fifty trays of white impatiens seedlings in her garage all spring. The lilies were on the brink of opening and she was going to plant them in a few hours' time, when it got dark. She was creating a 'white' garden – not à la the famous British gardener Vita

Sackville-West but à la PW Botha (the infamous South African racist) she told me with one of her ugly expressions. Sometimes I wondered why I bothered with her. Then I looked at her pinched, miserable face and I knew why.

Mrs Smythe had already planted the acanthus, wild iris, white aggies and then in the evening it was going to be the lilies and impatiens. 'It will be a triumph,' Mrs Smythe said as she attacked a tribe of blister beetles that were devouring her gardenia bush and started chopping the poor devils in half with her secateurs.[16]

It was about four-thirty the following morning when I heard a noise outside my window.

I had awoken in a hot sweat from a terrible exam dream where there were no Es on Regina's multiple-choice paper. 'Choose B!' I had yelled over and over again, but for some reason she couldn't hear me.

The rustling outside continued. It was probably Gregory, I told myself. He always took an early morning prowl around our house before hitting the apples. But when I looked outside I was just in time to see a man in a pair of boxer shorts (silky with red-and-purple hearts) slope past my window. It was Pops, and he had a pair of secateurs in his hand. He waved them at me and gave me a smile.

---

[16] It was a good thing they were not Buddhist beetles, because judging from the foul names Mrs Smythe was calling them, they would be coming back as lice next time around.

I smiled back. I was glad that Pops was up and about doing a bit of gardening. Granted, it was a bit early, but I had long ago learned that old people don't sleep as much as normal people. I wondered if Pops would be up for a game of ping-pong later.

Over breakfast I asked Pops how he had enjoyed his gardening and he looked at me like I was a nut. 'I slept right through. In fact, I've only just got up,' he said, all puzzled.

It was then that I got this bad feeling in my stomach. Because if there was one thing I knew without a doubt, it was that the guy who had smiled at me at four-thirty that morning was definitely Pops. I knew my own grandfather.

My stomach got worse when someone knocked on the door. It was Mrs Smythe and she was spitting mad. 'Some bastard,' she said. 'Some bastard,' she said again. 'Some bastard has deflowered my pride and joy.'

Pops looked very alarmed at this. It sounded to me like the kind of thing that the hot babes said in the sexy magazines Themba read, but when Mrs Smythe told us what had happened it was not nearly so juicy. She had woken up in the morning and gone outside to see how her St Joseph's lilies were doing. The big question in her mind was: Would they be open? And yes, the little darlings had all bloomed, but some bastard, some bastard, some bastard had chopped off all their heads.

I got the feeling I might know who the bastard was. What I didn't know at the time was that similar stories of deflowering and destruction were being told all over the Village. I learned about it ten minutes later when Mr Groenewald knocked on the door. He had someone with him. It was Mr Nathan Crawley from Number 21.

I knew Mr Crawley by reputation only. He was known as the rudest man at Nelson Mandela Gardens. People would bump into him on a walk and he would just ignore them or they would greet him at the braai and he would keep his head down.

But he was not really rude. Felicity Foxcroft, who knew him better than most on account of the fact that they shared the same dentist, had told me that he had a weird condition called prosopagnosia, otherwise known as face blindness.

Regina wouldn't believe it when I'd told her, but it is a real condition. People who are prosopagnosiacs can't recognise people by their facial features. What is even freakier is that some of them can look in the mirror and not recognise themselves. You can imagine that this must be really horrific when you're shaving every morning and there's some ugly old bloke you don't recognise staring back at you in the mirror.

As if having this weird condition wasn't bad enough, it couldn't be treated. Apparently, one out of every two hundred people have this condition and out of all the possible one hundred and fifty people at the Village, Mr Crawley (our very own prosopagnosiac) was the only witness to the vandalism. I was busy counting my lucky stars but I hadn't got to twenty when Mr Groenewald dropped the bombshell: While Mr Crawley had been unable to recognise the culprit's face, even though the man had been two metres from him, he had recognised the vandal's clothing. 'He was wearing a pair of boxer shorts with a purple-and-red heart pattern,' Mr Crawley said.

Now, if there was one item of clothing that was better known than Mrs Graham's red doodle-mesh thong, it was Pops' silky boxers. No one would ever forget the night of the Summer Ball when Pops'd had a wardrobe malfunction and pulled them down and flashed the butterfly tattoo on his arse.

Pops looked confused. 'But I've got a pair of silky boxers with red-and-purple hearts. They're my favourite,' he said helpfully.

Mrs Smythe, Mr Groenewald and Mr Crawley kept their eyes lowered.

I think my heart stopped at that point, then it was beating so hard I could hardly hear myself say, 'No, Pops. I sent them to the charity shop last week. They now belong to some poor person, not you.'

'No, that's not true,' Pops said, completely outraged. 'I was only wearing them yesterday.'

So I told him, no, he was mistaken. And that was my story and I stuck to it. Eventually, Mr Groenewald said he would call Inspector Prinsloo to come and investigate. We couldn't have outsiders coming onto the premises and damaging people's property.

When Mr Groenewald, Mrs Smythe and Mr Crawley had gone, Pops took me not so gently by the shoulder and pushed me into the bathroom, where he pulled out a pair of silky boxers with red-and-purple hearts from the wash basket. He shoved them into my hands, which was pretty sick-making because he'd had a good couple of days wear out of them and holding someone else's smelly old boxers isn't a helluva lot of fun, if the truth be told. 'Who are you?' Pops growled at me. 'You steal people's clothes and now you destroy their gardens and you lie about everything. I don't think I know who you are any more.' Pops was really mad-cross and sad and disappointed.

I turned away and crawled off to my bedroom where I lay on the floor feeling sick and miserable. I wished I could call Regina and ask her to tell me in simple English, not French or Xhosa, what she thought was going on with Pops. But I couldn't. At least, not until she'd finished her exams.

My head felt hot with all the worrying. As I fretted, I recalled Pops' miserable face as he'd shoved his boxer shorts into my hands and told me that he no longer knew me. I hadn't known what to say to Pops. Because I didn't know who he was any more either.

Things I Know:

Old People have
serious plumbing
problems

21

the BINGO INCIDENT

Mr Lawrence Blackman was the kind of guy who was always smiling. Like I would be passing by Chateau Blackman on my walks with Brutus, and five to one I would spot Mr Blackman in the garden examining his clivias. Smiling.

I use the word clivias with extreme caution because it's the kind of word that tends to get misheard and then conversations get misunderstood (words like masticate and thespian tend to suffer the same misfortune).

The thing with clivias is that they take precisely seven years to flower from the time of germination. And each shy flowering only produces a handful of seeds. Gardener's gold, that's what Mr Blackman called clivia seeds. And a bloke like

Mr Blackman really knows about gold because as the richest man in the Village he was rolling in the stuff. No wonder Mr Blackman was always smiling.

On this particular morning, the day after the judging of the Beautiful Summer Garden Competition (won by Mrs Smythe for her Apartheid is Dead theme, strikingly depicted by decapitated lilies), Mr Blackman was glaring at his clivias – in a smiling sort of a way. His mouth was pulled into a bare-toothed grimace and he was rubbing his Ray-Bans with the edge of his Lacoste golf shirt as though he couldn't believe his blue-tinted contact lenses. 'Only thirteen,' Mr Blackman said as he examined a floret of seeds on a yellow clivia plant. 'I counted yesterday and there were nineteen.' Then he examined a ripened floret of a particularly grand orange clivia plant. 'Seven today. I could have sworn there were sixteen yesterday.'

'Fifteen,' I muttered. And when he looked up I said a bit louder, 'Fine day. It is a fine day, isn't it, sir?'

Between ourselves, I knew for certain that there had been fifteen clivia seeds on that particular plant the day before because I had used eight of them to pelt my nemesis from the library, Andrew Cuthbert, from behind Mrs Smythe's loquat tree when he was out getting his post.

Mr Blackman said it certainly wasn't a fine day because some rotten cad had been harvesting his clivia seeds. He had been nurturing his gold for months and months until it had reached that perfect hue, which signalled the correct plucking time, and now half the crop was gone. It seemed that I was not the only one with itchy fingers for clivias at

Nelson Mandela Gardens.

When I feel guilty about something I tend to over-compensate, so I spent a good twenty minutes commiserating with Mr Blackman while Brutus dug a tunnel through his compost heap. To be honest, I felt like a total craphouse after he had finished explaining his 'every home a clivia home, every village a clivia village' vision to me.

It went like this: he and Mrs Blackman had been cultivating a private clivia nursery in their backyard for the last ten years and they hoped to launch their 'every … every …' concept the following year. This would involve planting five precious adult clivia plants in every garden at the Village and providing every resident with a Tupperware of germinating clivia seeds that could then be donated at maturation to the residents of other less-fortunate retirement villages in Port Elizabeth.

It was along the lines of an 'Each One, Reach One' concept and was designed to build bridges between old people in retirement villages all over South Africa (in addition to having great franchising opportunities – which Mr Blackman was still researching).

It had to be said that Mr Blackman was a great patron and a visionary – he was always looking out for ways for the folks at Nelson Mandela Gardens to enrich their lives.

Another one of Mr Blackman's big ideas was Bingo Night. Once a month, on a Saturday evening, Mr and Mrs Blackman hosted the Bingo Night. It was a huge crowd puller among the old folk. Mrs Blackman laid on a fat spread and then after everyone had stuffed themselves, and got a bit pissed on a couple of glasses of box wine, the games began.

The following night I would be attending my third Village Bingo Night, so I viewed myself as a bit of an old hand at it all. If anyone were to have asked me for a few tips I would have said the following:

Number One: stay awake – or as alert as possible.

Number Two: play with multiple cards – six is a good number (one card puts you in the game but it doesn't take you across the finishing line).

Number Three: don't sit next to Felicity Foxcroft, who, to put it delicately, is a spoiler and a cheat.

I had decided to share these insights with Regina the following day. I had invited her along on a sort of a date to celebrate the end of her exams. It was our second night-time date after the Summer Ball and I had wracked my brains for something special we could do together. Grace Foxcroft and Pops and a couple of the other folk in the Village had said that Bingo Night was quite the thing for a second night-time date, as opposed to cocktails at sunset on the beach (Mrs Smythe's silly idea) or a moonlit walk to see the Christmas lights at Happy Valley (Old Stutters – completely wacky!).

The next day Regina pitched up and we headed off to the Entertainment Hall, where I allowed her to give me a solid pasting at ping-pong. I thought that with my coaching she would become quite a decent little player.

Regina said that I seemed awfully quiet, was there

anything troubling me? I wanted to tell her about Pops and his hinky behaviour, but I didn't want to ruin our date. And things had sort of chilled between me and Pops, so I had begun to think that perhaps my mother was right about me, that I was just a needy worry-boots. So I told Regina I was just psyching myself up for the Bingo game. And, to be honest, it was true, I was aching to show her the ropes.

Pops, me and Regina arrived an hour before the actual games started so that we could save decent seats and also get our share of the lasagne, but it seemed as if everyone else in the Village had had the same idea and they were already at the buffet table like a swarm of starving cockroaches.[17]

I thought the Blackmans were pretty generous the way they put up the cash and fed everybody but Mrs Smythe said she had crunched the numbers and figured out that the Blackmans were making a tidy profit out of the Bingo Nights. In fact, she had it on good authority that Mrs Blackman used food that was way past its sell-by date – food that the supermarkets always offloaded onto the orphanages and old-age homes. I was getting used to the kind of things Mrs Smythe said by now and I wasn't going to let her ugliness spoil my second big date with Regina.

After cleaning out the buffet, Pops and me looked for a table, but it seemed that everyone in the Entertainment Hall had saved a seat for us. It was 'Oh, Randolph dear, I'm sure you and Regina will be comfortable here with us.' – Mrs Graham and Mrs Dearden – and 'No, Suzie, no! We were keeping this spot especially for Randolph and his little

---

[17] With respect to my late pet Donald.

friend.' – Mrs Barber and Mrs Brewer. What was it with these people? I wondered. It was as if they had they never seen a couple of kids on a second date before?Before Regina and I got pulled apart by the crowd, Pops suggested that we sit right at the front of the Hall at the Foxcroft's table, where everyone could see us. I agreed, but I made very sure that Regina sat between me and Pops as I wasn't going to have her being messed around by Felicity. On a previous Bingo Night I had watched Felicity remove poor Grace's buttons – which she used to cover up the called numbers – when she wasn't looking, and although Grace could never remember what numbers had been called, let alone what round we were playing, she got quite tearful that she never, ever won.

When Felicity got tired of teasing Grace, she took on the whole Hall. One of her favourites was to scream 'Bingo!' when she was nowhere near the full house of fifteen numbers. This always caused a lot of tears and excitement.

Pops had already bought a couple of books of cards for our table (Mrs Blackman charged fifteen rand a book to cover costs and to fund prizes) and I split our bag of bottle tops, that we would use instead of daubers, between me, Regina and Pops.

The evening was divided into ten rounds with ten minutes per round. It must be said that this was pretty much more than double the average time per round usually allowed, but Mr Blackman had learned to make allowance for repeating the numbers like twenty times for those who couldn't hear as well as they used to (everyone except me and Regina) – and for the fights that tended to break out when Felicity got up to her nonsense.

In addition, Mr Blackman always allowed a fifteen minute toilet break after five rounds for all those with weak bladders (once again, everyone except me and Regina) – there was always a real rush for the lavs at half-time it must be said.

One of the things I learned about old people during my stay at the Village was that they had seriously embarrassing problems in the plumbing arena. Themba tells some really hilarious stories about skidmarks and prairie dogging, but the stuff that went on at the Village was no laughing matter. In fact it made me sort of sad.

There was this one particular lady who said she was forever spilling tea in her lap. 'How clumsy I am,' she would say, looking miserable. And no one would ever say anything about her being a clumsy clot because most times she was never anywhere near a teacup.

Then there was this one time when me, Pops and Brutus were walking to the Entertainment Hall and we came upon a wicked smell in the vicinity of a panicked-looking bloke trying to wrap a cardigan around his waist. 'Ag, no, that damn Brutus,' I said, looking at the back of my shoe. 'What *has* he been eating?'

We continued with our walk, but a few minutes later Pops turned to me and said, 'Randolph, my lad, you make my heart glad.' And I knew from his smile that I had done something good, even though Brutus hadn't done anything at all.

I arranged my six cards in front of me and made sure that Regina's cards had enough space – Felicity always tried to cramp everyone's cards so that they weren't able to see the numbers (just one of her mean little tactics to try and gain an edge in the game).

I was halfway through explaining the rules to Regina just one more time when she said, 'I get it already, Red. Like Bingo isn't rocket science, okay?' And she smacked my hands away from her cards.

But to be sure, everyone was being affected by the tension in the Hall. The oldies were highly competitive. It was real nail-biting stuff. A bit like the poker showdown between James Bond and the bleeding eye guy in *Casino Royale*.

It had a lot to do with the cash prizes, which apart from the free food and booze, was the other reason why the Blackman Bingo Nights were such a hit.

There were some people, like the Robertsons, who relied on the extra few rand to supplement their income. If they scored big at Bingo, then it would be off to the casino the following morning with their cash stash in the hope that their luck would hold at the slots. Then, if it did, there was meat on the table five nights a week for that month, and if it didn't (ten to one they lost the whole stash and more) they had to hold on until the next Bingo evening for a good meat supper.

We were halfway through the fifth round (two wins to the Robertsons and one each to Old Stutters and Mrs Graham) when I noticed Pops sneak his hand over to Regina's side of the table. My hand had also been sneaking from my side to straighten up a bottle top here and there and on a couple of occasions to draw Regina's attention to One Fat Lady

(Number 8) and Never been Kissed (Number 17) – which she had missed in the first and third round.

I was just about to flash Pops a thank you smile for looking after my girl so nicely when I saw him take the bottle top *off* Droopy Drawers (Number 44) and slip it onto his own pile. I supposed Regina had made a mistake (and Pops was setting things right) and before I could think anything else about it I was distracted by the Robertsons' screams of joy as they sprinted home to their third win of the evening.

It was in the sixth round, just after half-time, when I noticed Pops' wrinkly hand emerging again – this time to remove two bottle tops from one of Regina's nearly full cards: In for a Poo (Number 72) and Your Place or Mine (Number 69).

My Regina didn't notice Pops' move and as Mr Blackman yelled 'Dirty Gertie' (Number 30) Regina leapt to her feet and yelled: 'Bingo!' But when she looked at her card and noticed that in fact 72 and 69 were still uncovered she went all red and blotchy and sat down saying 'sorrysorrysorrysorry' over and over until everyone got over their little annoyance and smiled at her again.

After that, I watched Pops' hand like I had seen tigers at the zoo watching the body parts of the people who had come to look at them. Lo and behold, Pops did it again. This time it was in round seven to Me and You (Number 2). I waited for Mr Blackman to make a couple more calls and then I slipped one of my bottle tops onto Regina's card to cover Number 2 again. But Pops was too quick for me. As fast as I covered, he uncovered.

In round eight Regina leapt up screaming: 'Bingo! I really have it this time. Bingo!' But when she looked down Dixie Lee (Number 3) was uncovered. She looked around the Hall and then looked at her card. 'I know I had them all. I had Dixie Lee, I know I did ...'

Good old Mrs Blackman came to her rescue. She compared Regina's card to the whiteboard where she crossed off the numbers each round as they were called and told the hissing Hall that Regina was indeed correct. Dixie Lee had been called. Regina Versagel was the winner of round eight.

It was that lousy rat Mr Cuthbert who made the next move. I suppose his eyes were sharper than most in the Hall from always having to keep an eye on the folk in the library trying to sneak out more than three library books. And he'd always had it in for me – and probably suspected me of the clivia seed peltings.

Before Mr Blackman could shout, 'Eyes down', to signal the start of round number nine, the old fart yelled, 'I saw old Randy do it. He's been messing with that young lady's bottle tops all evening. Playing silly buggers to try and spoil her game.'

And before I could stop myself I shouted back, 'It wasn't me, it was Pops!' Which to be honest was pretty much the worst thing I could have said. A bit like screaming, 'The Pope is a fudge-packer!' in the middle of the Vatican. Not only was I exposed as the meanest sort of cad – cheating my girlfriend out of a Bingo victory on our second date – but to cap it all I was trying to lay the blame on dear old Pops, one of the most popular guys in the Village. If I could have bitten off my tongue and fed it to Mr Swartz's mean cat Max I would have done so with a smile.

I looked around the room. Felicity (the blinking hypocrite) was staring at me like I'd walked over the white carpet in her lounge after having stepped in one of Brutus' little surprises. And she wasn't the only one, pretty much the whole Hall was looking at me like I'd slipped up in the plumbing department.

Pops didn't look at me at all. He sat at the table building a tower of bottle tops and when it toppled over, he shuffled the tops together and started again.

As for my Regina, she looked at me as though she couldn't see me at all. In fact, I know she couldn't see me because her glasses were misted up and her eyes were doing laps in two pools of tears.

I bit my lip and walked out of the Hall. I could feel Mr Blackman's eyes drilling a hole in the back of my neck. He made me feel like I'd taken ten years worth of clivia seeds and tossed them into the gutter.

Then I heard a voice. It was Pops. 'Can we play now?' he asked. 'Who's up for the next game?' And I wondered what sort of game my grandfather was playing.

Things I Know:

People shut you out
when they're feeling
like crap

22

the UNHAPPY CUSTOMER

My mother is the customer's biggest champion. She's always saying things like: the customer is always right, serve to exceed expectations, put the little guy in the front of the queue.

This is the kind of stuff she tells me and the other CEOs towards the end of the financial year when we need to budget for increased prices and screw Joe the Plumber for a ten per cent increase on the price of a burger. Then me and the other moguls run around telling the customers how important they are to us so they don't notice how we're ripping a hole in their pockets.

The good thing about having my mother as a business

coach is that I'm totally aware of my rights. I know that I don't ever have to put up with inferior service. I can always take my business elsewhere. And this was exactly what I told the lady at the telephone company when I called her for the fifteenth time about the shoddy service I was getting. Unfortunately, she told me if I wasn't happy with the service provided by the country's only fixed-line telecommunications provider, I could go elsewhere and good luck to me.

Being an unhappy customer was an understatement. I had called Regina Versagel twenty-three times since the Bingo Night. Here are a few of the scenarios I was not completely satisfied with, as explained to the Telkom lady:

I get through to Regina's mother on the landline who says she'll call Regina. Pause. Dial tone.

I phone and happen to get Regina on the line. 'Hi, Reg, is that you? Red here. I just want to say ...' Dial tone.

Then there's the late-night scenario when I just can't sleep because my heart feels like it has stage four bedsores. It's at these times I get Regina's father. Dial tone.

I thought Telkom had a lot to answer for and I explained this to the Telkom lady. If they would only, just only stop cutting the line until I had a chance to tell Regina that there had been a terrible misunderstanding ...

The Telkom lady told me to go the cellphone route and to please stop calling otherwise she'd put the cops onto me. This was all well and good, except when I called Regina's cellphone, it went straight to voicemail (again).

Pops was also having a bad service experience. His problem (or opportunity to excel, as my mother would say) was his Magimix, an old food processor he'd bought in France about thirty years earlier. It had been a loyal friend to him, chopping and slicing and shredding and grinding and puréeing and doing all those labour-intensive kitchen chores that housewives and foodie grandfathers hate to do by hand. But after thirty years of distinguished service, the heart of Pops' Magimix – that is the little motor that turns the vertical shaft to which the blades were attached – had packed it in. After much tinkering about, Pops identified the little piece of the motor that needed replacing and he called the Magimix office in Johannesburg to see whether they could sell him the part. Of course, they said. They would pop it into the post and it would be with him in four days. Oh, happy Pops! It had all been so easy. Too easy. Pops should have been warned.

Pops trekked off to the post office four days later, then had to go back the following day as it hadn't arrived, stood in a long queue and finally took possession of the magical motor part that would restore his Magimix to health.

Pops spent hours fiddling with the motor and then realised that it was the wrong part. The next day he was back on the phone to the Magimix office in Johannesburg and the manager was really apologetic. Oh *that* piece! Sorry, sorry, sorry. Our mistake. The right piece would be with Pops in four days.

This had been going on for seven weeks. Back and forward to the post office, fiddling with the motor and then back to the phone to say the piece was still the wrong piece, the right piece but the wrong size, right size wrong make, right make but not the right piece … And back and forward to the post office to send the wrong piece back and then back again to pick up the next piece that would make the motor work.

This is another thing I learned about old people. They never like to throw things away. They are always fixing and mending and darning and making do with things that I would have chucked out at the first crack. But Pops was uncommonly fond of that Magimix.

I had been made aware of this unhappy saga a few weeks back, after the fifth wrong fiddly bit had been dispatched back to Joburg. At that stage, Pops was still quite chipper and it wasn't long before he was back on the phone to the manager, all apologies for disturbing him and so grateful for his assistance and terribly sorry that they had got it wrong again.

This was the thing about Pops, he was always so pleasant. Always treating people nice. Always thinking the best of people, even when they were total idiots who were wasting his time and making him chop and slice and shred his fingers for nearly two months while the Magimix sat on the shelf like the Foxcroft sisters.

That Monday Pops returned from the post office with his ninth part. He then spent a soul-destroying morning trying to make it fit into the motor – right piece, right size, right make, broken in the middle because some idiot had stood on it as he leaped for the telephone thinking it was Regina giving him a call.

To be honest, as I watched Pops tinkering about with his Magimix I knew full well that he had about as much chance of making it work as Mrs Smythe had of making the liver spots on the back of her hands disappear by rubbing them with a wedge of lemon. And I have to admit that I felt just a tiny amount of pleasure at his frustration, as I was still a bit out of sorts with him over the stunt he pulled at Bingo Night. He hadn't even admitted to it and apologised.

But my spite evaporated when I saw the extent of his agony, so I phoned up the manager at Magimix in Johannesburg and told him that, unfortunately, some clot at the post office had evidently broken the magic piece. Would he be so kind as to send my grandfather another?

The manager sighed and said it was the last piece in the country and he would have to contact the head office in France …

Pops must have seen it on my face and before I had a chance to thank the manager and wish him well (and all the other things Pops usually said to his service providers) the Magimix hit the wall.

Pops mourned for a full afternoon while I moped around the house, staying close to the phone. But the only person who called was Felicity Foxcroft. When she heard my voice she sniffed and said, 'Oh, Bingo, it's you …' in a sarcastic sort of a way.[18]

Felicity was phoning to remind Pops about the 1820 Settlers' Club end of year lunch the next day. It sounded like something not to be missed. You had to be a member to attend the gatherings, but members could take a special

---

[18] Which I thought was a bit unfair considering she had such a bad track record as a cheat and troublemaker herself.

guest who was then allowed to join the Club if he or she met the approval of three other members.

Mrs Smythe went as a special guest about thirteen times until the Club Management caught on and told her she couldn't come back again unless she paid her annual membership fee. She paid up. No one argued with the Club Management, who were a bunch of tight-arses who had maintained an iron grip on the Club for as many years as Pops could remember.

The most exciting part about being a member of the Club – apart from the food (a set menu of potato salad, pasta salad, rice salad, a mince and potato casserole and then bread pudding for dessert) were the guest speakers.

Pops certainly brightened up at the news of the outing. He had been a member of the Club for five years and said the quality of the speakers was simply phenomenal. His eyes twinkled like the old Pops when he said this.

One month they'd had the manager of a company that exported ferns; another time they'd had a dental hygienist. And for the end of the year Christmas lunch the Club Management had secured a pest exterminator, or 'the Rat Catcher', as Felicity insisted on calling him. I could see that Pops thought this was going to be one gas of a lunch, so I tried to show some enthusiasm at being his special guest, although I would have preferred to stay home and wait for Regina to call.

It seemed like I had a lot of time on my hands to hang around the phone since Bingo Night. Four of my dog walking clients had bailed on me.

When I had gone around to pick up JR, Mrs Jacobson had said she was looking into finding a new role model for him. Then she'd relented and let me pick the fleas out of JR's ears and offered to show me her photograph album. But halfway through she'd stopped and said her heart wasn't in it. 'Randolph, my dear, I just don't know what to think,' she'd said and pushed a damp handkerchief into my hands.

Mrs Florence Guthrie had met me at the door and said that Friday (of the indeterminate breed) was feeling a bit off colour and would be working through his identity crisis at home alone today. 'Do you know who *you* are, Randolph dear?' she'd asked me sorrowfully.

And as for Princess, Mrs Clara Single just hadn't been home when I'd stopped by. Neither had Ouma Doreen. If there was one person in the Village I knew I could talk to about all the crap that was going on it was Oumo Doreen, but when I had gone round to her house I'd found a note on her door saying that she and Oupa Bas had gone to Malmesbury to spend time with their daughter. They would be back just before Christmas.

Things were certainly buzzing with excitement the next day when we arrived for the gathering at the Old Scouts Hall, six blocks down the way from the Village. All the members and their guests were wearing paper Christmas hats and the Club Management had also splashed out on some Christmas crackers, box wine and a Christmas tree. Totally festive.

Felicity had kept a place for us at her table but she was still kind of snippy with me when she greeted us (a sharp pinch on the cheek which she disguised as a fond squeeze). Captain Jack meanwhile gave me hearty slap on the back that contained enough force to down a Boeing. Only Grace Foxcroft was her lovely self. She behaved as though the Dreadful Bingo Incident (as it was being called in the Village) had never happened – which, for Grace, it probably hadn't.

First on the agenda was food. This is another thing I learned about old people: they like to eat three meals a day at set times. They want to eat lunch at lunchtime, which is at one o'clock. If you try and bring it forward by combining it with breakfast to make it brunch, they get cranky. And late lunch and dinner combos – sunners or dinches – are also not well received. Old people like to be fed on time at the same time, every day.

We carbo-loaded until the food ran out, then we pulled the crackers (Felicity cheated and kept my plastic ring with a genuine sapphire that I would have liked to have given to Regina – if she ever decided to speak to me again) and then it was the Rat Catcher's turn. Pops was right, it turned out to be a phenomenal speech. I wished, oh how I wished Regina had been with me.

The speaker, a Mr Freek Conradie, the acting manager from pest exterminating company *Vermin Beware*, cautioned us against using poisons to kill rats – for the sake of the birds. Instead, Mr Conradie advised us to use non-toxic bait mixed with Polyfilla. 'That will stuff 'em up real good,' he said, delivering the punchline and then waiting for the smiles and

251

applause.

Except the audience had just gorged themselves on an assortment of starchy salads and desserts. They shifted uncomfortably in their seats and stared at Mr Conradie glumly as they thought of the poor rats – and of their own traumatised plumbing over the next few days.

At the end of the two-hour speech, the occupants at my table all gave Mr Conradie a solid ten out of ten for entertainment value. He had managed to put most of the Hall to sleep. Some of those who had stayed awake had done unmentionable things like mini pukes into their serviettes as Mr Conradie had described the eco-friendly way to get rid of green flies and termites. A good time had been had by all.

On our way out (clutching our goodie bags of Polyfilla) we had to pass the wall of shame. This was a blackboard where, on occasion, the Club Management made important announcements and stuck up the names of all the members who had not paid their annual membership fees. It was a way of naming and shaming the bunch of tight-fisted slackers who never coughed up – the board was right at the exit where everyone could see it.

Pops walked past the board without looking. That's Pops. He refused to take part in things that might make another person feel embarrassed or humiliated. There were a hundred different ways to deal with things like this, without being petty and ugly. That's what Pops said.

I took a small peek, expecting to see Mrs Smythe's name or even Grace's (who would probably either have forgotten altogether or paid several times over), but there was only

one name on the Board. In BIG CAPITAL LETTERS. And
even though I called him Pops, I knew his name as well as
my own.

I called Pops back and pointed to the board. Pops stared
at where I was pointing. 'I paid it. I'm sure of it,' he said,
looking confused. 'I've paid for the past five years. I always
pay at the beginning of the year.' He grabbed his wallet out
of his jacket and flipped through his chequebook. He stabbed
a finger at a stub in front of the book. 'See, I paid it on the
twenty-sixth of January. See there.'

Pops grew hot and flustered. Then, as the indignity and
injustice of it all sank in, he went very red. He stormed up
to a couple of people standing in front of the door and shook
his chequebook at them. 'I paid. I paid at the beginning of
the year. How dare you!'

The one man (I think he was the Chairman of the Club)
tried to say something but Pops grabbed a pen out of his top
pocket and started scribbling in his chequebook. He then
ripped out the page and threw it at the other man I'd been
introduced to earlier who called himself the Chief Financial
Officer. This chap was gesturing and gibbering, but Pops just
flapped him away like he was one of Brutus' best fart bombs.
'I don't want to hear anything you have to say,' Pops growled.
'Take this. See, now I've paid twice. And you can take my
name off the Club membership list. I resign.' And with that
Pops grabbed my arm and stormed out, ignoring the bleating
behind him.

All the way up the hill to the Village, Pops raged against
incompetence and ineptitude, against rudeness and

uselessness and downright stupidity. It really wasn't at all like Pops, all this frustration and anger about something that really was just a mistake, a misunderstanding, a slip-up. Not something to have a heart attack over walking up a steep hill to the Village. I supposed it had all started with the Magimix and this was the last straw. That's all it could have been, a bad attack of customer rage fuelled by three helpings of bread pudding.

My mother has a few pointers on customer/service provider relationships. She always says that bad service can be dealt with if the channels of communication are kept open. If the service provider listens to the customer and if the customer allows the service provider to make amends.

When we got home, Pops went to lie down saying he had a headache and I checked on the phone to see whether there had been any messages left for me in my absence. The number five was flashing on the message counter. I nearly wept. My Regina had called.

The messages were all from the Club Management saying over and over again that Pops' name was on the Board because he had been elected to the Club Management Committee. Pops would be in charge of arranging the monthly speaker. A great honour. Could Pops please call? There had been a terrible misunderstanding. It had been nothing to do with annual membership fees. Was Pops all right?

I went through to my/his bedroom and told Pops, but he just turned his face to the wall. I despaired. Of this cross old man in my grandfather's body who wouldn't listen, and of ever speaking to my Regina again. I wanted so badly to tell her that the Dreadful Bingo Incident was all a big misunderstanding. That we could work things out if we kept the lines of communication open. But just like Pops, my Regina had shut me out.

Things I Know:

Everybody needs a
bit of magic in their
lives

23

MAGIC MOJO

My friend Themba says that desperate times call for desperate measures. I don't actually think Themba was the first bloke to say this. In fact, I think it was a chap by the name of Guy Fawkes, who then went on to invent a night where you party and let off crackers and wave around sparklers and try not to scare the dogs too much.

I was not entirely sure that firing off some rockets was going to get Regina Versagel to pick up her phone or answer my emails, but there was one thing I knew for sure, as sure as I knew that Captain Jack was using Felicity Foxcroft's Dark and Lovely hair dye on his moustache, and that was that I was in desperate need of some love mojo.

This realisation came to me moments after I finally managed to run Regina down outside the Internet cafe. Minutes before I had been reading an email from my mother titled Making Your Own Magic. The newsletter was all about making your own magic (as per the title of the email) and my mother emphasised that you needed to mix the right magic ingredients to ensure certain outcomes. At the end of every paragraph of inspiring prose, Mom had written the words: *Yes we can!*

My mother wrote about combining the correct amount of intangible magic (hope, energy and ubuntu) with those tangible ingredients (cash, marketing, good product and excellent service) to produce those magical six figures on the bottom line. I had to hand it to my mother, she really knew where I was at.

After reading the email I glanced up and saw Regina backing out of the Internet cafe as though she'd forgotten something or wanted to avoid someone. I managed to catch up with her about four blocks down from the cafe. Hell, that girl can run fast.

'Red, what is it? What do you want?' she said when she stopped sprinting. Her face was terribly tired – but not the tiredness you get from running four blocks, it was another tiredness, the one that comes with too much sadness.

The honest answer was 'You, only you ...', but I used the second option on my list of honest replies and said, 'I want to talk to you. I want to explain ...'

Regina snorted. A tiny, breathy, horse-like snort, which

made my ribs ache as my heart expanded. She shook her head and said sadly, 'Red, I just need some time to think. Please, I don't want to be mean, I just need . . .' And then she dropped her eyes and stared at the pavement.

I allowed her to walk away because it came to me just at that moment: what Regina needed, what we both needed, was some love mojo. Some magic that would bring us together again and make all the misunderstandings go away.

My mother's email made me think about the time that Themba had taken the magic route – not that he's a client of my mother's, he just came to it on his own. Themba had the hots for this girl (he has the hots for all the girls, but there was this one in particular he was very perved up about). He wasn't getting anywhere fast with this hot thang, but he'd learned from her Facebook home page that she was crazy about blond guys with blue eyes and great tans. This would have been bad enough for me, but any fool could see from just looking at Themba that he wasn't even in the race.

Themba talked about Jikking his hair and getting blue contact lenses – he already had the great tan – but Buster said that this would just make him look like a negative version of the albino henchman Zao in *Die Another Day*. Anyone else but Themba would have slit his wrists or gone on to number two on the hot thang list. But not Themba. He resorted to desperate measures. These were prescribed to him by one of his uncles who, as luck had it, was a sangoma, a genuine African mojo man. For three weeks Themba was not allowed to bath (or wash his hands or brush his teeth), he had to wear a dried piece of goat testicle around his neck and he had to drink sea water before going to bed at night. And he could only eat raw meat.

After one week of observing these rituals that would make him an irresistible babe-magnet, Themba got sent home from school to take a bath and floss his teeth (and a week's detention for wearing inappropriate jewellery). Needless to say, he never did get the girl.

I wasn't up for the whole sangoma thing, but there was this one old bloke in the Village who I thought might be able to help me. His name was Mr Buzzer Goodwin (Number 31) and he was what some medical practitioners sometimes call a homeopath (and most other medical practitioners call a dagga-kop).

Mr Goodwin (call me Buzz, dude) was a keen gardener. He had a huge herb and veggie patch in the front of his house and he also kept a few plants that he called his 'special frost-sensitive babies' inside. He hid these on the enclosed porch out of sight of prying eyes, eyes like Mrs Smythe's, for instance.

Buzz always had people coming and going from his house, usually early in the morning or just after dark. It was as though some people didn't want other people (Mrs Smythe) to see them toing and froing with those little parcels in their hands.

Felicity Foxcroft was one of Buzz's most loyal patrons and she didn't care who saw her. Before she and Captain Jack had got it on, Felicity mostly used to consult Buzz about the pain in her knees. Buzz would give her some dried-up bits of leaf from one of his special porch babies and that would do the trick.

Felicity used to tell me (as she stuffed the leaves into a clay chillum) that without Buzz she would be in constant agony – his herbal remedy just took the edge off the pain that came when the bones grated away at each other in her knees.

But since Captain Jack had appeared on the scene, Felicity had been in and out of Buzz's house like a honey bee chasing pollen, sourcing what she called her and Captain Jacks's love mojo, a mixture of man root (ginseng) powder and a secret something that Buzz refused to reveal to anyone (probably oysters). Whatever it was, it seemed to be making Felicity and Captain Jack tired because they took a lot of naps and didn't go out much.

I left Pops snoozing on the sleeper couch (lazy bones!) and made my way to Buzz's pad. Buzz seemed pleased to see me. 'Hey, dude, you should have come yesterday, we could have done a family consult,' he said, peering at me over his John Lennon shades.

Apparently Pops had been around the day before to pick up a little something and that's all Buzz would say on account of patient/doctor confidentiality.

'So what can I do you for?' Buzz asked, turning down the Leonard Cohen album that was playing on his stereo. Then he peered at my face. 'Oh, yeah, oh man, yeah. I can see the prob ...' he said and then made a jeez-ouch expression and said he had something that I could wash with three times a day that would dry them out.

I said, no, cool man, Buzz, but apart from the zit muti I

need something to bring me and Regina back together again. I need your strongest love mojo.

Buzz said groovy. He had just the thing in mind. He'd recently supplied it to Mrs Smy ... And then Buzz said, sorry, man, this thing that he had put in his tea that morning had made his tongue as loose as a goose.

I left Buzz sewing a patch on to the pocket of his bell-bottoms, clutching my zit remedy and a potion of clear liquid he said I had to dab behind my ears. As soon as Regina got a whiff of it we would go as wild as Marianne and Mick at Redlands in '67. And, he said, of course I should bath and brush my teeth, did I think I was living in the Sixties?

Back at home I found Pops sitting buck naked on the couch. He was wearing his underwear on his head and talking to his shoe. It was one of a pair of old slip-slops that he used to wear in the garden. They were never very clean and it was certainly the last shoe I'd want to try and have an intelligent conversation with. 'Hey, Pops?' I said.

In response he offered me a cigarette. Not that there was anything in his hand, but he first tapped his right hand on his left and then waved his hand at me. 'Take one, it's my last but I'm trying to quit, Tony.'

I knew Pops had smoked back in his glory days when he and his best pal Tony Ballito worked at a Pool Hall and were as tight as Mrs Smythe when it came to tipping, but unless I was going nuts my name wasn't Tony Ballito – and I didn't smoke.

I told Pops I'd pass and went to the bathroom to assess the situation and to wash my face with Buzz's special face wash that smelt like Grace Foxcroft's sock drawer.

It was when I was carefully patting my face dry (no rough rubbing, it spreads them) that I noticed blood all over the towel. My heart felt like it was going to do a Mr Collins on me and seize up and I gave a whimper and shut my eyes. I knew I was going to have to open them sooner or later and when I did I noticed that the blood looked more like paint. Which was a good thing. And when I touched it, I could feel it was paint, which was even better. But I didn't have more than thirty seconds to wonder what it was that Pops had been painting, or to wipe the paint off my hands and face when there was a knock at the door. I peeped out of the bathroom window and saw that it was Mr Groenewald and Andrew Cuthbert from the library. They looked as mad as mad bears with sore heads.

I made it to the front door as Pops was waltzing into my/ his bedroom with a blonde stripper. That's what it looked like from the way he was moving, although I couldn't have sworn that she was blonde.

I opened the front door as Pops closed his/my bedroom door and before I could smile politely, Mr Cuthbert took one look at the red paint on my hands and face and started shouting. 'You, you, you,' he yelled. He was fit to burst with fury, like an enflamed, monstrous zit.

Mr Groenewald meanwhile didn't say anything. He just gripped me by the ear and led me away from the house, down the path and towards the Library. A trail of red paint stopped just outside the building. I managed to wrench my ear back and looked up. *Red Rules OK!* That's what I saw on the wall, in red paint. And then a big peace sign. On the wall. In red paint. I shook my head. *Red Rules OK!* What did it mean?

What it meant was that I was in it up to my eyes and that I would whitewash the wall all day 'if that's what it took to get the graffiti removed from it, ruddy vandal!'

It also meant that everyone who took a stroll to the library, went to hang up their washing in the Drying House or popped into the Entertainment Hall for a game of ping-pong saw me whitewashing over *Red Rules OK!* All day. Then a whole bunch of other people with a sudden passion for fresh air decided to take a little wander past the library as news of the Dreadful Graffiti Incident spread like cold sores at a kissathon.

And then there was my Regina, on her way to Felicity's house for a poker lesson with her and Captain Jack. I couldn't bear the look on her face.

At the end of the day, when the library wall was as white as Ouma Doreen's false teeth after a good bleaching, I went around to Grace Foxcroft's house. She was the only one who ever seemed pleased to see me in those days after the Dreadful Bingo Incident. She sat me down in her lounge and got my hands busy with ball of wool she was untangling. Then she stopped and took my hands in hers.

I wasn't in the mood for her nonsense, but I let her examine my paint-spattered hands. She turned them over and examined the shape: I was emotionally sensitive and aware of the feelings of those around me, Grace said (everyone hated my guts). My low-set index finger told Grace that I had experienced rejection (Regina couldn't stand the sight of me). My thumb showed Grace that I had strength of character and the ability to manage difficult situations (except life).

Grace stopped when she got to the long lifeline on the palm of my hand. She traced the line and gazed at me. 'Randolph, my dear, there are many unresolved issues in your life. I suggest you get some closure.'

I went home to have it out with Pops. Things were getting out of hand. I was down to two dog-walking clients (Brutus and Beefie) and I hadn't had a clothes-fitting or a cake-tasting or a milkshake-testing in days. I had fallen from favourite Village grandson to despised Village leper. Pops had to tell me what the heck was going on.

Pops was lying on his/my bed and he said that he had a shocker of a headache. He felt like he'd drunk a gallon of renosterbloed – Captain Jack's favourite breakfast tipple of brandy, Red Bull and coffee beans. Pops blamed Buzzer Goodwin. He should have stuck to Disprin and not tried Buzz's homeopathic headache powder.

I was on the phone to Buzz faster than a person could say what the hell did you give my grandfather you miserable dopehead quack, he's been behaving like a lunatic on acid.

But Buzz said, no way, dude. He'd given Pops his usual headache remedy, which consisted mostly of ground ginger. But according to Buzz, the way Pops had been behaving sounded like he'd been chewing moonflower seeds. Just a teaspoon of seeds would send Pops to Mars in a basket, Buzz said. It was a miracle that he had landed again. But there was no ways Pops could have got it from him by mistake. He hadn't touched the stuff since the night Jimmy Hendrix had been taken out by the military-industrial complex. The bastards.

I checked the kitchen and found a little brown packet of powder smelling of ginger next to a cold mug of tea. There was no sign of moonflowers. Or moonflower seeds. Or anything else that could have sent Pops flying over the moon.

Before I went to bed (the sleeper couch on the stoep – Pops was hogging my/his bed) I poured Buzz's love mojo down the kitchen sink. In my heart I knew that even if I had showered in the stuff and shaken myself dry all over Regina, like my godson Brutus after a dip in Old Stutters' koi pond, I was going to need a lot more than Buzz's magic to make things better again.

Things I Know:

Sometimes you have
to trust someone

24

the CHRISTMAS BOX INCIDENT

A couple of weeks before Christmas the Christmas fairy went around the Village collecting for Christmas stockings. It wasn't really a Christmas fairy, it was a crazy old lady who went by the name of Mrs Lizzie Potter (no relation to the chap with the broomstick) and there were no Christmas stockings, just discarded cardboard boxes that Mr Groenewald got from the liquor store.

My mother would say that this was first-class marketing: making people think they were getting a Christmas stocking full of goodies from the Christmas fairy when in reality it was

an old liquor box full of junk nobody had any use for anymore
(from a crazy old lady nobody had any use for anymore).

Crazy Lizzie went around the Village every couple of
days, ringing doorbells and when someone opened the door
she would chant a little rhyme:

Christmas is near, full of goodwill and cheer,
We are blessed to be sure, so give to the poor,
Yes, allow them the chance, to sing and to dance,
Give to the poor, don't you dare shut your door.

A lot of people were very generous and gave as much as they
could to those less fortunate than themselves. Take the poor
Robertsons, for example. They weren't in any position to
give away much, every tin of baked beans was a tin away
from them having to eat a pot of cabbage soup for supper,
but they gave in other ways. Mrs Robertson would spend
the year unpicking bits of knitting: old blankets, buggered
old jumpers that were past wearing and the odd sock. Then
she would knit. There were booties and gloves, beanies and
scarves and covers for hot-water bottles. And by the middle of
December every year, Mrs Robertson would be in a position
to fill each Christmas box with all the items she'd knitted.
She said this meant that she could sleep easy, knowing that
the poor people of Govan Mbeki squatter camp weren't going
to freeze that Christmas.[19]

---

[19] Though with PE having an average summer temperature of twenty-
five degrees they were bound to be pretty toasty whatever they were
wearing.

Then there were people like Mrs Smythe, who was rolling in it and saw the Govan Mbeki Christmas boxes as a spring-cleaning opportunity. Out with the box of stale Weet-Bix, the rice with the weevils, the dented tin of pilchards she'd bought goodness knows when. As soon as Crazy Lizzie pressed that doorbell, Mrs Smythe would be at the door with her collection of goodies.

In contrast, the Blackmans were a couple who liked to give. They really went big. For the adults there were bars of fruit and nut chocolate, Quality Street sweets, packets of Camel cigarettes and sheer pantyhose. For the kids there were superior lucky packets, filled with toys that would last the whole of Christmas day.

Apart from the gifts, the Blackmans would always make a hefty cash donation to the doshbox that Crazy Lizzie liked to spread among the poor, so they could buy candles on Christmas Eve when their electricity got cut off.

But on the Friday morning I opened the door and saw Crazy Lizzie for the first time (and heard her catchy little chant) I thought for one moment that I had been chowing down on some of those moonflower seeds Buzzer Goodwin had told me about. Crazy Lizzie was quite a sight. She liked to dress in character. There was the wand and the gauzy pink fairy dress and the big round red circles on her cheeks which made her look like one of those killer dolls in the horror movies.

She did the chant for me and then asked if Pops was in. 'Your grandfather loves to give. In fact, he always gives too much.' I think she chanted it. She pretty much chanted everything she said.

I didn't tell her that Pops had gone over to Mr Groenewald's office to give him a piece of his mind about the way the Christmas lights were being kept on in the Village all night (or what a mean and grumpy old man my grandfather had become since he'd emerged from his weird trip into space). Instead, I told her I would get some things together and she could pick them up the next day. And I would contribute a good slice of my dog-walking cash to the doshbox. Not that I saw much more coming my way. I was down to walking one client a day – my godson Brutus. 'Randolph, my dear, all boys go through bad time,' Mrs Collins had said when I'd picked him up a few days before, her chins wobbling. 'You'll come through, I know – at least, I hope you will.' And it seemed that the rest of the Village was holding their breath for me and hoping too.

Crazy Lizzie made me cross my heart and hope to die and then she waved her wand over me and said she'd be back.

I felt as much in the mood for Christmas as I did for being given a bed bath by Andrew Cuthbert. If Pops was acting cross and mean, I was acting sulky and depressed. Because I was. About everything. About Pops' strange behaviour and Regina not talking to me and everyone else in the Village except Grace Foxcroft thinking I was a little turd. I moped around the house until Pops got home and I told him about Crazy Lizzie.

'Not this year,' Pops said. 'You do it for me. I don't feel like it this year.'

Then Pops said he was tired out and went to lie down, so

I got busy with Number 42's contribution to the Christmas boxes. Crazy Lizzie had us in her sights.

I thought about the Blackmans, and how they always gave so much, and Mrs Smythe, who never gave anything that mattered, and I gave the Govan Mbeki squatter camp my favourite branded T-shirt (*I'll Kill for Puma*). They also got three pairs of Levi's and my Fanta frisbee. I hung back from giving my best pair of shoes because best pair or not I think wearing another bloke's shoes is about as much of a turn-on as wearing his jocks.

I went through Pops' cupboards as well. He had this spot on the top shelf where he kept things that he wanted to give away to someone who would appreciate them – he was always giving his stuff away. There were a couple of shirts that had grown too big for Pops and some trousers that had gone a bit saggy around the waist. Actually, there was a lot of stuff – Pops had really taken the summer slimming fad on board.

By the time Crazy Lizzie was back the next day, I had two of our own liquor boxes full of stuff to give her. She chanted that Pops had been more than generous, as usual, and that there would be a riot over my Puma T-shirt in the Govan Mbeki squatter camp on Christmas day. When she said that I felt sort of good, in fact, better than I'd felt in a long while. And when I tossed a whole wad of my dog-walking wonga into the doshbox I felt even better.

It didn't seem Pops was of the same opinion. When I told him what I'd done, he went sort of ballistic, and after yelling at me for a while about stealing his stuff he went and did a sulk session in my/his bedroom – refusing to listen as I tried to explain that I'd only done what he'd asked me to do.

It was a couple of hours after midnight, as I was throwing myself about in agony on the sleeper couch on the stoep, thinking about never seeing Regina again and wondering how Pops had survived sleeping on this crappy sleeper couch for more than two months, that I heard a noise. It was the sound of an old bloke shuffling past my window and down the path towards the Entertainment Hall to go and reclaim his shirts and trousers from where Crazy Lizzie had stored them. I figured this out by the time we were about halfway there (as I shadowed Pops down the path).

Getting into the Hall was easy. It took a screwdriver and a hammer and a bit of geriatric brute force. Then Pops was inside and having his way with Crazy Lizzie's boxes. I watched through the Hall windows as Pops chucked things about – pantyhose and chocolates and Mrs Smythe's weevil-infested rice. The stuff went everywhere.

After a good five minutes of mayhem, where Pops ripped and tore and made a right mess of everything, he shoved some notes from the doshbox down the front of his shirt and slunk out of the Hall with a bag of his clothes.

Just as I was making my way back around the Hall, to follow Pops home, I saw the light of a torch shining down the path that led to Mr Groenewald's cottage. The chances were that it was the man himself and that he was going to bust me for breaking and entering unless I hit the road very fast. Which I did, making as little noise as it is possible for a bloke to do when he falls over a huge metal garbage bin.

I did a mad sprint home, with Mr Groenewald panting behind me, and I'd nearly made it when I saw a ghost floating down the pathway towards me. I got such a shock I felt like I was having an enema on the spot.

When I started breathing again I realised that it was only Grace on a very early morning stroll. She nodded sweetly at me as she passed. 'A little chilly isn't it, Randolph, for such a fine summer's afternoon,' she said, clutching her long diaphanous gown around her. Silly old bat. I just had to love her.

'You never saw me,' I hissed and threw myself behind Mrs Dodge's Shasta daisy bush just as Mr Groenewald huffed into view. He stopped in surprise. 'Miss Foxcroft, what are you doing walking around at this time of night? It isn't safe,' he said, waving the torch around. 'You didn't see anyone come this way?'

Grace smiled. 'I haven't seen a soul, not even Randolph.'

I remained behind the Shasta daisy bush until just before sunrise, when the sprinkler system came on (soaking me through). Then I crawled home and slept, hoping that things would look better in the morning. They didn't. The sky was overcast and the birds were making sharp frightened noises in the trees outside and there was a damp feeling in the air. But of course it wouldn't rain. It never did, even if you wished like crazy.

I considered the various scenarios: The first was that I would be nailed for breaking into the Hall and wrecking the Christmas boxes and plundering the doshbox. The second was that I would be nailed for breaking into the Hall and wrecking the Christmas boxes and plundering the doshbox. The third was that Grace would prove an unreliable witness and while most people would know it was me they would have to give me the benefit of the doubt.

No matter how I looked at things I knew one thing for sure: I was destined for twenty years behind bars at Jackie Selebi Prison in Grahamstown. I felt like I was drowning. I needed help.

My mother always tells me (and the other CEOs) that asking for help is the sign of a true leader. There is no shame in it. So I chucked my swimming trunks on under my trousers and threw myself down the hill to the Internet cafe, where I spent three hours writing a letter to my mother. I told her everything. Well, not everything. I left out Regina; that was too painful. The room grew dark as I typed and I typed. The air was heavy with moisture. And so were my eyes.

I told my mother about all the weird stuff Pops was doing and how anxious I was. And as I wrote the email and recalled the strange incidents that had taken place over the past couple of months I'd spent with Pops I couldn't help snotting up the keyboard.

I am feeling desperate. I don't know what to do. Please help me. Your loving son, Randolph. That's what I said at the end of the email. And as a last act, before sending it off, I wrote *HELP!* in the subject line.

I'd just finished cleaning up my face and the keyboard with a bit of A4 paper from the printer when an email popped into my Inbox. It was from my mother. She had heard my cry for help!

I read through the seventeen page email twice. It covered every possible crisis, from cash flow problems to bankruptcy, but in the end there were always only three solutions to each problem: I either had to extend my time frame, invest more money or get more people on the job. There was no mention from my mother of Pops or any of my other troubles. At the end of the Out of Office email, my mother said that she was on vacation until after Christmas, but that in the event of an emergency I could speak directly to her office manager. She gave an email address.

I was trying to grab myself another piece of A4 printer paper, to start mopping up my face and the keyboard again, when I heard a noise behind me. It was Regina. She said, 'Red?'

It was all too much. I grabbed my rucksack and ran for the beach where I spent some quality time hard-tackling a couple of sand dunes. Then I stripped down to my costume and spent the next hour beating up on some waves, feeling glad every time I was thrown back against the shore by a real dunker. I was hurt. I felt sore. I was glad. And I wasn't alone.

Regina sat watching me. She sat on my beach towel as though she belonged there.

Finally, I spat the sea water out of my mouth and walked out of the sea as casually as a guy could when the crotch of his costume is packed with sand.

I felt the first spit of rain on my skin and looked at the sky. The clouds hung dark and heavy over the sea. A flash of light cracked across the sky. It was going to rain.

Regina got up and handed me my towel. 'So, Red, don't

you think a girl has a right to know why her boyfriend is acting like a psycho?' she asked.

She'd said the boyfriend word. One word not two. That was who I was. Her boyfriend. Not some miserable little shit who stole from the poor and buggered up peoples' things and who should be kept away from the dogs in the village for being a dangerous influence and a lousy role model. I was Regina Versagel's boyfriend.

There was a rumble of thunder and the sand spattered gently at my feet as the rain began to fall.

I took the towel and started rubbing my arms and legs, but Regina grabbed the towel out of my hands, turned me around and started rubbing my shoulders. 'The thing is, Red,' she said, 'I've been thinking. The creep that's been doing a whole lot of mean stuff at the Village couldn't be you. Not *my* boyfriend.'

She'd said the beautiful boyfriend word again. I stood there, unable to move or to breathe as the rain drizzled down and Regina rubbed hard down my lower back and then started on my sides. 'You see, Red,' she continued, 'I know you. I knew you from the first moment I met you. You don't hold any Christmas box surprises for me.'

Regina then turned me around, pulled me down onto my knees and started rubbing my hair. 'I got a bit hurt and confused and needed time to work it out. But I know I could never have been wrong about you.'

She rubbed and rubbed at that hair of mine. Then she stopped rubbing. 'So, tell me what's been going on, Red, so I can help.'

I looked up into those strong, loyal green eyes and took the towel from her and pretended to carry on drying my hair. I kept my head down, rub-rub-rubbing away at my hair so madly that she wouldn't see how I was shaking and snotting up my towel.

Then it bucketed down. And I stopped trying to dry my hair. I just gave up. And I told her everything.

Things I Know:

You can feel really
lonely in a crowd

25

the CHOIR INCIDENT

It rained for three days.

On the first day everyone was out in their wellies, chattering on the pathways under their brollies and talking cats and dogs about how much rain it was raining. Mr Groenewald had a rain gauge in the shape of a gumboot, which he kept outside the Entertainment Hall, and everyone was down there at least ten times a day to check it.

At first it was raining moderately (0.25 inches of rain an hour), but then it came down like it did on Noah's ark (0.50 inches of rain an hour).

'Look Randolph, my boy, look,' everyone was saying,

pointing at the gauge. Then we were inside the Hall, playing ping-pong and Rummikub and clutching ourselves with delight. It was raining and we couldn't stop talking about it.

And everyone was talking to me too: 'Randolph, just go outside and check the rain gauge ...', 'No, *surely* not 0.60 inches an hour ...' and 'Randolph, could you shake out my umbrella ...'

Even Mr Groenewald was talking to me. It seemed like the rain was washing everything fresh and new, and me along with it.

On the second day, Mrs Collins got a cough and Debbie Brewer couldn't wash her curtains and started coming out in allergy bumps. Grace Foxcroft's clothes smelled worse than a wet sheep and all the dogs were going stir-crazy without their walks. And still the rain came down.

Then, on the third day, everyone started talking about how much they wanted it to stop raining. The gutters weren't holding up and Mr Groenewald's rain gauge boot was leaking. It was enough rain.

And at last, in the early hours of the fourth day, it stopped raining.

I had ten days left at Nelson Mandela Gardens before I was to jet off and join my parents in the capital of Thailand. I would arrive the day after Christmas, which was fine really because the people of Thailand don't celebrate Christmas.

My parents aren't all that big on Christmas either. Mostly

they give me some cash and tell me to go and buy my own presents and get stuff to fill my stocking. Which is pretty cool if you think about it. I never have to lie awake on Christmas Eve wondering what's going to be under that tree. Because, first of all, we never have a tree, and, second, I know exactly what's going to be in the presents at the foot of my bed because I wrapped and put them there myself. There are none of those sleepless nights and hysterical early mornings running through to the fireplace to see if Santa's polished off the beer and cookies. Quite a relief really.

I think the second best person (barring Pops) to spend Christmas with would be Grace Foxcroft. You'd get to open a lot of presents and eat Christmas lunch a good couple of times over if you played it right. But the first best person to spend Christmas with would be Regina, my girlfriend.

During the three days after the rain stopped I spent practically every moment I could with my girlfriend, Regina (whatever way I say it makes me feel just as good). It was her school holidays, so she could come to the Village whenever she wanted. She usually spent the mornings with Felicity Foxcroft and I had her (Regina, not Felicity) for the afternoons.

We did a lot of time on the beach, where she tried to teach me how to surf properly with a board. She said she was really just handing me the tools for survival because in Thailand the waves got so big that they could wipe out small villages. Wicked!

Things between me and Regina had been perfect since that miserable day on the beach where I'd spilled my guts and most of the contents of nose. I'd told her everything about Pops and the last couple of months. Right from the beginning, just like she'd asked.

I'd told her about Pops stealing the clothes from the Drying House and wrecking the gardens for the Beautiful Summer Garden Competition and all the other crazy stuff – the headaches and the weird moods and the loss of appetite and all the things he'd been saying and doing that weren't his normal style.

There, on the beach, I hadn't been able to use the right insane, crazy, barmy, mental, lunatic words to describe his behaviour. They had scared me too much. So, eventually, I had tried the one Felicity used when she couldn't bear to say the word which meant that Grace couldn't remember things any more unless they happened fifty years ago: doolally tap.

It had a fun sound to it and it didn't make me think of a disease. Pops had gone doolally tap – it sounded like some kind of dance. But when I said that word, Regina had looked at me with a frown which had wrinkled her nose and made her mouth turn down. It was her sympathetic look, the one she gave me when I'd wiped out body surfing in the waves and left the top layer of my skin on the sand. 'Red, if you think your grandfather has gone mad, say it,' she'd said. 'It's a serious thing. Don't hide behind words. My teacher at school says if you can say it, then it's easier to deal with. We can deal with it together.'

I had hardly been able to think about Pops and how freaked out I was after that, because all I could hear was the together word she'd used to refer to me and her. And since then we had been dealing with things together.

Me and Regina had kept an eye on Pops and watched for any sign of him going nuts again. And if and when he did, we'd deal with it. Together. But for the past few days Pops had been behaving like his normal self. A little tired some days, a little cranky when he said that his head hurt, but on the whole he was my Pops. Perfect.

I tried not to think too much about leaving Regina and Pops and everyone else at the Village when I went to the capital of Thailand. Because if I thought about it I started realising that there were a whole bunch of people I'd probably never see again. Like Bruce and Sylvia Collins and some of the others who wouldn't be able to hang on until I could get my parents to send me back for a holiday.

I know Pops felt the same way about me leaving because when he wasn't snoozing on the stoep, he spent as much time with me and Regina as he could.

On one of those days, me and Pops spent the afternoon practising for one of the highlights of the festive season, which would take place at 7 p.m. sharp that Friday night. This was when the Happy Echoes Choir wandered around the Village, calling in on the residents and singing them their favourite Christmas carols.

Regina was going to be singing with us too, because even though she and I had only been members of the Choir for a few days, Mr Donald Frankish (he was the choir master) had told us 'the more the merrier'.

There was also a Mrs Frankish (Cynthia). She was the deputy choir master and played the piano. Well, she played when it suited her, and it only suited her when the carols were what she called 'traditional' and not some of the 'new-fangled nonsense' Mr Frankish came up with.

Mrs Frankish said that anything that was composed after 1900 was modern rubbish not fit for the human ear, but Mr Frankish contended that they had to move with the times to stay relevant. To get back at Mrs Frankish, he wouldn't conduct when she played something that he termed 'old fashioned'.

So when the Happy Echoes Choir was practising a modern carol, like for example 'Adam Lay Ybounden', by a chap called Boris Ord, who Mrs Frankish loathed with a passion, she wouldn't play the piano. Mr Frankish would try to keep us all together (and singing in tune) by banging on the table with his stick and waving his arms about. But it was almost always a bit of a disaster because all the old folk didn't know the modern tunes. And I was a bit in the dark myself, it must be said.

Then, when we were practising something everyone knew, like 'Once in Royal David's City', Mr Frankish wouldn't conduct us. Then it was up to Mrs Frankish to stamp her feet on the floor as she hammered the tune out on the piano.

It was damn hard to try and do two things at once, a bit like rubbing your nose and the top of your head in opposite directions at the same time, and either Mrs Frankish ended up sounding like she was playing the piano with her feet or we sounded like we were singing 'Adam Lay Ybounden' instead of one of the good old favourites.

The Frankishes had been at this argument for as long as

they had been married, which was forty-five years. The only reason the two of them were still together was because they liked arguing with each other about this so much. Or so Mrs Smythe said.

So there Pops and me were on Friday afternoon, in the Entertainment Hall with the rest of the choir members, going though our paces one last time before we went public at 7 p.m. Regina couldn't make the last rehearsal as she'd gone Christmas shopping with her mother – she said she was buying a present for a very special boyfriend, wink wink.

We were singing 'Whilst Shepherds Watched Their Flocks', which is a great old tune and a special favourite of Mrs Frankish because it was composed some time in the Renaissance. Regina and me liked it a lot too because we changed the words to *While shepherds washed their socks by night*, which was rather fun. But it was not so much fun alone and I wished Regina were with me.

Anyway, there I was with Pops and we were singing about the Shepherds watching their flocks and all of a sudden I saw Pops go quiet. Then he bent over, holding his head in his hands and began rocking from one side to the other. Even though Mrs Frankish was sort of playing the tune half right, in between hammering the floor with her feet, Pops was rocking to a tune of his own. It was getting really confusing and I could see that some of the other choir members weren't sure if they should be following Mrs Frankish or Pops.

Then, just before we got to the end of the third verse, Pops started howling. I was hoping that he hadn't got a set of rude words of his own because shepherds could be doing a whole lot of things and some of them weren't as polite as washing socks.

I belted out, 'And this shall be a sign!' really loudly, to try and cover for Pops, but it was no good. Mrs Frankish stopped playing and everyone grew silent. Except for Pops; who was still holding his head. Tears were streaming down his face.

Themba has this creed: make no apologies; give no explanations. I don't think it's an original. In fact, I'm pretty sure he stole it off some American arms dealer or someone like that, but there are times when such a creed is useful and this was one of those times. I ignored the weird stares from everyone, put my arm around Pops and walked him out of the Hall.

By the time we'd got home, Pops had stopped howling and was whimpering, 'I can't stand the noise! I can't stand the noise!' over and over again, like he was in terrible pain.

I thought it was a good thing that Pops hadn't said this in front of the other choir members because it was show time for the Happy Echoes Choir in barely two hours time and that kind of talk can really break a team's spirit.

I got Pops some headache pills and left him lying on the sleeper couch on the stoep while I went to make him some tea (and took phone calls from the Frankishes and fifteen other choir members enquiring after Pops). As I waited for the kettle to boil I called my girlfriend Regina to tell her what had happened. I wanted us to talk about Pops' strange behaviour, together, like she said we could. But Regina's father said that she'd already left to go and sing Christmas carols with her spotty boyfriend (which was me).

When show time came around, Pops said that he wasn't feeling himself (figuratively – not literally) and that he couldn't face the performance, but to send his sorrys to his fellow choir members and to enjoy it for him. I said not a chance, I wasn't leaving him, although I felt badly torn between seeing my girlfriend and staying home with Pops. But Pops was adamant. He said I couldn't let the side down. 'Go, on Randolph, my boy, sing loudly for me,' Pops said, pushing me out of the door, 'I'll be fine, really.'

I caught Regina at the Entertainment Hall and we spent the next hour with the Happy Echoes Choir singing our hearts out for the residents of the Nelson Mandela Gardens Retirement Village.

We sang 'O Little Town of Bethlehem' for Grace and Felicity Foxcroft, who gave us home-made fruit punch with the kick of a donkey. I told them that Pops wasn't figuratively feeling himself while Regina ploughed her way though the fruit. Felicity looked worried but Grace just asked again where Pops was. Eventually they said they would join the sing-song and maybe pop in at the house on the way and try and cheer him up.

We sang 'The Holly and the Ivy' for Mrs Smythe. She gave us Glühwein with a difference and looked concerned when I told her that Pops was feeling out of sorts. She eyed Grace and Felicity and said that if Grace was popping in on Pops she would join us and maybe look in on him too.

I managed to catch Regina's ear between songs and mentioned to her that Pops had acted a bit weird at choir practice. He'd said that he couldn't stand the noise. Could we talk about it, together?

Regina giggled and whispered between gulps of Glühwein that Pops was spot on. Old Stutters sang like he had a cat stuck in the back of his throat.

I said yes, but it was still a bit strange, didn't she think?

Regina said she'd think about it and let me know after another glass of Glühwein. That girl could really sink a drink, it must be said.

When we got to Mrs Klingman and Gregory's house we sang 'Ding Dong Merrily on High', and even though they didn't come out of the house, I knew they were listening because I saw two shadows jumping around behind the net curtains.

At Number 87 Mrs Collins and Brutus came to the door and listened very politely while we sang 'Adam Lay Ybounden' and then Mrs Collins asked if we would sing a real Christmas carol for Mr Collins, who couldn't come to the door, so we gave him 'Away in a Manger'. Mrs Collins said it was the perfect choice because all the cattle lowing around the manger confirmed her belief that heaven was a place full of God's creatures. She watered us with Long Island tea, which tasted nothing like tea at all.

I was starting to feel a bit anxious about Pops – I suppose it was Mrs Collins going on about heaven and Mr Collins being so poorly – so I took Regina aside and told her that apart from Pops' flaky behaviour at choir practice he'd had a head sore enough to burst. I was really worried about him. What did she think?

Regina steadied herself against me and said she thought

that she needed to lie down herself otherwise she was probably going to fall over. 'I'm really sorry, Red,' she said. 'I'm letting you down, but I'm feeling kind of woozy and I'm just not focussing properly. Do you think I could come around tomorrow and we can really deal with this properly?'

She looked pretty mortified and I squeezed her hand and said, 'Sure thing, Reg. It can wait.' And I really hoped it could.

When we got to my house, that is Pops' house, the lights were all out, but I knew Pops was lying on his sleeper couch on the stoep, so we gave him the three verses of 'Silent Night'. There was no peep out of him, though, and the lights stayed off.

I am not sure if it was the Long Island tea or the fruit punch with the kick or the Glühwein with the difference, but I also started to feel a bit strange after that. So I held my girlfriend Regina's hand tightly and hoped that she remembered what she had said about us being together. Because even though I was with my girl and the Foxcroft sisters and Mrs Smythe and the Frankishes and fifteen members of the Happy Echoes Choir, I didn't think Pops was with me any more and I felt kind of alone.

Things I Know:

Fire burns

26

the FIRE

Pops didn't leave his sleeper couch for two days. He lay there, stiff as a corpse, staring at the ceiling (which, as ceilings went, rated zero on the fascination charts). When I asked him what he was doing, he said he was thinking about things. And when I asked him what things, he told me things like global warming and the war in Iraq and all the people who had been killed in car accidents and in the last two world wars.

It was a good thing someone was thinking about Iraq, because that was the topic for my last assignment for the year and I hadn't been applying myself too well. When it came to choosing between Option One: writing essay and

Option Two: playing ping-pong and hitting the beach and surfing with my girlfriend Regina, the second option always, always won. It's a funny thing that!

I'd managed to cobble a few thoughts together in the days following the Christmas Carol evening. I'd been at a bit of a loose end after Regina got grounded for life (read four days) for marinating the back seat of her mother's brand-new car with a cocktail of Glühwein and punch – I wasn't even allowed to speak to her on the phone.

In the meantime I just hoped that Pops would stay quietly on the couch until me and Regina got a chance to decide, together, what to do about his worrying behaviour. It was making me quite anxious, it must be said.

When Pops finally did get up (on the third day), it was to do one of the things he loved most in the world – and it was not writing my essay. No. He washed his car.

A lot of people think that washing their car is a drag, so they take it into one of those big car-washing places and while their car is being washed they drink skinny cappuccinos or do the grocery shopping. Not Pops. He wouldn't let anyone touch his car. He'd had it for like thirty years and he knew every inch of it like he knew his own body. He even kept two plastic bottles of water and a towel in the boot, so that if you went to the beach and your feet got all sandy, you could wash them off and dry them before getting back into the car. That was how Pops looked out for his car.

I once asked Pops what he called his car. 'It's a car, not a person,' he'd replied, looking at me like I was mad. 'It's just a machine. Why would I give it a name?'

That was the kind of person Pops was. He didn't give dead things names, which if you think about it, is a really a wack thing to do. Like Themba calling his school tie Tiger, on account of the fact that it represents his manhood (or so he says) and he is untamed and wild like a fully grown tiger. But Pops may as well have given his car a name, because, if the truth be told, Pops loved this car like an old friend.

It was not as though the 1981 Beemer was much to look at. It was sort of gold on the outside and leather on the inside. And I know I'm not a car person, like real boys are supposed to be, but I can't think of anything else to say about it.

Themba is definitely a real car person. He says that the kind of car you drive tells a girl how you're going to do it. It's an extension of your whatsit, so to speak. For example, if you drive an Audi, it's a given that you'll be steady and reliable and you'll get the girl there in one piece. Whereas, a sports car tells a girl it's going to be a crazy, exciting night full of fireworks. And it doesn't matter if she lives to tell the tale or not, because it's a one time thing anyway.

But when I looked at Pops' BMW, I didn't see Pops' whatsit, I just saw an old car that had seen a lot of years. It was a car that said it wanted to read a book and chat to you over a glass of milk and then maybe take a doze in front of the television after the weather report.

I watched Pops rub her down gently with soapy water and then dry her off with a soft cloth. Then he took some polish and shined her up all over. When he'd done with her on the inside, he drove her back into the garage, but as he came back into the house he was shaking his head. 'She's leaking oil,' he murmured. 'Pouring oil all over the garage floor.'

Pops said he couldn't risk the ride down to the garage where he got his car serviced once a year, so he called his pal the mechanic who said he'd stop by in the afternoon to take a look-see.

The mechanic (a Mr Howard Greybe) spent half an hour looking over the car. Then he started her up and took her for a spin around the Village. When he got back, him and Pops spent some time on the stoep talking. As he left, he grabbed Pops' shoulder in a firm manly gesture of consolation and shook his head a couple of times. I gathered the news was not good.

Pops told me that Mr Greybe had said that it was the end of the road for his BMW. If the motor didn't seize up the next time he was out on the road, it would happen sooner or later. The oil leak was just like a person who'd had his legs chopped off – the blood drained from the body faster that it could get replaced. That Beemer was catching the next taxi home to the scrapyard in the sky.

Pops didn't eat supper with me. He spent the evening in the garage tinkering around in the Beemer's insides. He used a laundry bucket (that he normally used for washing his socks) to drain the oil out of the engine, then he tinkered some more and replaced it. Then he used another laundry bucket (for white shirts) to catch the oil as it flowed out again. He was in there for hours.

When Pops finally came back inside again he looked like one of those surgeons from a television medical series who's been in theatre for eighteen hours and then lost the patient.

He didn't say anything and went to bed. And so did I.

I lay there thinking about Pops not sleeping, thinking about his beloved Beemer. I kept awake with Pops, thinking about that car. The car in which he had driven my mother, his daughter, to school all those years ago. The car in which he had taken his daughter, my mother, to the beach and to the drive-in for a double feature. The car in which he had taken his wife and my grandmother, my mother's mother, to the hospital. The car in which he had taken my mother, his daughter, to the airport, leaving a freshly dug grave for a woman who'd never come back from the hospital. I fell asleep thinking about Pops' memories of that car.

I don't know what it was, but around two o'clock in the morning something woke me. I resisted it like mad because I was having the most fantastic dream. Me and Regina were on this giant surfboard and I was standing behind her, holding her around the waist. We were cruising on a wave and the wind off the sea was blowing her hair into my face. It was kind of whipping me in the eyes like wet seaweed, but I didn't mind because I'd caught a strand of it in my mouth and it tasted all salty like popcorn. Regina turned around and her glasses were all misted up with salt water and she was covered in spray and I was just about to ... and then I smelt smoke.

I lay in bed and I sniffed again. It was the smell of rush-hour traffic: smelly exhaust fumes, overheated engines, burning oil and ... smoke. My eyes started stinging and this time it wasn't because of Regina's hair.

I got out of bed and stumbled through to the stoep. I was sort of groggy from sleep and my eyes were burning from the smoke, but whichever way I looked at it the sleeper couch on the stoep was definitely empty. Pops wasn't there.

I tried to call out for him but the smoke was making me feel kind of dizzy and it was hurting my chest. I took short, shallow breaths, gulping the smoky air like a dolphin beached on the shore. Breathe, Randolph my lad. When things get bad, just breathe, Pops had always told me.

Suddenly I heard a cry from the open door next to the kitchen. I stumbled through into the garage, the smoke hitting my eyes something wicked, making them tear up and burn. Holding my hand over them, I peered through my fingers into the garage. It was dark, but through the haze I could still see a guy hunched over the side of the Beemer. It was Pops. Tears were pouring down his face and as I watched, he moaned and lit a match, flipping it into the petrol hatch. But as he did this, the match went out. So Pops tried again, this time lighting three matches at once.

I was feeling kind of strange. My mind wasn't working properly. I shook my head, trying to clear the fog, but it felt like my brain was exploding. There was oil all over the garage floor and a pile of crates in the corner of the garage filled with Pops' home brew had somehow caught alight, flames devouring the boxes and smoke billowing up towards the ceiling, but Pops didn't seem to notice.

I called out to Pops and he turned around. 'Go away.

Leave us alone,' he shouted as the flames licked hungrily against the bottles of ginger liquid behind him.

'Pops, you must get out of here,' I screamed. 'Come, Pops, please. Stop doing that.'

But Pops ignored me and lit another match. My head felt like it was going to burst. I stumbled over to where Pops was standing and grabbed the matches out of his hand and threw them against the garage wall. Then I tried to pull Pops towards the door, but he fought me like I was attacking him.

We struggled, me pulling Pops towards the door and him pushing back, until he pushed me over. Then, as I looked up at him from where I lay, there was a huge explosion from the direction of the crates of beer and Pops fell backwards onto the garage floor.

I got onto my hands and knees and crawled over to where he was lying, a couple of metres away from me. The garage floor was burning hot. I could feel the hot oil under my hands and the heat of the flames on my face. My hands were on fire.

Pops was very still. I reached out for him and pulled him towards the door leading to the kitchen. His clothes were alight and I tried to beat the flames out, but my hands were burning and arrows of pain were shooting up my elbows.

In the kitchen I looked around, half blind with the pain, then I grabbed the kettle off the kitchen counter and threw it at Pops. It bounced off him, spilling hissing streams of water onto the floor.

Flames and smoke were still pouring out from the garage, so I began to drag Pops across the kitchen floor. We had to get away from the smoke and fire. We needed air. But there was no air. He was too heavy.

I was finding it hard to breathe and I felt incredibly tired, but I knew I had to get Pops to the stoep. As the breath started leaving me the smoke and the flames followed me from the garage to kitchen. I wanted to scream at the fire to leave me alone, but there was no breath in me. I sucked smoke into my lungs and pulled Pops along the floor towards the lounge.

If I could just get him to the stoep I could open the door to the garden and I would be able to breathe. I pulled and pulled, but Pops was a dead weight in my arms.

Eventually, we reached the stoep. I tried to open the door, but my hands weren't working properly any more. They weren't my hands. They were blocks of pain.

Just grab the handle. Just pull, I told myself. I grabbed the handle and I pulled on it, but it wouldn't give. I stared at my hands. They looked as though they were covered in bubble wrap. Like someone was posting my hands abroad and had wrapped them in red and pink and black bubble wrap. But even though I was really tired and it was dark and I couldn't really see properly, I knew my hands weren't really wrapped in bubble wrap.

I couldn't breathe. I was burning from the tips of my fingers to under my armpits. I was done. The fire had won.

Then I saw it. The panic button next to the door. I pushed it. I pushed it again and again and again until it made its *eyawa-eyawa-eyawa* sound that went on and on and on.

A few minutes later I heard a hammering on the stoep

door and then a lot of crashing. Hard fingers dug into my arms and I screamed in pain as I was dragged out into the night. I gasped in the cool night air. I could breathe again.

I raised my head from the grass and I looked around me. Behind me the house was burning. Pops lay on the grass, but he wasn't moving.

Things I Know:

You have to let go of
the ones you love

27

SIXTH SENSE

Me and my friend But are down by the harbour waiting for the boat. No kidding, my best friend in the capital of Thailand is a guy called But with just the one T. If he had two Ts and lived outside of Thailand, like in America, it would probably be a real problem for him. But ... I mean, however ... in Thailand there are lots of guys called But.

People in Thailand call their kids all kinds of cool names. I'm sort of used to it now. When I first got here, a year ago, I used to email Themba all the time about the names of people I'd met: Kum and Pong and Pee and Nit. It all made Randy sound really mild. And as they call me Landy or Led, it's even milder.

A lot of people in Thailand are simply called by a letter of the alphabet. Like B or D or T. My housekeeper, Mrs Shinawatra, tells me that it's to confuse the spirits, who are always looking to cause mischief with people. It kind of spreads the risk a little when there are twenty Ps in a room (you just can't be sure which of the buggers you want to mess with, if you are an evil spirit that is).

Me and But have been waiting for the boat for over an hour. To kill time, we buy some noodles from the noodle guy at the food stall in the Soi next to the harbour road. I've become quite a whiz at eating with chopsticks. The trick is to hold the carton close up to your face and then just shovel in the noodles. It's not easy handling chopsticks with gloves on, but the only time I take them off is when I take a shower or bath. The rest of the time I wear gloves made out of the thinnest cotton; they allow my skin to breathe and make sure that I don't sweat too much. Without gloves, my hands look pretty disgusting. Even I want to throw up when I look at them.

Themba says that I should get some gloves made especially for bedtime. He said it could be quite a turn-on, sleeping with your hands covered in silk or satin or whatever the fabric is that girls get their underwear made out of. I told Themba I would ask for a pair of gloves just like that for Christmas, which is only a few weeks away. A pair of white silk gloves. And I also told him that he should ask for a pair too. It's not fair that only people with damaged hands like me and the late Michael Jackson (RIP, buddy) should have all the fun.

Not that Christmas is a big thing in Thailand, a lot of Thais being Buddhists and all. However, my father and mother are going to town on it this year because last year was such a non-event. They have asked me for a wish list of Christmas presents and are going to give Mrs Shinawatra the cash to buy them. And she has to wrap them too, which is pretty cool.

My parents said they wanted it to be a special Christmas since this is probably the last year that Pops will spend Christmas with us.

We (But and me) are hoping that next year Pops will be spending Christmas with us as Tata Young's sister. We don't actually know if Tata Young has a sister, but she's the hottest singer in Thailand and is regularly voted one of the sexiest one hundred women in the world in *FHM* magazine. Me and But don't stand a chance, so we'll settle for the sister, if she has one.

As she'll actually be Pops reincarnated, I think I'll stand a better chance than But, on account of the fact that Pops knows what kind of guy I am. When we meet it will be like she/he has known me all his life, which she/he has really.

Buster says that Tata Young is nothing. Halle Berry beats her hands down because she was voted *Esquire* magazine's Sexiest Woman Alive. He also says that the way I'm talking about Pops kicking the bucket and coming back as a celebrity's sister sounds a bit sick to him.

Buster may have a point. However, death isn't such a big deal here in Thailand. People kind of take it in their stride. They know they'll see each other again next time around.

Pops is also taking it all in his stride. Actually, he's taking it in big jumps and leaps and summersaults. He cashed in his shares and is blowing the lot on the longest farewell party a guy could have. In fact, it's been going on since he got out of hospital eleven months ago.

The minute he walked out of the Chris Hani General Hospital in Port Elizabeth Pops turned to me and said, 'Randolph, my boy, it's party time.'

It must be said that he didn't look much like a party animal. For a start he'd lost all his hair due to all this toxic medicine he'd been taking to keep his tumour under control.

That tumour. It had been the size of a tennis ball when they'd examined his head after he had burned down his house at Nelson Mandela Gardens. It had started out like a small pea, but it had grown into a grape and then a plum and then a golf ball and then finally a tennis ball. It had squeezed the hell out of his brain. No wonder the poor bugger had been acting so strange.

The doctors had told Pops about the tumour a few weeks after the fire. He'd turned to them and said, 'Now that's a relief. It's a ruddy tumour. I thought I was losing my mind.'

Then, when they'd told him that it was just a matter of time, he'd said to them, 'Then you best let me out of here. I don't want to waste any.'

However, they had kept him in hospital for a couple of weeks while they zapped away at the tumour, trying to shrink it back to a decent size. And also because he was a bit battered from the fire. So was I. Well, it was mostly my hands. They really did take a bit of a beating.

I don't like thinking about all the stuff that happened to my hands. I was a bit cut up when the doctors told me how badly they had been damaged. But hell, I never was going to be a Beethoven or a Picasso. And if I'm completely honest with myself, I was a pretty lousy ping-pong player. It's not as if beating Pops and Felicity Foxcroft put me right up there in the same league as those Olympic champs Ryu Seung Min and Wang Hao – I mean, even Regina could whip me playing with her left hand.

Regina. My girlfriend Regina Versagel. I look at my watch and see that she's now two hours late. But tells me that it's always like this: the tourists always get caught up shopping in Singapore and then leave late for the capital of Thailand.

But my whole body is aching and tingling. I just can't wait any more. Come on, come on, come on! I look across the stretch of water but I still don't see it – the boat that's bringing them from the ocean liner up the Chao Phraya river to the capital of Thailand.

Regina's on that boat. Along with Pops and Grace and Felicity and Captain Jack and Mrs Smythe and Marjorie and Buzz and Crazy Lizzie and the Blackmans and Mrs Collins (Mr Collins and Brutus went on ahead a few months back, so Mrs Collins is alone now) and Old Stutters and about fifty of Pops' other friends from the Village. They've been cruising for the past two months and from all accounts they've been having the time of their lives. They are all the people Pops said he wanted to spend his last cents on before his time ran out. Oh, and me. He said he also wanted to spend a bit of time with me. And Regina.

My girl joined them in Singapore, but she'll be staying with me for six weeks over Christmas. It's the best time for her to be in Thailand, when the north-east monsoon is blowing cool and dry and the temperatures average about twenty-five degrees. And it never rains, not even the weatherman in Thailand dares to mention rain over Christmas. But during the summer, Thailand gets more than its fair share of rain and everyone talks about it a lot. I have learned the Thai word for rain (*fohn*) which is also a verb (but then it figuratively means to sharpen one's skill – something an Expert like me can appreciate). And I have also managed to learn how to say I love Regina (Legina) in Thai (*pom ruk koon,* Leg) and Regina, you are very beautiful (Leg, *koon suay mak*). It took me about five weeks to learn how to say these two phrases perfectly – how I missed Mrs Collins and her expertise in languages.

Actually, I've got a whole lot of stuff organised for Regina. In the first week I'm taking her to the James Bond Island where they filmed *The Man with the Golden Gun*. Buster says Regina will go mad for it. He says that if he lived in Thailand he'd go there all the time and have his photo taken in front of the island. There are more than fifty souvenir shops on the stretch of beach facing the island so there's tons to see and do, Buster tells me.

If there's time, I'm also going to take her surfing at a beach called Bang Tao on Phuket Island. I only went there because of the name, but I quickly found out that it has some of the best waves anywhere. It's actually for experienced surfers but I kind of want to show off a couple of my moves.

Surfing is the one sport I can actually do without using my hands too much.

Themba says that I'm going to have to get over the hand thing, because there's another sport that I'm definitely going to need them for (he always gives a dirty laugh when he says this). He's been sending me all sorts of what he calls 'educational material' because he says that by the end of the holiday I'm going to know exactly what colour underwear Regina wears. He says he can sense these things.

I should have put Themba out of his misery and told him that I already know. I acquired this knowledge the day before I left Port Elizabeth for the capital of Thailand last year.

I was sitting with Pops on the stoep at Grace's house (where he was squatting while his place got rebuilt) and we were talking about stuff. So I asked him the question that had been bugging me for a long time. I sort of felt I had to know the answer in case the tumour got Pops before I could see him again. 'Why have you always warned me against women with red hair who wear black underwear?' I asked him. 'What is wrong with these women?'

Pops had looked at me from under Grace's gardening hat, which he had borrowed to keep the sun off his shiny head. 'The problem, Randolph, my boy,' he said, 'is that there's nothing wrong with them. Nothing at all. They are absolutely perfect. Take your grandmother for example ...'

I thought about my grandmother. My grandfather's Boadicea. Fierce and extraordinary.

'She was the most perfect woman in the whole world,' Pops continued. 'After her, you know, there could never be anyone else for me. And that, my boy, is the big danger. These women ruin you for any other woman.'

I thought about what Pops had said. And then I thought about Regina. 'So, how do you know that Regina is one of these women?' I asked him. 'How can you be sure? Be sure that she wears ... them? The black knickers?'

Pops smiled. 'I could see it in the face. It was the expression in the eyes. That's how I knew.'

This amazed me, it must be said. Here was a guy who could tell the colour of peoples' underwear just from the look on their faces and the expressions in their eyes. Amazing!

Some people are born with extrasensory perception. The regular guy in the street calls it a sixth sense. Experts call it synaesthesia. It's a really cool brain condition which morphs two of your senses to give you a sixth sense and in some cases it allows these special individuals to experience taste sensations in association with different cities. Like I say London, you taste potato. I say Rome, you taste tomato. Or it allows the person to see colours with numbers or letters (Z is the colour of iced tea, seven is the colour of broccoli). There was this one guy who tasted Kentucky Fried Chicken when he said the Lord's Prayer. And now my own grandfather had his own unique brand of synesthesia. It was a trick I desperately wanted to learn. 'So, what was the expression in her eyes? What could you see in Regina's face?' I asked.

Pops took off Grace's hat and rubbed his head. 'No, Randolph, my boy, it wasn't what I saw in her face,' he said. 'It was what I saw in yours. It was in your eyes. That day you came back from the Internet cafe, where you first met her,

I knew it had happened. And that you were ruined forever.'

When Pops said this his face got all scrunched up as though he had terrible toothache. If I had consulted the three people in the world I know who are true experts in their fields I would have received very different interpretations of the nature of Pops' expression. Buster would have said that Pops was experiencing the kind of agony that James Bond felt when he had his goolies whipped by the baddy in *Casino Royale*. Themba would have said that it was the expression that guys get at that very moment they're doing it. And my father would have said that the source of Pops' pain was chronic dehydration – that he obviously wasn't drinking his eight glasses of water a day.

However, I knew without a doubt that what Pops was feeling was that weird sort of pain which comes from intense joy. Knowing as he did, that like him, I was one of the lucky ones.

I knew this because I had The Knowledge. I was an Expert in Old People.

the END

ALSO BY EDYTH BULBRING